Nc

June Bassett &

3

92

Nys

D1527854

THE END OF
AN ALTRUIST

THE END OF AN ALTRUIST

MARGARET LOGAN

St. Martin's Press   New York

Design by Basha Zapatka

Library of Congress Cataloging-in-Publication Data

Logan, Margaret.
    The end of an altruist / Margaret Logan.
      p. cm.
    "A Thomas Dunne book."
    ISBN 0-312-10459-6
    1. Women interior decorators—Massachusetts—Boston—Fiction.
2. Women detectives—Massachusetts—Boston—Fiction. 3. Boston
(Mass.)—Fiction. I. Title.
PS3562.04478E5   1994
813'.54—dc20   93-39586
                                                  CIP

First Edition: February 1994

10 9 8 7 6 5 4 3 2 1

For Jan, John, and Mary Logan

THE END OF
AN ALTRUIST

1

If Olivia Chapman knew anything, it was that nature had designed her to work at full tilt, answerable to one person only: herself. This morning, though, she'd dragged out of bed with none of her usual zest for the tasks ahead. Too much had gone wrong lately at Chapman Interiors, all of it outside her control, no solutions in sight. And money running lower by the day.

Breakfast was oatmeal topped with wheat germ. You had to at least start with real food. Spooning it in dutifully, she imagined the simpler lot of the 9 – 5 hire, gd. salary, 3 wks. vac., full bnfts. And, paramount, a boss. Male.

She saw him clearly, the man for this lousy mood. Not a Prince Charming—she hadn't believed in that stuff since she was sixteen. Her boss would be a can-do bulldozer. Granite jaw, thick neck, florid. Buttons about to pop, he's put on weight and can't find time to buy new shirts that fit. (Shopping's sissy.) He charges around, spews fusillades of orders, lays out action plans. She's to do what she's told, nothing more. (Women—girls, he'd say; gals—aren't built for thinking.)

An action plan misses its mark? Turns a puddle-sized glitch into a raging monsoon flood? No problem, he'll take the heat. That's what bosses are for. Count on it, kid. Don't worry your pretty head.

Olivia lived over the store, Chapman Interiors occupying the first floor of the narrow brick townhouse she and Philip, her husband, had bought some fifteen years earlier. Because it had been a much-abused rooming house on Joy Street, at the top of Beacon Hill's unfashionable north slope, the price had been right. "Are we up to it?" Philip had wondered. "Day after day on the crest of Joy?"

Renovating, Olivia had saved the winding staircase with its coffin niches, the pre-1850 moldings and mantelpieces, and gutted the rest. What resulted was an upside-down plan that had served the Chapmans and their two sons very well. On the fourth floor, where Olivia was finishing breakfast and inventing her dream boss, walls had been demolished and skylights opened to make a large, airy space for cooking, eating, and hanging out. A circular staircase led to a roof deck, tiny because it was squeezed by the skylights and an architectural code that kept modern additions invisible from the historic streets. There had been a family wrangle, the boys siding with their father for a bigger deck and no kitchen skylight. Olivia had won by wheeling in heavy artillery: "You guys want me to keep cooking or what?"

The things we used to argue about, she thought, stirring her coffee. As if we had all the time in the world.

Early as it was, sun poured through the disputed skylight. Another hot day, much too hot, everyone was saying, for May. Meeting one or another of her neighbors on the street, Olivia had begun to hear a bass line of millenarian foreboding. However carefully these men and women continued to groom themselves, to fight plaque, watch cholesterol and maintain aerobic capacity, doom-laden concepts—"greenhouse;" "ozone layer"—crept into even casual exchanges.

Olivia's air conditioner had been running for weeks. Central AC, though, had lost its solution status and become part of the problem. Central AC was greenhouse, ozone, a piper to be paid, the mechanical equivalent of a cigarette habit.

I'll shroud the skylights, she decided. If I want sun with my coffee, I'll drink it on the deck.

Instantly she felt better. Action, however puny, serves the soul. Wallows in global anxiety do not. Nor would a wallow in the essential frivolity of interior decoration. Enabling Mrs. Sullivan to adorn her drapery rods with hand-carved pineapple finials was no stupider than lots of other jobs. Building aircraft carriers, say. Or manufacturing attack rifles. Or devising ads for pantyhose—Philip's biggest account before he quit the agency to set up shop as Boston's first Green adman.

Their plans, their wonderful futures! As soon as he had signed up enough environmentally benign clients to begin making money, she would shut down Chapman Interiors and go back to school—graduate work in art history, probably, though Philip had pushed architecture. "The math," she'd protest. "I'll tutor you," he'd promised.

The coffeepot was empty. Time to suit up, to attack Mrs. Sullivan's missing finials.

Imre, the old-world woodworker Olivia had discovered and made too busy for everyone's good, claimed the finials had dropped into some black hole at UPS. The shipping receipt? Also lost. Lies, probably, but confrontation would be a mistake. Early on, a lost mantelpiece (and its lost receipt) had prompted Olivia to say, mildly, "Listen, Imre, if you haven't finished the thing, just tell me." Magyar honor, grievously offended, had taken months to heal.

At the Hamrick job, another kind of mess. The painter the Hamricks had insisted on using—a man unknown to Olivia—had taken his deposit, prepared some surfaces, and disappeared, losing Olivia her place in line with her wallpaper and carpet men. Ellen Hamrick was for hiring a new painter, paying, of course, a new deposit. Over my dead body, Bob Hamrick had yelled, and the fight was on. Right in front of Olivia.

The language of this cross fire—Ellen was a bubblehead, a spendthrift living in a dreamworld; Bob was a control freak with a miserable little bean-counter soul—clarified what was really afoot. Couples like the Hamricks were a shelter-biz occupational hazard. They had turned to a decorator to distract themselves from what they really needed—a marriage counselor. Or a divorce.

Olivia had wanted to disappear, let them make this grim discovery on their own. But the project was too big and had taken too much of her time to give up on. She had to break in, loud, bright, confident. "House painters keep close tabs on their competitors. I'll make some calls, see what's with your guy. Also, if I ask as a special favor, maybe one of my regular painters would be willing to . . . No, Bob, of course not. Not a penny more than the original budget."

Then there was the chintz for the Maddens' summer house. Olivia had just learned that delivery, delayed once already, was going to take an additional three weeks. The Maddens' house-warming invitations had been printed, sealed and addressed. Still jittery from the first delay, they'd go ballistic over this new one.

Altogether, a half-dozen jobs hung like this, crucially short of completion. Josie Spangler, Olivia's assistant, could normally be counted on to help leave the countless messages, to nag, threaten, throw real and contrived tantrums, but Josie had left a week ago to pursue true love in New York City.

Olivia had yet to advertise for her replacement. It was almost summer, decorating's fallow season. She could manage alone until fall. Also, Josie's New Yorker might not pan out, in which case the best assistant she'd ever had would return to Boston.

There was also a deeper reason, kept to herself, Philip at its root.

Unbidden—self-preservation forbade a conscious summons—his face floated before her, a pale hologram. Last Saturday had marked the end of the second year of the coma he'd been in ever since his motorcycle had been sideswiped by a drunk in a pickup.

Philip's last words to her, a merry cry before he roared off, were part of the horror: *Remember this when we're old and gray.* He'd found a buyer for the Harley. A man who flogged items like pantyhose required the solace of a hawg; Boston's first Green adman did not. After all their fights over the monstrous machine, it was that simple.

The drunk, sixteen years old, had no insurance. Philip had only life, not disability, insurance.

Two years. An impossibly long haul, because it was really two years going on three, or five, or ten. Life expectancy on feeding tubes was apparently no more predictable than the other version. The specialists—early on, Philip's parents had flown in specialists at the drop of a hat—did agree it was unlikely that he felt any discomfort. They also agreed on the horrible name for his condition: *persistent vegetative state.*

Recently Olivia had caught herself feeling surprised it had been *only* two years. Her former life, her life with Philip, had begun to seem more remote than that.

This remoteness did not derive from faulty memory. Olivia remembered very clearly, especially the rituals of the unbooked weekends they'd begun to guarantee themselves once the boys were away at school. Pajamas by eight on Saturday night, soup-and-sandwich dinners on trays, a black-and-white classic on the bedroom VCR. Next morning they'd fall upon the Sunday papers, as famished as if stranded for months in Tibet or Timbuktu. Eventually one or the other would declare a need for exercise. Country bicycling this usually was, Olivia refusing to deal with the Harley. After exercise they'd soak in the same deep tub, decorating their trim, oxygenated bodies with Vitabath froth, a prelude to lovemaking—the central marvel of their marriage—that unfailingly left them elated and grateful.

Now, despite this clarity of detail, her recollections had become partial. Missing was the physical, the elating and marvelous ways her neck, breasts, hands, feet, fork, had responded to this one man for so many years. It was as if her body, on its own, without her permission, had renounced such sensations. A change unutterably scary and sad. It told her, more persuasively than anything yet, that Philip was dead.

Sometimes she could admit quite clearly, at least to herself, that she wasn't rushing to replace Josie because she was looking forward to lighter expenses and a reduced workload. To Philip's final death, in other words. To the day when she'd be able to defy his parents' delusions and her own last residues of hope and—another horrible phrase—pull the plug.

She gave herself a shake. Get a move on, she ordered. Not aloud. She tried to avoid talking aloud when alone. Bad enough to drink alone. Lines must be drawn.

"That green is good on you."

Olivia jumped. Absorbed in writing a killer fax to the chintz people, she hadn't heard Dee's approach. "You startled me. Anyway, it's teal."

"You're welcome. I like to start my day with a compliment too."

She smiled at him. Dee, Diego Quintero, Philip's friend since Yale and now the second-floor tenant of her rearranged house, was looking pretty good himself. His striped shirt looked fresh from the box, his pegged and pleated cotton pants fit perfectly. He'd cut his ponytail—"too mainstream." His dark hair was now combed high on top, narrow on the sides.

"I'm liking that haircut more and more," Olivia said.

"My Latino Trendo? Thanks."

"De nada."

Dee was what he called wetback faculty. No benefits, no status, no security. The money sucked; you had to overschedule commitments to survive. On an old, theft-proof clunker of a bicycle he shuttled from institution to institution, teaching literature, freshman comp, and fiction workshops. In between, he wrote short stories, some of which had been published in various quarterlies. One, about a man dying of AIDS, had won an award. He and Olivia had quarreled over it. She thought he'd ripped off Philip, he'd insisted every syllable was an act of homage. "You're not the only one who loves him," he'd finally blurted, causing them both to burst into tears.

"What's today?" she now asked. "B.U.?"

Dee raised his eyebrows. "B.U.'s been over for ages. You're living in the past." Hearing what he'd just said, he froze. "Oh God. I didn't in a million years mean Philip."

"I know."

"Actually, a friend's picking me up. We're going to the beach. Want to come? No, really. Why not?"

"Too much busy work. Who's the friend?"

"Kevin."

"Uh." Olivia would never understand men, never. Gay or straight, show them a dumb, pretty blond and they lose all sense of proportion.

"I know, but he's so cute. Forget him, think of the fresh air and sunshine. Put roses in your cheeks."

"It's tempting, but I can't. Among other disasters, Imre's at it again."

"The hairy hound from Budapest? You're too nice, is your problem. You're smart, your markups are merciful, and you've got perfect-pitch color sense. Also great legs and a face Burne-Jones would've died to paint. So why's this lying Green Card allowed to push you around? Makes no sense."

More, Olivia had been gesturing, more! Now she laughed. "Too *nice? Me?*"

"I was speaking comparatively." Spotting her sample of the Maddens' chintz, he plucked it up with theatrical distaste. "My dear! What on earth?"

Chin on fist, Olivia tried to see the pattern freshly. Muddy browns, pinks, and greens on a curiously strident cream background. Birdcages, birds in flight, and botanically improbable flowers linked by vines that evoked slow, painful strangulation. "I serve my clients' tastes," she said, "not mine or thine."

"Well, a slipcover, a throw pillow, what's the dif? A man running for his life might not even notice them."

"Sorry. It's the whole room. Draw draperies and all upholstery. Quite a big job, actually. New kitchen, new baths, some complicated construction problems. Going like clockwork until Mrs. Madden managed to penetrate the Design Center and find this. All on her own, the instant I'd turned my back. Two hundred and twenty yards I had to order."

"Ever read *The Yellow Wallpaper?* Charlotte Perkins Gilman? A woman goes bonkers from vines no worse than these. Better send your Maddens a copy. Like a surgeon general's warning. These are litigious times."

Olivia's phone rang.

"Coming at that precise moment," Dee intoned, "Mrs. Madden's call caused the conspirators to exchange a guilty look."

She giggled and picked up the phone. "Olivia Chapman."

"Oh good. This is Jane Griscom. Am I disturbing you? Oh good. I was talking to your mother-in-law the other night—she and my husband are old friends. She said you might be able to help us with some furniture."

"I'd be glad to. What sort of furniture are you considering?"

"Oh, we don't want to *buy* anything. I'm sorry, I didn't make that clear, did I? It's an inheritance from my aunt. She collected furniture as a hobby. Well, more than furniture, actually. All kinds of little things."

Olivia rolled her eyes for Dee's benefit. "I see. And how can I help you?"

"We want to sell it, but we have no idea where to begin. Sally said you sometimes do appraisals for people like us. Unless you're too busy?"

Dithery as the woman sounded, Olivia trusted Sally Chapman's radar. There had to be money somewhere in this deal. And she loved appraisal work. "I'm never too busy to look at a new collection. Where's it stored?"

"Stored? It's right here in Cambridge. In our house."

"Would you like me to stop by, then? I've just had a cancellation, as a matter of fact. I could see you this afternoon, if that's not too short notice."

"Today? Oh."

Olivia waited.

"I'm not sure my husband can get away, is the problem. And he's hard to reach."

"Suppose we say two o'clock, tentatively. If that doesn't work, you can call me back and we'll find something better."

"Fine. Well. Goodbye for now."

"Just a sec. I'll need your address."

Laughter. Olivia's lubricant and social, Mrs. Griscom's flustered.

Telling Olivia how to find the house was a laborious process. "I've made it sound more complicated than it is," Mrs. Griscom finally said. "Basically you want to get half-way up Harding Hill. Look for the house with the meadow."

"Meadow," Olivia confirmed. "Unless I hear otherwise, I'll see you at two."

"Country?" Dee asked when she'd hung up.

"Harding Hill. Less than half a mile from Harvard Square. Ever been there?"

"Sure. Ritzy little enclave. I thought you said 'meadow.' "

"She said 'meadow.' "

"Ecology. How Cambridge. What's the name?"

"Griscom. Sally knows them."

"*Jonathan* Griscom?"

"My God. You think?"

Excited, Olivia grabbed the phone book. Dr. Jonathan Griscom, Nobel laureate, tireless crusader for social justice, willing talk-show guest, spouter of quotes, sound bites, and op ed pieces, would never have anything so elitist as an unlisted number.

She found his and Jane's names and the Harding Hill address. "It's them," she said.

"Golly. Can I tell Kevin? He swears by *Leaves* of Life.*"

"No you cannot. Dr. Griscom sells organic food?"

"You're thinking of the store. That's his son's. Dr. Griscom wrote the book the store was named for. It was America's first asterisk title." Dee sketched in the air. "Referred you to a list below—fruits, grains, sprouts, and so forth. Eat veg, is the basic idea. The son sells meat and fish but he plays the old man's luster for whatever it's worth. Keeps racks of the paperback right by the cash registers—like a health food *National Enquirer.*"

"Funny, Philip was going to pitch that store. Wait. It's coming together. Mrs. Griscom told me Sally was an old friend of her husband's, and Philip said he and the food-store guy used to play in the same sandbox. Huh. Small world. Can you get a Nobel Prize for a food book?"

"Not yet. He discovered a leukemia cure. There was some controversy, remember? No? It was a particular kind of childhood leukemia—a strain that hits northern Europeans. Swedish children, in other words. Given the natural bias of the Nobel committee, folks wondered if the good doctor's choice of research had been a trifle calculating. *Leaves* of Life* came out much earlier, back in the sixties. A pioneering effort. Controversy there, too. It included a long list of research projects commissioned by the beef industry, the egg industry, the sugar industry, like that. It won't surprise you that there was an absolute match between what these funding industries sold and what other learned scientists—Griscom's colleagues, remember—deemed essential for good nutrition."

"The things you know, Dee."

"I read the paper. Plus, El Comandante was in beef before he switched to more lucrative crops."

El Comandante was Dee's father, living in suspect luxury in Peru. Dee, convinced he had to be in drugs, wouldn't touch a single tainted centavo.

Now Dee was struck by a thought. "You're aware that *Leaves** of Life came from *Leaves of Grass?* Walt Whitman?"

"Yes, Dee. He was on the reading list." Philip's list, Olivia meant, of essential books. Given to her on their fourth or fifth date, right after she'd given him a list of essential works of art.

"How did you like him?"

"Whitman? Too much ego. Clubs you over the head."

Dee laughed. "Sounds like Dr. Griscom."

2

Meadow had Olivia expecting something out of Andrew Wyeth, tall plumey grass dotted with wildflowers. Sally's hasty briefing—Olivia had caught her on her way out the door—hadn't prepared her for what she found: tufts of rank weeds, thickets of briar, and seedling maples. Here and there were beer cans, burger wrappings, pieces of yellowed newsprint.

The house itself, like its neighbors on the curved, tree-shaded street, had been built to exhibit affluence and conventional good taste. But the white trim, meant to enliven the gray of the granite walls and slate roof, had needed paint several seasons ago, and the front door, once dark green, was as patchy as camouflage.

"Oh good. Come right in. My husband's not home yet, but I expect him any minute."

Jane Griscom—"Jonny's third wife," Sally had said—was tall, as tall as Olivia, and thin to the point of scrawny. Her smile showed clean, flawless teeth and tense neck cords. A red plastic band scraped her straight hair, auburn threaded with gray, back from her face. She wore a plain white T-shirt tucked into a worn, madras wrap skirt and red rubber thongs—attire that, anyplace but Cambridge, would cause Olivia to suspect a breakdown of her mother-in-law's fiscal radar.

The spacious living room Mrs. Griscom led Olivia into went with the rubber thongs. Planks laid on concrete blocks and plastic milk crates sagged under haphazardly piled books. The vinyl cushions of cheap "Danish" sofas and chairs were bandaged by silver duct tape. Wooden wine crates served as end tables. Shag carpeting, a drab green and much stained, covered the floor along with a remarkable assortment of pillows and hassocks. Some were beautiful, made from Navaho or kilim rugs, handblocked prints, embroidered leather. The other grace note was an abundance of cheap, functional lamps, arranged for reading.

Mrs. Griscom moved to a set of double doors and shoved them open. "Some of it's in here. There's more down cellar."

The center of this smaller room was piled high with cardboard packing crates. Around the walls Olivia could see a Sheraton-style camelback settee, an assortment of armchairs with carved frames, a funky Gothic loveseat, a blocky wing chair that was enough of a low-rider to be the real thing, and various pieces of American country furniture—blanket chests, bureaus, chairs, and small tables. If the painted finishes were original—at first glance they seemed to be—these might be quite valuable. But what most excited Olivia's interest was blocked from full view by the packing boxes: a carved bonnet top illuminated by sun from the uncurtained window. It had the glow of primal mahogany—dense, close-grained wood that could only have come from an old-growth tree.

"Is that a desk back there? The kind with a bookcase on top?"

"Yes, exactly. And little drawers for stamps and paper clips. It's funny you spotted it right away because that was Aunt Martha's favorite. She bought it way back in the depression. My favorite's right here—this table."

She put her hands on either side of the shallow drum top and turned it like a steering wheel. Four secret compartments lined with pale green velvet opened like petals. "Magic," she said, her smile remembering a time when it really had been.

Five hundred dollars, Olivia called it offhand. The marquetry

13

top, a wreathed grapevine done in several lighter shades of wood, was pretty, but the legs were machine-lathed. Still, with auctions you never knew. The fun of those compartments might start a bidding war.

"It was in her bedroom," Mrs. Griscom said. "The lamp that stood on it had grapes too. Part of the magic was that sometimes she'd put a little present for me in one of the compartments. But before I was allowed to look, she always took the lamp off. For safety's sake."

Olivia hardly dared ask. "Were the grapes done in stained glass?"

"Why yes. How clever of you to guess. The packers must have put it in one of these boxes."

Not necessarily a real Tiffany, Olivia reminded herself. But that mahogany bonnet promised authenticity elsewhere.

The smell in the room was, powerfully, dog.

"She taught Latin," Mrs. Griscom went on. "In the Duxbury high school. Do you know Duxbury?"

Olivia did. Cranberries and ship captains. Many antique houses, many attics crammed with nice old things.

"She never married," Mrs. Griscom went on. "She must have told me a million times that someday her treasures would be mine, and now they are. She died last month."

"I'm sorry."

"Thank you. She was close to ninety, and sick, but I can't help missing her. She was all I had for family. My last blood relation, I mean."

Olivia murmured sympathetically, then asked how the collection had been formed.

"Auctions, I think. I know she went to loads of them. She used to say she had three passions, Latin, auctions, and dogs." A fond laugh. "She never had fewer than two dogs, sometimes more. She brought them home from the pound and named them after famous

Romans. Luckily, well, not luckily, but you know what I mean, they all died before she did."

"They must have been well behaved. I don't see any signs of chewing."

"My husband disapproves of pets," Mrs. Griscom said, as if conscience required this interjection. "He says that people who lavish love on dogs and cats are afraid to love people. But I think if he knew Aunt Martha as well as I did, he'd say she was the exception that proves the rule. I know she loved me."

Olivia smiled. "Of course she did. Look what she left you."

Taking this as a literal command, Mrs. Griscom stared at the magical marquetry table. She might be seeing it for the first time.

She might also be having second thoughts about selling something that had figured so powerfully in her past. Before Olivia could test that possibility, Mrs. Griscom frowned and gave herself a shake. "How much is all this worth, do you think?"

"I can't say yet. A lot depends on provenance—where a piece came from, who owned it, if that's known. And how original it is. If that desk, for example, has its original hardware, and if it's American, not English, you can expect top dollar. I don't want to raise false hopes, but with signed, handmade American desks, top dollar can be over a million."

"A million *dollars?* Goodness. I had no idea. Who has that kind of money to spend on *furniture?*"

"It's a rich country," Olivia said, shrugging. "Did your aunt keep records? What she paid, the when and where of each purchase?"

"Would it have been a loose-leaf notebook? I seem to remember—I'd have to look through her papers. They're down cellar."

"I'd love to see whatever you find. Can you give me a rough idea of what's in the boxes besides the grape lamp?"

Mrs. Griscom had to think. "Old toys? Yes, and those funny little mechanical banks—you know, the little man dances when you put in a coin. Quilts. Oh, and bird carvings. Dozens of those. Aunt Martha loved birds. Paintings. One of a little girl she set great store by. Everything very old-timey." She laughed in depreciation. "And sort of cracked and, I don't know, *rusty.* I hope you won't be disappointed."

Holy shit. Was this a cache of unrestored Americana? Hidden treasure, some of it quite literally worth its weight in gold? It was all Olivia could do not to grab the closest carton and rip it open. First, though, she'd better set the hook. Make sure that she, and she alone, was commissioned to usher these marvels into the public eye. "Let's go sit down so I can lay the selling process out for you. Essentially, you have two ways to go—auction and private placement. There are advantages to both."

Olivia sat on a sofa next to a starburst of duct tape. Mrs. Griscom was about to take the other end when she had a thought. "Maybe," she said with doom in her voice, "we should have something to drink. Shall I make lemonade? Or iced tea?"

Anticipating a major dither, Olivia was brisk. "Thanks, but I just finished lunch. Now, why don't I start by explaining what I can do for you and how I figure my fees. Then, if we're still in business, we can move ahead to the rest."

"In business?"

"Sally did mention that I do this for a living, didn't she?"

"Oh I didn't mean *that.* Oh gosh, of course not. It's just that we should probably wait for my husband. Since it's his idea."

"The sale?" Olivia guessed.

Mrs. Griscom snatched up a pillow, hugged it to her chest. "We have no use for these things, you see. My husband—we both have strong feelings about material possessions. About the pain and misery materialism causes in this world."

Ah yes, Olivia thought. Poor Aunt Martha, shuttling from auction to auction, a driven creature, never satisfied, never content. And more poor tortured souls gathering in the wings, victimized by their lust for a mechanical bank, a quilt, a special painting of a little girl.

Innocent of such contradictions, Mrs. Griscom was chattering away. The proceeds from the sale would be used to set up a charitable foundation. There was need, crying need, everywhere you turned. Until now, the Griscoms' efforts to help had been financially inadequate, and, possibly worse, not directed toward any defined goal or coherent plan. The foundation would change all that. With the foundation, they could begin to make a real difference.

The front door banged open. "*There* he is," Mrs. Griscom cried, the light in her face positively bridal.

Jonathan Griscom was a gusty breeze, a charge of energy bowling into the torpid afternoon. His dark hair, home-barbered and tousled, showed no gray. His eyes were a deep, alert blue, their whites strikingly clear. He wore threadbare, rather grubby, chinos and a T-shirt like his wife's. On his feet were Birkenstock sandals and elderly black socks that sagged around his ankles. Over one shoulder he carried a transparent plastic sack which he set down carefully before shaking Olivia's hand. The sack contained a great deal of green-striped computer paper. Olivia also spotted milk and juice cartons, spent teabags, orange peel, an apple core.

Griscom kicked a hassock into position opposite the two women and folded his long, lean body down. Big feet wide apart, arms propped on his thighs, he leaned expectantly forward.

"Tell Mrs. Chapman about your trash, Jonny," his wife invited, her smile still bridal.

"We're doing a little environmental theater at the medical school. We'll carry these bags for a week, adding in more personal trash as we accumulate it. We'll wind up with a weighing and recycling ceremony—and, hopefully, some media attention."

Greenhouse. Ozone. "I like it," Olivia said. "Says that reduction at the source will get the trash problem off our backs."

Griscom grinned. "Perfect. I'm going to quote you."

Olivia grinned back. Not every day a Nobelist dubs you perfect.

"Unfortunately," Griscom continued, "the administration has barred us from dramatizing the major problem—the mountains of

17

trash the hospitals generate day after day. I'm not talking red-bag, of course, the stuff that's routinely incinerated, just the gowns and whatnot that go to ordinary landfills. You get it, don't you? If these items are supposed to be safe for landfill, why aren't they safe for our demonstration bags? On the other hand, if they *do* contaminate landfills, why are we, an institution devoted to the healing arts, committing a clear health hazard? But of course the throwaway mentality, as you've probably noticed, Mrs. Chapman, isn't susceptible to logic."

"Never mind, Jonny," his wife soothed. "You'll make your point."

"Hopefully. Well. I'm stealing this time, so let's get started. What do you think of all these things we've been landed with, Mrs. Chapman? Can we turn them into money?"

"Oh yes. I'll know more when I can take a closer look, but I think you can be optimistic. Americana's hot."

"Imagine, Jonny, the big desk might be worth a million dollars."

" 'Worth?' "

His correction was almost teasing, but her face fell. She looked like a little kid who knew in her bones she'd never get it right, never ever in a million years. No matter how hard she tried.

Olivia grabbed at a change of subject. "Another nice thing, you'll get a tax break."

"No, the taxes are all settled," Griscom assured her. "Aunt Martha's lawyer paid them out of her life insurance."

"That's the inheritance tax," Olivia said. "But since you're donating the proceeds of the sale to a charitable entity, you get to claim the deduction."

Neither Griscom catching on, Olivia spelled the goodies out. "Legally, the furniture is a capital asset, same as a block of IBM stock, say. Whatever it sells for, you can deduct against your income tax. And remember, you get to deduct the appreciated value. What your aunt originally paid is irrelevant, even if it was very little."

Griscom laughed, a boy's incredulous whoop. "I'm sorry to be so slow on the uptake, Mrs. Chapman. It's just that on my salary . . . well. Tax deductions aren't much of a motive around here."

Later Olivia would decide that his long, sweeping arm, indicating the shabby room, the ugly stained carpet, had been too prideful. At the moment, though, any skepticism was beyond her. From the first, when Griscom had leaned expectantly forward on his hassock, she'd felt little nudges, tugs, of sexual attraction—burst, by now, into hot, wet bloom.

He was, of course, a man who expected adoration, took it lightly for granted. So what? And so what if the ground at his feet was heaped high with worshippers already smitten?

She cleared her throat to explain about the tax code's carry-forward provisions.

"You sound thirsty," Griscom said. "Me too. I'll make us some lemonade."

Mrs. Griscom jumped to her feet. "I'll do it, Jonny. You and Mrs. Chapman talk business."

Get a grip, Olivia told herself. Speaking with deliberate care, her voice weirdly hollow in her ears, she outlined the different merits of private placements and auctions.

When she'd finished, Griscom restated her final point. "The commission is identical, then. Whether we pay it to you or an auction gallery."

Olivia saw no reason to tell him that any gallery she'd recommend would pay her a healthy finder's fee. "That's right. And for appraising, I charge by the hour."

"Would you consider contributing those hours? For the benefit of our foundation?"

He'd hiked himself to the very edge of his hassock, his knuckles almost brushing her tense knees. His smile was unutterably sweet.

"I'd have to think about that," she said.

"Oh, but is thought really called for? Haven't we moved past that? Aren't we in the realm of the heart?"

Let's do it, Olivia heard clear as day. Let's get down, not another word, fuck ourselves silly. Everyone else has loved it and you will too.

Appalled, thrilled, she faced it. The first man she had wanted since losing Philip was so close to her that the smell of his hair and sweat saturated her every breath. Alone with him, she'd reach out her hands, pull that lively, merry face into her lap, her breasts. Slide beneath his weight onto the hideous carpet.

A surge of raw, confident vitality ran through her. Where to take this delicious yearning—she had, suddenly, a revulsion against joining the adoring crowd at Griscom's feet—was a detail, to be dealt with later, after she'd calmed down. For now, she needed to tend to business, to set the hook Griscom had inadvertently handed her. To clinch a deal that, if the desk really was eighteenth century, would pay her sons' tuitions for years to come.

"But I've already made my contribution," she said.

His most endearing smile yet. His smell was driving her crazy.

"You have?" he said. "I hadn't heard."

"Your wife's not entirely happy about selling off her inheritance. I pretended not to notice, but I could have. I could have gotten her excited about keeping it. We could redo this room and set up a nice little parlor behind the sliding doors. A special little room just for herself."

"Never. Jane doesn't have a materialistic bone in her body."

"She'd probably tell herself she was only respecting her aunt's memory, but she'd do it."

"You're very sure of yourself, Mrs. Chapman."

"I've been in this business a long time."

"You have? Is it—how do I want to say this?—challenging enough for you? Satisfying?"

"Yes."

"I don't think I believe you. Why's that, do you think?"

Olivia lifted a shoulder, smiling but saying nothing.

Griscom moved back, away from her knees. He's evaluating me,

Olivia decided. Appraising the appraiser. Against the tumult just past, the mildness of her own feelings—a trace of boredom, let-down—amazed her.

"If it were my decision," she said, all helpful and friendly, "I'd go for an auction. The wholeness of the collection, on top of its hidden-treasure aspects, will boost each item. It's crucial to pick the right gallery, of course. That's a bit of an art in itself. I'd be glad to scout around for you, get them vying for your business. What with Mrs. Griscom's ambivalence about selling, I'd feel bad if I couldn't be confident of achieving the highest return possible."

"You two must be parched," Jane Griscom said, ice tinkling as she rejoined them with her tray. "I don't know how it can take so long to squeeze three little lemons."

"Your timing's perfect," Griscom said. "Mrs. Chapman and I have just finished striking a deal. She's going to find us the perfect auction gallery and do our appraisal, too. The whole shebang."

3

Jonathan Griscom arrived at work the following morning with a spring in his step. His testing was at a particularly delicate and interesting crossroads. Tonight, if he slept at all, he'd nap on a cot next to his lab bench. Such a vigil, exciting in its own right, also evoked the glories of the past, the night watches that had culminated in his great prize.

Along with this bounty, a delicious new ambition colored his day. Some women were "if," many more were "when." Olivia Chapman, his morning boner had convinced him, was a "when."

He'd no sooner entered his office than the phone began to ring. It was his private line; he'd given Olivia the number yesterday, watched her write it in her notebook. Hardening again, he picked up the receiver.

But it was only Arnette Murfin, an altogether different kettle of fish. She sounded upset, her voice thin and high. "That drug house cross my street? It gone—clear to cinders. They saying one a them addicks done it—nodded off smoking and things. And that woman on the third floor, had three kids? All of them's gone. Burned alive."

Griscom said the things people say to convey shock, outrage, pity. He'd been dreading something like this. And, on another level, waiting for it.

Couldn't have happened at a worse time, though. Much as he wanted to run right over, work on her before she numbed down, it was out of the question. He tried to explain about his tests in terms she'd understand.

"*Uh* huh," she said when he stopped talking.

Funny how they always gave it that skeptical inflection, even when they believed you. "I'll call soon as I can get loose," he promised. "In the meantime, you'll be talking to people, won't you?"

"Talk till I turn bright green don't mean they listen."

"I know. But try, all right? It's really important to keep trying."

By midmorning the next day the tests had inexplicably fizzled into a dead end. Disappointed, baffled, Griscom called Arnette to say he'd be there around noon and left his assistant to set up the next sequence.

Arnette lived in the Woodside section of Roxbury, once a stable, if not uniformly thriving, Jewish community—home, in fact, to some of Griscom's brightest classmates at Boston Latin School. Today, it was a crumbling backwater, ignored by the larger city except as a metaphor for failure, despair, and violence.

Arnette's second-floor windows offered a good view of the charred wreck opposite. It had been a double version of Arnette's three-decker, frame-built with a center stairwell. Long ago, its original clapboards had been plastered over with patterned asphalt shingles. Perversely, these grotesque parodies of weathered white cedar had resisted the flames.

It was their second resistance. Several years earlier, the six families living in this building had been burned out. Although that fire had been minor compared to this one, the building had been boarded up by the realty trust that was the owner of record. An arson investigation drew a blank; so did the city's feeble effort to discover real, as opposed to paper, ownership. Within days, various squatters broke in, most recently a group of crack processors and dealers in this and other drugs. They had escaped this fire with their lives and, Arnette was gloomily positive, "every smidge" of their product and equipment.

The dead mother and her children had been squatters too, their legal residence, the address the woman's check was mailed to, a relative's home on the other side of Roxbury. No one had ever squatted opposite the death-trap apartment, the previous fire having devoured most of the roof on that side. This gaping hole, although Griscom did not make the connection, had intensified the inherent draft of the central staircase and contributed greatly to the ferocity of the fire. As an arson-squad spokesman later expressed it, "These unfortunates died of fire one as much as fire two."

Talton, Arnette's three-year-old grandson, was tugging at the doctor's pants. "Candy," he stated, too sure it would be forthcoming to ask. "Candy."

Intent on explaining the street's passive acceptance of the fire, Arnette paid the child no mind. "They scared and things," she said, "but they ain't *that* scared."

Griscom let his frustration show. "Four innocent human beings burned alive isn't a call for action? I'm having difficulty with that, Mrs. Murfin."

"Like I say, they was *new*. People been *round* Wardell Street see that house gone, they ain't thinking 'bout no poor woman and her babies. They saying good riddance to them dealers."

Talton gained a handhold on the doctor's pocket and tugged more purposefully.

Now Griscom noticed. "I forgot your treat, Talton. My mind was on the fire and I forgot. I'm sorry."

Arnette slapped at the child's head. "Ain't I told you no begging? Ain't I?"

Talton let out a single yowl, relinquished the pocket, and stuck his thumb in his mouth. It struck Griscom that he didn't know Talton's last name, that he always thought of him as Talton Murfin. Which, of course, he might be, his mother, according to Arnette, having had a final falling-out with his father several months before his birth.

Griscom squatted, knees cracking, to apologize at eye level. "Next time," he promised, "I'll remember."

Talton looked away and sucked harder, uncomfortably reminding Griscom that a fatherless child had little reason to trust male promises.

It was cooler today, a faint breeze fluttering Arnette's curtains. Griscom could smell burnt wood. He wished he had a camera: the blackened timbers framed by the filmy white of the curtains, Arnette's powerful, dark, erect form, her head wrapped in an African-looking turban. The room's walls and ceilings, she insisted, were filthy with soot. She'd already washed and ironed the curtains and would start on the rest once Griscom left. Arnette was maniacal on the subject of clean. Tragedy notwithstanding, when she'd opened her door to him this morning her most urgent demand was that he explain "that mess," his plastic bag of personal garbage—which, shaking her head at the fathomless peculiarity of white people, she had ordered left out in the hall.

How this strict, energetic woman had produced kids who were such losers mystified Griscom. You couldn't even lay it on a derelict father; Mr. Murfin, a school janitor, had been faithfully in situ until his children were past their teens, then carried off by cancer. Arnette's daughter, Talton's mother, had split over a year ago, lost to drugs, possibly dead. Both of Arnette's sons were in prison, one for armed robbery, one for murder. Talton's two sisters, also being raised by Arnette, were in school right now—or at least were supposed to be. Kimi and Kinesha. All three grandchildren had different fathers, none of whom provided any form of support.

This male irresponsibility troubled Griscom less than the defection of the children's mother; Arnette had made it clear she was far from the only Woodside grandmother left holding the bag. No question, drugs, cocaine especially, had exploded the complacent axiom that black women, come what may, will shoulder the burdens of family. The unbroken chain of female toil that had sustained Woodside's fluid (in trusted company, Griscom would say African) social structure had been snapped past discoverable mending. And worse ahead. Kimi and Kinesha, absent a miracle, would breed at a pathetically early age; in Woodside, Griscom had begun to realize, primiparity was a rite of passage roughly analogous to a Harding Hill girl's first evening date. What guarantee did Arnette have that Kimi and Kinesha wouldn't defect too, leaving behind a third batch of babies for her to raise?

Arnette had come to Griscom's attention some six months earlier, when the intern who was treating her blood pressure happened to mention her spunky one-woman rent strike. Her objective, the intern told Griscom, was to force her landlord, the same real-estate trust that owned the burned house, to install sprinklers or at least a centrally wired alarm—safeguards which, in low-occupancy buildings, were not required by the city code. Curious to see what kind of woman would risk eviction in a city so woefully lacking in cheap housing, Griscom had told the intern he'd like to meet her. Shortly afterward, he'd started paying his weekly visits.

Griscom's hope, freely expressed to the ardent young gathered on the Harding Hill pillows and hassocks, was that others would join Arnette's rent strike until every last slumlord in Woodside was forced to accept his or her responsibilities. And this would be just the first round, the sapling that would grow into a giant oak of activist ferment. Empowered and energized by its own successes, Woodside would turn itself around.

Because so many of the young disciples were hatchlings of smug, Reagan-era blindness, he'd had to lay out the dynamics of social change in elementary detail. Grass-roots strategies, he'd made them see, were the only way to go. Witness the dismal failure of top-down strategies like public welfare and every other creation of the social-service mafia. Volunteerism? Good vibes for the volunteers, but look at the target group. Where's the real, lasting change? Where are the attitudinal and behavioral shifts that will challenge the system, render the volunteer unnecessary and obsolete?

"Compared to Woodside," he'd remind his rapt audiences, "I'm rich beyond the dreams of avarice. I can write checks, hire alarm installers by the dozen. Or I can grab some tools and tap tap tap, do the job myself. To what end, though? Do people of color really need fresh proof they're helpless without white intervention?"

Arnette Murfin, tough break, had turned out to be one of those individuals whose superiority inspires resistance and defensive mockery rather than emulation. An early indication of this was embedded in her request that Griscom wear, when visiting her, "your doctor coat, and you know, your ID and things. For security." From Kinesha and Kimi, Griscom learned more. Wardell Street, they told him with much giggling and innuendo, had met Arnette's trumpeted claims of her new friend's eminence, his Nobel prize, with raucous disbelief.

To giggle along with them would undermine their grandmother's authority, but Griscom certainly saw the funny side. How had Arnette learned so much about him? He'd told the intern who treated her to keep mum. Over the years he'd learned that even simple people tend to invest the Nobel with miraculous powers, and he'd prefer his contacts with Woodside unhampered by myth.

He supposed there was no escape. A household word was a household word, even in darkest Woodside. Then Kinesha, eight and cool, set him straight. "Gramma have her doubts on you. She ax the information lady at the hospital."

A little disappointed, Griscom nodded his approval. "Makes sense to check out a stranger."

Kimi, six, blurted out the rest. "Gramma scared you putting *moves* on her."

For reasons he never examined, Griscom resolved then and

there to turn Arnette into an agent of social change. Later, when he was alone, he considered her sexually. She wouldn't, of course, be his first black, but the others had been middle-class, educated women, professionals of one sort or another. With Arnette he'd expect major differences.

That, however, was very much "if," and very far down the road. For the present, their relations were formal. He wore his white coat and ID badge as she'd requested and always phoned ahead to see if his visit would be convenient. He was "Dr. Griscom"; she, unfailingly, was "Mrs. Murfin."

In recent weeks, he'd seen signs that the power of his quiet, steady attention was bearing fruit. Some of Arnette's neighbors had started to respond to the respectful nod-with-eye-contact he'd chosen to establish a benign street presence. And this morning, one of the old geezers gathered on milk crates in the vacant lot had actually said, "Morning." A civil greeting from a contingent normally given to snickers, wild rollings of eyes, mooing, grunting simulations of animals in rut—Griscom counted it a real breakthrough.

Now he glanced at his watch. If he intended to get any lunch today, he'd better make tracks. "Help Wardell Street *use* the fire, Mrs. Murfin. If they're ever going to slam the door on the man with the rent book, now's the moment. Help them understand that, will you?"

Arnette said she'd do her best and Griscom said goodbye. He didn't risk squatting down to say anything to Talton. Talton might snub him, and Arnette, maniacal on manners, would slap him again.

Out on the street, approaching the vacant lot, Griscom continued to regret his failure to remember the candy. Such an easy, automatic thing; Maria, everybody's favorite technician, kept an oversized snifter of the stuff right in plain view. You had to pass it whenever you left the lab.

Preoccupied, he almost missed Cyrus's question. The skinny old gent was the ringleader of the milk-craters, probably because he'd lived on Wardell Street most of his life. Griscom had asked Arnette whether he was Mr. Cyrus or Cyrus something-or-other, but she, a relative newcomer to the street, didn't know and—their baffling lack of curiosity about such matters!—had yet to find out.

"What you toting there, Doc?" Cyrus asked. His smile showed teeth so broken and discolored Griscom's own mouth ached to see them. "Garbage?"

"Exactly. It's something we're doing at the medical school. The idea is to make people aware—"

To make people aware. Jonathan Griscom's last words on earth were a miraculously apt epitaph had Cyrus or anyone else in the subsequent confusion been able to recollect them. But it was past noon, and the bottles twisted into their brown bags had worked their easeful magic. What the milk-craters could later attest to were the drama's broad strokes, not its fine points.

A late model sedan, big, dark, American, had swung around the corner fast, spitting bullets like blue Jesus. The car then streaked for the next corner, rounded it on two screaming wheels, and disappeared. More screaming issued from the mouth of Jamal Sutton, who had been dropped to the sidewalk by a bullet in the thigh.

Seconds before, Jamal Sutton had emerged from his building, five doors down from Arnette's when you counted the vacant lot. On his front stoop he had paused a moment to adjust his belly bag and squint at the sky through shades the iridescent blue of a tropical butterfly. Then he'd started walking toward the vacant lot and his car, a Fiero he was about to exchange for a newer Mazda MX-6, ketchup red. Belonged to a brother he knew, a dude doing long time at Walpole. The cash difference, plus six monthly additional payments, would go to his mama. The bro owed her, Jamal guessed.

The words that came to him had set his fingers snapping:

Cash morn flash wheels
be yo need?
Jamal's old Fiero
just yo speed!

Two men, then, had paused momentarily on Wardell Street in the Woodside section of Roxbury. Had Jamal Sutton preened and hip-hopped a bit longer, or had Jonathan Griscom's bag of garbage not prompted Cyrus's curiosity, it is likely that only one man would have been in the path of the bullets. Which, though? The two-bit crook and pimp or the Nobel laureate? The survivor, cursing and writhing on the ground, or the pale, silent, unmoving other, his white coat garishly collared by the blood gushing from his neck.

Cyrus Grier, as the newspapers would later refer to him, once had loved Jamal's mother hopelessly; he'd known the boy since babyhood. Leaving others to call 911 or crowd gaping around the doc—famous doc; gon be hell to pay on *this* one—he kneeled to lift Jamal's head and offer him a drink from his bottle.

"Don't be gulping, now," he cautioned, but Jamal ain't never taken one lick of advice his whole life long.

Choking and coughing, Jamal managed to tell Cyrus what he wanted him to do: sneak away his belly bag and keep it safe until he got back from the Emergency.

In the distance, sirens. "Come on, man," Jamal pleaded. "An easy hundred bucks."

"Deal," said Cyrus. Later, alone in his room, he saw what was making the bag so fat—two thousand dollars in fifties and twenties. No new bills, the twenties particularly worn and dirty. *Local* money. Cyrus had to give consideration to drugs. One thing: them two peaky hoes Jamal had for a string didn't turn no twenty, fifty dollar tricks. Ten they lucky.

He pocketed his own fifties, the cleanest of the lot, shoved the bag deep under his mattress. Wide awake with thoughts of his windfall and what it might buy, he nonetheless stretched himself out for his usual afternoon nap. Law come poking and prying, a man be needing the help of his routines.

4

Dr. Griscom is survived by his wife, Jane, his daughters, Francesca and Anne, and his sons, Benjamin and Gordon. Our reading eye slides smoothly over the obituary formula unless (or until) we, too, know firsthand what it is to be a next-of-kin survivor of sudden, violent death. Such survivors bear a special burden: they can never find release from the moment the dreadful news first struck. They will remember everything—the weather, the clothes they wore, who was with them and, in terrible detail, their own identities, the self they were at the time. Every personal inadequacy and flaw will remain precisely fixed, forever defeating the process of erasure and revision we normally rely upon to adjust our histories, make us more tolerable to ourselves.

In downtown Boston, Francesca Griscom, Dr. Jonny's eldest, stepped into an empty elevator with her husband and partner, Boyd Pierce. They were returning from lunch, a late one, just the two of them. Even though they'd talked business most of the time, Chess was impatient to get back to her desk—to get back, she noted treasonously, to real work.

Boyd took his wife's hand. "We must do this more often."

"Mm," said Chess. Then, to save fuss, stuck on a smile.

Boyd, as usual, missed everything but the smile. He lifted her hand, gave the palm a moist kiss.

The elevator stopped at the twentieth floor. Before the doors opened Chess had reclaimed her hand and wiped it dry on her trim flank.

Griscom & Pierce Ventures was just the two of them, their secretary, and the occasional temp. To the partnership, Boyd had brought an initial capitalization of thirty million dollars—money he'd inherited. Chess contributed her excellent brain and ready access to Jonathan Griscom's vast, productive network of friends and colleagues. Though intangible, this access meant more to the partnership's success than the Pierce millions. Every venture capital outfit has money to invest; only Chess could confidently expect to get through to the top whenever she wanted. Even cold calls met no obstacle. "I was talking to my father last night," she'd say to a leading researcher in therapeutics, "and he told me about the interesting new work you're doing with synthetic carbohydrates." Openings like that reliably got Griscom & Pierce in on the ground floor, where equity is cheap and profit high.

One pesky cloud: secretarial turnover. Colleen, their latest, was new. Like her many predecessors, she'd been given permission to play a small radio for company.

Today, the instant her employers entered, Colleen switched the radio off.

"That volume's fine, Colleen," Chess said. "Don't worry, we'll tell you if it's too loud."

Pudgy little Colleen turned bright red. Not beautiful herself, she fervently believed in beauty, in its power to bestow good and deflect evil. She had gushed about her new bosses to her girlfriends. "My whole first day, I was like, what are they, models? Movie stars? Plus which, she's got this really, really famous father."

Who was dead, the radio had just finished saying. And they, the poised, glamorous pair standing before her, knew nothing about it. Colleen broke down and started to cry.

After Chess had heard, through the girl's sobs, enough to understand, she separated herself from Boyd's embracing arm. "Hold my calls," she said. Then she walked carefully to her office, shutting the door behind her.

Slumping against her desk, she stared at the blow-up that decorated one wall. In grainy black-and-white, it showed her and Dr. Jonny in his lab. He was dropping dye onto a slide; she, an intent ten-year-old, monitored closely. Hopeful entrepreneurs always got the message: Griscom & Pierce are right at home with greatness.

She'd shut herself in here to be alone with her tears, but no tears were coming. All she felt was the terrible pressure of things to be done, people to be seen. Daddy, she whispered. Daddy.

When that snapshot was taken, she abruptly realized, he was almost the age I am now. And Jonno is exactly ten.

Her son—Boyd's son too, though she rarely thought of him that way—had been named for his grandfather. Her daughter, Susan, was eight. The hoped-for bond across the generations had not yet materialized. Chess had made the mistake of complaining about this to her mother. "What did you expect," Isabel had jeered, "fishing trips? Two little kids—where's his audience?"

Stop that, Chess warned herself. Think like an adult. Like a mother, not a daughter.

Tonight, she and Boyd would leave early. From somewhere, she would gather the strength to tell the children what's happened. No, that's crazy. This isn't a simple family tragedy, this is news. Nobel Winner Slain in Drive-by Shooting. The kids'll hear about it in school, won't they? Unless we go right now and pick them up? Is that what we should do, pick them up now? Before anyone can say something to frighten them?

She stared bleakly at the girl in the photograph. What had she comprehended, at ten, of death? Of hideous, terrifying violence?

34

There was a tap on her door. She said come in, and Boyd did. His face, his entire stance, proclaimed his helplessness. A dreadful tiredness surged behind her eyes, dense, oppressive, like a head cold coming on. A wailing noise filled the room. Until Boyd came to her, until his shirtfront was blotting her wet face, she didn't know she was making the noise herself.

Twenty miles to the west, Barb Griscom, second-eldest Benjamin's workhorse of a wife, heard the news from Joe Bartholomew, a colleague at the high school where she taught social studies. Amid her shock and horror she felt an arrow of pain in her belly. On the side with the fibroids.

"Barb?" Joe asked. "You OK?"

"Almost," said Barb.

"Maybe you should lie down."

"I've got a class."

"So be ten minutes late. I'll go tell the office."

She thanked him and made her way, in a dream, to the teachers' lounge. The bell having rung, it was empty. She dropped into one of the shabby old chairs and took a deep breath. The thick stink of cigarettes grounded her, woke her up.

Women with ovarian fibroids, the gynecologist had said, can have trouble getting pregnant. He'd spelled it out clearly: "If you're planning to have children, don't procrastinate."

Ben had procrastinated about his father and lost his chance to make up. Forever. And if Dr. Jonny had cut Ben out of his will, she had lost her chance for a baby. Forever or might as well be. They were barely surviving as it was, and the moron voters had just said no to taxes that would have given her a raise, long overdue. Much worse, this vote virtually promised cuts in staff. Nothing would make the morons happier. Trimming the fat, they called it.

They could trim her.

She had to stop this, pull herself together. Scrabbling through her tote bag, she found pencil and paper. TO DO, she wrote in shaky capitals, then, CALL BEN.

But when? She checked her watch. For the next fifteen minutes (she knew Ben's schedule as well as her own) he'd be in their tiny apartment giving Karen Schwinde a voice lesson. After a half-hour break, more private lessons, an unbroken stream of them. At six, exhausted, he'd tear off to direct the weekly rehearsal of the Charles River Community Chorus, his sandwich supper in one hand as he drove.

You had to do it, didn't you? Barb furiously accused her father-in-law. Just plain had to pick the busiest day of his week.

Ten minutes, Joe Bartholomew had said he'd tell the office. She'd already used up five. If she waited until Ben was finished with Karen she'd be nearly twenty minutes late and twenty minutes was almost half the entire—

Quit that, she said aloud. Calm *down.*

Come to think of it, Ben might not direct tonight. By then, news of the shooting would be all over the place, so the chorus would know not to expect him. He'd complain because the concert was coming up, every minute of rehearsal time vital. And he'd certainly point out there wasn't a whole bunch of love lost. Still, he'd have to see that people would take it amiss if he didn't cancel.

The chorus knew, of course, that he was Dr. Jonny's son. Ben wasn't above using his father's stardom, and why should he be? His tenor section—tenors are scarce everywhere—was widely envied by other choruses. "I'm the only one," he'd told her, "who's got Dr. Jonny's name roping them in." His bitterness obliged her to demur: "Aren't they above that kind of thing?" "No one's above that kind of thing," he said with bleak finality. "No one in the world." And Dr. Jonny's fame didn't hurt when it came to private students either.

But where was her *head?* Wouldn't the private students expect Ben to cancel too? Of course they would. She had to make that clear to him when she called. "Who cares how it *looks?*" he'd scoff.

"If I cancel I won't get paid." "I know, honey," she'd soothe, "but they won't like it. It'll make them too uncomfortable."

Was there a middle path? Suppose she didn't call him at all? Certainly Ben would never turn on the radio; he hated the news, couldn't stand those loud, hysterical voices hyping up the traffic jams and whatever. OK, so there he is, his break's over, the next student, Don Kelly, comes in, works on his upper register, pays, goes home. What's wrong with that?

She had the answer immediately. Don might, this very minute, might be hearing about Dr. Jonny. And Don was shy, Barb knew, so painfully shy he hadn't been able, his first lesson, to sing a blessed note. Would a man like that call into a house of mourning to ask if his lesson was still on? Never. He'd just stay away, leaving Ben to worry that he'd lost interest and would soon drop out, taking his twice-weekly fee with him.

But death makes everyone shy. What if *all* the students stayed politely and uncommunicatively away? She'd come home to find Ben devastated, hardly in a state to hear more bad news. And it *was* bad news. The will, the eventual loss of Dr. Jonny's fame, and of course the fact that, despite everything, a father is a father. Ben was bound to—No. On that point she could predict nothing. That area of her husband's heart had always been closed to her.

In the thick of these swirling probabilities, a sudden clarity: Isabel. Ben's mother, barging in ahead of her.

Not even stopping to check the time, to see if Karen Schwinde's lesson was safely over, Barb grabbed for the phone.

At the eastern edge of Cambridge, two geographical and a million sociological miles from Harding Hill, third-eldest Gordon was in the office of his store, winding up a chat with a young salesman for a new line of organic lotions and hair products. Leaves* of Life sold *food*, he'd tried to make the kid understand. Yeah, yeah, markups and margins, he didn't need any reminders on that score. But monetary temptations took you only so far, and he, Gordon, had concluded that a single aisle devoted to health and beauty, vitamins, and the occasional irresistible novelty item was enough. As it was, nonfood products kept inching beyond their designated territory. "Check it out yourself," he invited the salesman. "First they sneaked around the end of the aisle near the registers, then both ends, and now they've claimed the far end too. They're like, I don't know, some kind of *lava*. They've got a life of their own. Unless I put my foot down the whole place'll turn into a New Age head shop."

The salesman, a sweet Oregonian, a true and tender believer who'd been doing his cross-country sales tour on a Greyhound pass, looked glum, beaten.

"Call me in six months," Gordon said as he walked the kid to the door. "Your stuff's good. If one of our present suppliers goes belly-up, you'll be at the head of the line."

"Really?" the kid asked.

Gordon patted his back. "You have my word."

He had just settled down to his spreadsheet when Darla came in. "Hi, Fudge," he greeted her.

Darla had worked at Leaves* of Life since last summer, as a staffer, then manager, of the extensive deli and takeout counter. Her Sesame Chicken (free-range) with Green and White Linguine was a consistent top seller; her new Potato Flan with Kielbasa (one hundred percent chemical-free) was almost as popular. Just after Christmas, she had moved into Gordon's house.

All this time and she still hadn't gotten used to the way his face, his whole self, would light up to show how happy he was to see her. (He lit up for everyone, she knew, but so what? Gordon was special, different. She, too, should strive to be different, try not to dwell on the same old jealous resentments.) "Hi, Gordon," she said.

"Something wrong?"

"Yes."

He pushed back from his computer terminal and stood with his arms wide. "Hug first."

Her breath caught in a little sob. Gordon had taught her all about the healing powers of touch. After she'd started using his techniques with her deli crew, productivity had soared. Now, in his arms, breathing the fresh, clean smell of his hair and skin, she fiercely willed to him every ounce of strength she possessed. Dr. Jonny was his inspiration, his ideal. No son ever loved a father more.

Gordon groaned luxuriously, giving himself over to the deep pleasure of being held by a woman who worshipped him. Then, slowly, cell by cell, he disengaged.

They stood apart. "Thank you, Fudge. Now. What's happened?"

The enormity of what she was about to do to him hit her with a terrible force. What if he ended up blaming her? Forever more associating her—associating her touch!—with this devastating moment?

Anne, the baby of the family, lived in a small, grubby apartment five blocks from her brother's store. Rising late, she'd gone out to buy the *Phoenix,* intending to circle five or six of the tabloid's Help Wanted ads before her three o'clock appointment with Dr. Schultz. Her therapy session would go better, she knew, if she arrived with this show-and-tell in hand.

Midday, the paper still lay unread. Anne had, however, settled upon a plan: eat something, then the ads, then kind of race to the Square, arriving at Schultzy's right on the dot of three.

She turned off the TV, went to the kitchen, switched on the radio, and opened the refrigerator door. That leftover macaroni? Mix it with ketchup, slab on some cheddar, brown it in the toaster oven?

Preoccupied with her preparations, the sound of her father's name made little initial impression; like all of Griscom's children, she was used to hearing it broadcast. Oh boy, she thought idly, what's he mouthing off on now?

At length the transfixing truth penetrated and made its fearsome claim. Frowning slightly, eyes unfocused, Anne engaged with every word they said. When "a distraught eyewitness" spoke, she, too, felt distraught. The report of "concerned police at the scene" filled her with concern.

"Dr. Griscom, he was a *friend*," Anne heard some total stranger say. "He really *cared* 'bout Wardell Street."

"That was Arnette Murfin," said the announcer, "the Woodside grandmother whose rent strike first drew Dr. Griscom's attention to the area. Mrs. Murfin has lived on Wardell Street for ten years. In other news at this hour, shipyard workers at General Dynamics in Quincy—"

Other news? How could there be any other news? Angrily, Anne silenced the hateful blather. Then she slammed the refrigerator door shut and scooped up Bunwerl, her rabbit, pet, familiar, fetish, from his unheeding nap on the floor.

Bunwerl does not exist!, her father would yell into the screaming residues of her nightmare. She was five; the nightmares had begun the year before. *Open your goddamn eyes! The room's empty. See? See? No Bunwerl! No such thing.* Bonita, her mother, protected by her pills, slept through everything. Night after night it all fell on Dad.

She carried the rabbit into the living room, sat in her favorite chair with him in her lap.

"Dad's dead, Bun," she whispered into his fur. "Dead and gone. Stone cold dead in de market. Doornail dead. I'm a norphan. Little Norphan Annie."

Tears stung, spilled over.

Bunwerl, not liking the wet dropping onto his fur, struggled free and hopped behind the avocado plant. After awhile, Anne hoisted herself up, went to the bathroom, blew her nose, and threw cold water at her face. Then she went back to her chair to wait until it was time for Dr. Schultz.

Pretty lucky, having your weekly appointment the very day your dad gets blown away. What were the odds of that? Six to one? Or seven? Whatever, you'd have to call it lucky. Course, if she'd been one of Dad's *friends* instead of just his kid, she could have therapy as often as she wanted. Twice, three times a week. Every day. Why not? Last week she'd had to beg Schultzy to give her a little extra, please, please, just this once, just ten minutes, *please.* Times like that, even every day wouldn't be enough.

He really cared 'bout Wardell Street. Oh boy. Oh boy. There'd be some kind of memorial service, with all the Harvards and all the *friends* milling around. Dad's gang, all *concerned.* Not to mention *distraught.* End of the handouts, boys and girls, no more free lunch. Have to find yourselves a new Candyman.

She eyed the phone. Should she call someone? Wait and see who called her?

If this was a normal family, her first call would be from Gordon, her super-successful big brother. In a normal family he'd say to himself, gee, the poor little thing, stuck in that hole with nothing but want ads and rabbit turds for company, maybe I can comfort her.

Gordon, though, loved Dad. Purely and truly looooved him. If he was going to call someone, he'd pick someone who'd be as busted up as he was. Probably he was rushing over to Jane the Plain right this minute.

How about the other two, Isabel's kids? (Knock, knock. Who's there? Isabel. Isabel who? Isabel ringing?) Anne doubted she'd ever hear from Ben. He'd always acted, at those awful family dinners Dad used to inflict on them, like he'd forgotten who she was. And Chess would call only to issue orders on the funeral or something. She had that Hitler side. Look how bossy she'd been when Bonita checked out.

Bonita. Where else did the dead exist besides in their children's dreams and nightmares? Could Bonita be trailing along out on some astral plane, about to bump into her husband for the first time in, what?

Anne counted on her fingers. Twelve years. Her mother had been dead twelve years. God. The kid next door was twelve, and

41

he was like a real person. You could talk to him, have a normal conversation, use the same kind of words you'd use on anyone.

Lady-in-waiting, Schultzy sometimes called her. While it was going on, the days passing each other and all, it hadn't seemed an especially long time, but when you looked at the kid next door . . .

Bunwerl, nick of time, hopped up and cocked his head at her. His cutest look. She wiggled her bare toes, enticing him to play, to distract her. The phone didn't ring.

Bicycling west along the river path, headed for the Griscoms' Olivia felt terrific. She and Jane would spend the afternoon unpacking, finding who knows what treasures. Then, first thing tomorrow morning, she'd begin her systematic appraisal.

The sky was blue, the air clear, the temperature under eighty for a change. The sun seemed friendly rather than baneful. On top of these felicities, Imre had called to say he'd "found" Mrs. Sullivan's pineapple finials.

The Griscoms' meadow had collected some new trash, which reminded Olivia of Jonny's (they'd all parted on a first-name basis) plastic garbage bag. The nutty selectivity of the man's environmental awareness, along with a sudden, sharp memory of his big feet, his lanky, boyish moves, made her flush. He wouldn't be here today, Jane had said. Good thing. How would she concentrate?

Smirking like a fool, she locked her bike and started up the walkway.

Jane opened the door. At the sight of her frozen, pale face, Olivia's heart gave a guilty jump. *She knows*, she thought, *she's seen straight into my lustful and adulterous soul.*

"Oh lord," Jane cried, her voice wobbling. "I completely forgot. I thought you were Gordon. Oh here he is now."

Olivia turned to see a white van with a green Leaves* of Life logo turn into the driveway. A tall, barrel-chested man with a full beard and sunstreaked ponytail got out.

"This must be a bad time," Olivia began, but Jane, with a terrible wail, ran past her to throw herself into her stepson's open arms.

Feeling horribly intrusive, Olivia tried to leave unnoticed.

Jane put out a hand to stop her. "Oh Olivia. It's awful. Jonny's been killed. We have to go to him."

Killed? Olivia couldn't believe it. She wanted an explanation. To demand proof; who, what, why, when, where? "I'm so sorry," she said instead. "So very sorry. Go, of course. Unless—can I drive you someplace? Or do anything else for you?"

"Gordon?" asked Jane.

Gordon had dug out a bandanna and was blowing his nose, mopping his eyes. "Thanks, but I think we're all set. Gordon Griscom," he added, sticking out his hand.

"Olivia Chapman," she said. Three Wasps doing their manners in the sunshine. Something—outrage, protest—bubbled dangerously at the back of her throat. She swallowed hard.

"I'll call you as soon as I can," Jane promised.

Gordon bundled her into the van and they were gone.

5

Olivia rode back to Boston on automatic. Reaching Charles Street, minutes from home, she spotted The Sevens, the closest thing Beacon Hill had to a neighborhood bar. Home, it struck her, was an empty house. The last thing she needed was to be alone in an empty house.

She braked, too suddenly for the bike messenger coming up fast behind her. Swerving out of the way, he flung his summary over one lycra shoulder: "Asshole."

Normally good for mouthy riposte, Olivia kept it shut. Enough violence in the air already. Besides, she'd been at fault. She locked bike and helmet to a parking meter, ran her fingers through her hair, and went inside.

Some bars achieve comfort with deep upholstery and muffling surfaces. The Sevens, small, dark, and shabby, comforted with its air of timelessness. Even strangers sensed its atmospheric permission to loosen up and, if the spirit moved, let fly. Rudeness, crudeness, and other lapses, at The Sevens, were readily forgiven. (Not, however, forgotten. A penalty of timelessness.)

When their sons were young, Olivia and Philip had dropped in here every couple of months, whenever the rest of their life felt clogged with getting and spending, with Cub Scouts and the Tree-Planting Committee. The townie regulars tended to be plain-spoken, especially concerning liberal orthodoxies. Eavesdropping on them was astringent. Olivia and Philip would arrive weighed down by their multiple roles—parent; citizen; professional. Leaving an hour or so later, they were reduced (or was it restored?) to identities that felt lighter, more fundamental. Sexier.

The red walls, the battered, uncushioned wooden booths and fake rusticity were just as she remembered. She also remembered the bartender. His mustache looked droopier. Gravity's steady tug. There was a CD jukebox in place of the old one.

The lunch crowd having returned to work, the place was nearly empty. Three young men clustered at the far end by the TV which was tuned to the Red Sox, the volume low. Two older men, one in paint-spattered whites, the other in a shiny shirt the color of the Kraft caramels Olivia had loved as a child, occupied independent positions closer to the door.

Kraft was holding the bartender in close conversation. Olivia seated herself midway between him and the painter. The bartender gave her a courteous nod without, she thought, any recognition. Fine. She and Philip had been outsiders here, their deliberate choice. Get into names and life stories, Philip had said, and we might as well join some damn club.

TV. Would they have interrupted the ball game for a news bulletin on Griscom?

"So am I right?" Kraft was demanding of the bartender. "There's gotta be some reason they can't get with the program?"

"I guess," the bartender said.

"No, I mean, whaddaya think? You personally."

"I'm not one to generalize."

"What I think, this country was settled by immigrants. French like me, well, French-Canadian, Italians, Germans, Irish, what-ever—all immigrants. Jews. Say what you like on the Jews, at least they behave themselves, right? OK. So basically, why did everyone come here? For a better life than the old country, right? A chance to make something of themselves, and God bless them for it. OK, who stayed home? The rejects, right? Your stick-in-the-mud types, no initiative. Now with these colored, what you get is the exact opposite. The ones who left the old country—Africa, whatever—were slow and dumb. Too slow to outrun the slave traders and too dumb to hide their asses. And that, my friend, is the basic reality we hafta deal with in America today."

"Slow?" said the painter. "Ever watch track and field? Carl Lewis? Flo Jo? Jackie Joyner-Kersey?"

A call for fairness or baiting a loudmouth? Olivia wasn't sure.

The bartender asked Olivia what he could get her.

"Vodka and tonic. Anything but Absolut."

"Anything but? That's a new one."

"They spend that much on ads, how much can be left for the product?"

The bartender seemed to like this. When he set her drink in front of her she asked him if there'd been anything on the news about a doctor getting killed.

"Sure was," Kraft butted in. "A real shootemupski over in Woodside. Broad daylight, what they call a drive-by. Bang, bang and they're outta there. And guess what? No one got the plate number. Surprise, surprise."

The back of Olivia's neck prickled. Kraft's racist diatribe had been inspired by the attack on Griscom. "He was in Woodside?"

"Hafta wonder, huh. They had this big old colored girl on. The doctor was her friend, she said."

"More like a friend of the neighborhood," the painter corrected.

Kraft's laugh showed what he thought of this theory. "They kept saying what a brilliant scientist he was. All those brains, why don't he have the sense to stay outta Woodside?"

"Wait," said Olivia. "Were they shooting at him or someone else?"

Kraft shrugged. "Who knows?"

"They hit a black guy too," the painter said.

"Means nothing," said Kraft. "They coulda been after the doc and winged the nig by accident. You think these people care what they do? Look how they handle their kids, for chrissake. Little kids eight, nine years old selling crack and smoking it—they're animals! What's a famous scientist to a buncha animals? I mean, we're talking war zone! Wall the whole place up, I say. Finish themselves off quicker that way." He raised his empty beer glass. "Give me another. The lady too."

Pretending she hadn't heard, Olivia dropped money on the bar and slid off her stool. Some things are worse than an empty house.

She went straight to her desk. Get some work done, distract herself from the shock and horror.

No dice. Focusing on the Hamrick's fugitive painter was beyond her. Even the pleasure she usually took in her office—the apple green walls, the art deco Chinese rug, Stickley chairs and other thirties stuff she'd lovingly and cheaply collected before their revival—seemed empty.

She slumped disconsolate, tired to the bone. The weekend was coming up, and with it, her turn to visit Philip at Arlington House, the nursing home she'd picked because it was kindly, clean, and near a subway stop. She and Philip's parents alternated weekends. The period when all three had gathered together at Philip's bedside had ended conclusively about a year ago, the day they'd settled Philip's transfer from Mass. General to the nursing home. They had adjourned to the lounge of the nearby Holiday Inn for what Flip, Philip's father, called white bullets—vodka on the rocks. It may have been too long since lunch, their stomachs vulnerably empty. And of course they were shaken by the implications of the transfer, from healing to custodial care. Whatever the reason, in the middle of the aimless chatter that occupied their second round of white bullets, the terrible buried question had burst loose: *Why wasn't it you?* Not in words so succinct, of course, but near enough and clear enough. And it had been additionally clear that by "you," Olivia had meant Flip, Sally had meant Olivia, and Flip had meant Sally. All three knew themselves guilty, all three knew themselves maimed. The silence lengthened until Sally, in her committeewoman voice, suggested they start alternating their visits "in lieu of darling Pip's move." Flip, for once, didn't correct his wife's usage.

But the visit to Philip wasn't what was making her tired. Next week Abbott and Ryland would be home, wanting Olivia to be mom. She would try, go through the motions. Cook things. Do what she could to moderate their ragging and bickering. And she'd remind them of their filial duty to visit Arlington House. Abbott, once again, would flatly refuse to go and flatly refuse to discuss his reasons. Ryland, once again, would pay his father one grudging and insultingly brief visit. Then, before Abbott left for his fishery job in Alaska and Ryland for his junior counselor job in Maine, the brothers would have a knock-down, drag-out fistfight, a raw-knuckled spate of chaos and havoc that would make mockery of all their mother's efforts, all her conscientious trying.

I can't, she despaired. Can't be a good mom. Can't put out because nothing's coming in.

She hadn't felt love for Jon Griscom, only lust. But lust, too, offers bright sprigs of hope and future. Snatched away, it leaves an abyss.

Bleak grief doubled her over. Hugging herself, she sank cross-legged to the floor and wept.

Later, empty of tears if not entirely calm, she went out to buy groceries. Trudging back up the hill, she wondered if Dee were home yet.

She listened outside his door. Dee's friends, as a rule, required more energy than she had right now. Hearing no talk, she knocked.

"Uh-oh," he said when she took off her sunglasses.

"Vodka, thanks," she said.

"Tonic?"

"On the rocks."

"Is it Philip?"

"No more than usual. Vodka, please."

She fell into one of Dee's leather armchairs—he'd bought them from a bankrupt health club—and lifted her feet onto its ottoman. The room had seating for four only, each chair with some form of footrest. It was Dee's conviction that five was a noisy crowd and that blood pooling in the feet starved the brain's wit center. How nice this leather smelled. How sweet to shut your eyes, slide low in its cool smoothness.

"Lime?" Dee had a tray, the lime right there.

"Just plain." A white bullet.

Dee pursed his lips. Unadorned booze, in his book, was one of the ten signs of alcoholism. Rather ostentatiously, he poured himself a Dos Equis with a nice high head.

Olivia drank, felt the bullet hit its mark, drank again. "You been listening to the news, Dee?"

He hadn't, so she told him what had met her in Cambridge and the little more she'd learned since from the radio. "To me," she then said, "the worst is that no one knows whether he was killed on purpose or because he was in the wrong place at the wrong time. That's the operative phrase. I must have heard it twenty times by now. If I were Jane I'd be out of my mind. At least with Philip I *knew.* I didn't have to wonder what he'd done to incur a hit man."

"What could he have done? Griscom, I mean."

"Drugs, I guess. You have to suspect drugs for everything these days. And doctors have such easy access to them."

"Was that on the news?"

"No. No one mentioned drugs in The Sevens, either. At The Sevens, we discussed racial inequality." After explaining Kraft's theory, she offered a confession. "Philip and I used to lap that stuff up."

"You did? *Philip* did?"

"Maybe it was milder then. I hope so. We treated it like theatre. How come you gave Philip the benefit of your doubt? Instead of me?"

"Oh, you know. Lingering regard for the hero of my impressionable youth. Besides, Philip always stuck a tint of rose in his specs. You're tougher. More willing to take it in straight shots."

"Speaking of which." She raised her empty glass.

"Help yourself."

This was a refusal to assist her downward plunge into alcoholism. Dee had his standards.

"I'm not so tough," she said when she returned from the kitchen with her fresh drink. "I had to run away from Kraft."

"Tougher than Philip isn't necessarily tough enough."

"I see."

"You've yet to concede, for instance, that humankind is an evolutionary error. A warped monkey."

Olivia used to think Dee said things like this because he would never have children. Now she wasn't so sure.

"Abbott and Ryland will be home next week," she said, not entirely changing the subject. "How am I going to keep them from tearing each other to pieces?"

"How did your mother keep you and your brothers from tearing yourselves to pieces?"

"She didn't. John beat me up and I beat James up. By the time James got big enough to overcome our age difference I was big enough to use psychological warfare. But there's no comparison. My brothers and I *had* to fight. It was our sole means of self-expression. I've told you the house motto, haven't I? 'If you can't say something nice, don't say anything at all.' Jesus! I mean, repression came ahead of food and drink. Ahead of *oxygen*. Whereas Philip and I, in *marked* contrast, have been excellent parents. We wouldn't repress if our mouths were full of it. Ryland and Abbott have no *cause* to fight."

"We've had this discussion before, you know."

Of course they had. How else to exorcise the muted, penny-pinching household she'd grown up in, to probe puzzles still unsolved. Had her father, with two children under three, reenlisted for Korea because another baby, poor old posthumous James, was on the way? And had he been an early, inglorious casualty because his life no longer interested him? Olivia's mother, repressively smoking the three packs a day that eventually killed her, had refused any discussion, and now there was no one left to ask.

"Sorry to bore you," Olivia said to Dee. A lie. What were friends for?

"I'm hardly bored, just noting that it's a rerun. You insist that your sons open themselves to cozy, cuddly, family feelings they simply can't risk right now. Not with Philip gone and you—don't ask! The last thing they want is to start thinking closely about *you*."

Olivia sighed. "You're right. We've had this conversation before."

"And, as before, you deny reality. The essential and total randiness of teenaged boys—"

"I deny nothing of the kind. Philip—"

"Don't interrupt. Your sons, I was saying, may very well assume their young and attractive mother is similarly awash in incessant and disobedient randiness. What, they must wonder, does she *do* about it? What will prevent her, untethered and unserviced as she is, from falling without warning into its powerful grip? Whereupon . . . but here their imagination fails them. Aghast, the filial heart slams shut, the portcullis drops on *all* feelings—at least as long as you're around, rubbing their noses in your aforementioned youth and attractiveness. But of course they're too young and normal to stifle their feelings entirely. Eventually they blow. Have a fight."

"I see."

Dee gave her a close look. "Oh, go ahead. Call me a flaming gynophobe."

"Huh?"

51

"I concocted this whole scenario because women terrify me, mothers worst of all."

"A low thrust. I won't dignify it by argument."

"Just checking. Kind of thing we minorities need to do from time to time. You want to help Abbott and Ryland? Lay off on making them visit Philip. Don't even mention it. They mention it, make sure they understand it's their choice to go or stay away, not yours. And if you can, lay off on the rest. No dinner with Sally and Pip, no gallant little mom coaxing the boys to the fireside for three-handed bridge."

"The fireside? It's summer, Dee."

His shrug was very Latin.

Olivia drank, pondered. "Got it," she then said. "Thanks, amigo."

"De nada. Did you notice I made black beans? Those Cuban ones you like?"

"Thanks again. I'd love to."

"One last word of wisdom? If it really was your mother's fault you and your brothers fought all the time, she may have done you a favor. Rotten world like this, a woman should know how to use her fists."

6

Jonathan Griscom's funeral had been private, family only. Everyone else, from grieving colleagues to star-struck strangers, would have to wait for the following week, when a service would be held at Harvard's Memorial Chapel.

Meantime, extra details of police spread across Woodside, interrogating and ransacking house-to-house. For the uniforms, nasty work; for residents, the baleful insult of invaded privacy. Some householders, turning their rage inward, suffered humiliations that went very deep, all the way back to slavery. Others, young men for the most part, fought back by taunting the invaders, throwing rocks, bottles, and bricks. Squad cars left unguarded were speedily torched; retaliation left broken heads and stomped kidneys. Night after night the frantic wail of sirens—fire, ambulance, police—rent the stifling air.

For all its thoroughness, the search led nowhere. Having nothing concrete to report, the media fell back on Woodside's reaction to the invasion. "This the U.S.A. or Nazi Germany?" "They tore my whole place up and for what? Gunman hiding his piece in my chifforobe?" Older residents took particular offense at the reiteration that Griscom had been in the wrong place at the wrong time.

"You telling me a man of goodness and peace ain't *allowed* on Wardell Street? Why ain't you saying no *dealers* allowed?"

There was, in addition to the type of weapon fired (a dirt-common MAC-11 assault pistol) only one other piece of hard news. It involved Jamal Sutton, the other victim in the shooting.

After being treated at Boston City Hospital, Jamal had been taken to the police station to give his statement and endure some questioning. Told to stay available in the extremely likely event that he'd be wanted for more questioning, he had arrived back on Wardell Street just before six and was observed by several people, including a police officer, entering the three-decker where he had his apartment. A little later, Cyrus Grier was seen going into this building and, shortly after, leaving. Around sunset, Gloria and Teneer, Jamal's hookers, had walked around from the apartment they shared a few blocks away. They, too, had stayed only briefly and were seen leaving without the paper bags they'd carried in.

Two days passed before Jamal's upstairs neighbor decided that the unbroken silence below, nothing from Jamal's massive sound system, not so much as a toilet flushing, was strange. Was he lying down there dead? Had the gunmen slipped in to finish the job, cut his throat in the night? The neighbor called 911.

The police kicked in the flimsy, hollow-core door to find Jamal gone. Half the hangers in his closet were empty, and so were his bureau drawers. The bathroom, too, showed signs of packing—no toothbrush, deodorant, or shaving gear. Burglary was unlikely because the stereo and TV hadn't been touched. Jamal's open, screenless back window was only a five-foot drop to a rat-infested alley that ran the length of the block. Despite long service as a neighborhood dump, this alley, at night, was passable by someone seriously motivated to flee unseen.

Once again, the police questioned Cyrus Grier. Had Jamal been there to receive his visit? "Well sure. Lying on his bed, but doing pretty good." What had prompted Cyrus's call? "Just friendly. I knowed that boy a long time now. Me and his mama used to keep company." Had Cyrus laid eyes on Jamal since that visit? "No I ain't, now you mention it." So then, being a family friend and all, wasn't he worried? "Pssssh. Wasn't nothing but a biddy little hole in his leg. Sides, his car sitting right there and all." Did Cyrus have any idea why Jamal might have left town? "Morn likely he scared. You take a bullet, ain't you scared too?"

If a man with a leg wound chooses to hoof it instead of driving away in his car, that man probably wants time to hide himself well before anyone notices he's gone. Gloria and Teneer were questioned closely on this point. Each woman said much the same thing. Jamal had telephoned to demand beer and food. "We carried him some ribs and a nice chicken," Gloria amplified. "He say he don't wanna see our ugly faces no more—not till he up and walking." Neither woman had been surprised by this rough dismissal. "Jamal ain't never been a man to *do* for," explained Teneer.

Again, though, the police work produced no results. No witnesses or informants were inspired to come forth. No motive for the shooting emerged, and, still, no certainty which man had been the intended victim. The idea began to circulate that there had been no designated target. The purpose of the shooting, this theory ran, was to intimidate, to halt, for instance, Wardell Street's complaints to the police about the drug trade.

If so, the warning was working. Calls to the Drop-a-Dime hotline, reporting drug activity, were way down. Reporters couldn't pry loose anything on the subject of drugs or crime in general, including, of course, the shooting. Only on the subject of police brutality and the trashing of civil liberties was there comment, a roar of protest both within and without the beleaguered neighborhood. Alan Dershowitz made his statement. So did the Civil Liberties Union.

Finally the search ran out of houses and stopped. The story's next development was given minor play: Arnette Murfin ended the one-woman rent strike that had first attracted the Nobelist to the neighborhood. An alarm company had showed up to wire her house. "They give us a good strong system," Arnette told reporters, "heat and smoke both. And they got work orders for the rest of Wardell Street too." The reporters asked the installer, an independent contractor, who had hired him. The installer gave them the name of the realty trust that was the owner of record. Only one reporter tried to find out exactly who had ordered the fire alarms and why. She got nowhere, the realty trust's most concrete manifestation being, apparently, an answering service.

Several journalist forays covered the story itself. What was it about this particular murder that continued to grip the public's attention? One emerging view was that Bostonians, consciously or not, consider brainpower no less central to their sense of hometown identity than the Red Sox, the Celtics, crazy drivers, Irish pols, Durgin-Park, Filene's Basement, and the swan boats. And why shouldn't they? Between MIT and Harvard, the Boston area, over the years, had claimed a lion's share of Nobelists. Winners of the other big prizes—MacArthur, Wolf, Pulitzer—were equally thick on the ground.

But there was more to it than that, the thumb-suckers asserted. The shooting had shaken everyone, even citizens normally wary of pointy heads and ivory towers. The doctor, it must be remembered, was famous not only for his intellect but also for his altruism, his moral goodness, his rigorous attention to environmental and social issues. The rest of us, wanting the best for our children, tell them to study hard and be good. The message of that afternoon in Woodside was a grim one indeed: head, heart, and conscience, however perfected, are no defense against savagery. If a giant like Griscom can be brought down so easily by the forces of darkness, what hope is there for common folk?

The mayor's anguish had a special twist. Having surmounted the prejudices of his Irish townie roots, he had long crusaded in behalf of black Boston. He and Griscom had met several times; he had used Griscom's name to add clout to some of his interracial initiatives. How could such a man have loosed his police on the women and children of Woodside?

An astute columnist tried to explain. "This is vengeance—the angry reaction of a man who has striven to love his neighbor and had it thrown back in his face. Hell, we're told, hath no fury like a lover scorned. Especially one who has managed to love despite growing up amid racial views that would not distress an Afrikaner on the far right."

The mayor, of course, would attend the memorial service. So would the governor and a raft of senators and congressmen, national as well as state. With all the celebrities expected, Harvard had enlisted extra police for security. These would be Cambridge police. Boston, deep in the hole for the overtime required to toss Woodside, would be spared at least this.

Abbott Chapman came home from school Wednesday night; Ryland would not arrive until Friday. Thursday, the day of the memorial service, Abbott rose early and Olivia late. Mother and son met at the breakfast table, which was unusual. On vacation, both boys were famous sack hounds, known to sleep until one or two in the afternoon. "Glands," Philip had explained with the tranquil authority of one who'd been there. "It passes."

Had the gland phase, Olivia wondered, passed for Abbott? Certainly he looked different. His hair had been cut in a version of Dee's Latino Trendo that—Olivia wouldn't have predicted it—was extremely becoming. He'd grown an inch or more. His jaw, neck, and shoulders were heavier, stronger looking. Even unshaven—he must need to shave every day now—he was still too young to seem a man. Still, boyhood, physically anyway, was clearly over. And another change—he'd been downright chatty all through their juice and Raisin Bran, alertly curious about the famous man's murder.

Olivia told him what she knew, admitting it wasn't much. "Dr. Jonny—that's what people called him—expected to be liked," she concluded. "I found myself going along quite happily. He was . . . compelling. Full of life. Jane Griscom's different—one of those good hearts you admire without much inclination to take things further."

Olivia was dressed for the memorial service. Her mother-in-law would be picking her up in a half hour, a plan Sally had sprung late last night.

Abbott was frowning. "If they're not really friends, how come you're going to this service?"

"Your grandmother's orders. She and Gramps were old friends of Dr. Jonny's. She got herself in trouble by doing her manners— telling Jane Griscom to please call on her if there was anything she could help with."

"Anything, darling," mimicked Abbott in falsetto, "anything at *all.*"

"Turns out Jane had just the job for her. She's to stand by to offer a special welcome to Arnette Murfin—the woman Dr. Jonny was visiting—and anyone else who shows up from Woodside."

"Grammy's dealing with *Woodside?*"

Olivia giggled. "See why she roped me in?"

"Wild. Maybe I'll come too."

Oops, Olivia thought, time to back off, behave, be a proper model. "It's funny to think of Grammy getting hoisted. But the rest isn't funny. Not really."

"No, Mother, it's not. And you really didn't have to say so, either."

"Sorry."

"You do that all the time."

"What?"

"Correct me. Treat me like a little kid."

"Sorry again."

Olivia had made orange walnut muffins, Abbott's favorite. His shoulders hunched, his scowling face loutishly close to his plate, he munched in unnoticing, unforgiving silence.

At length Olivia stood, smoothing the skirt of her black dress. "Now that the skylight's covered," she said, "I've been having my coffee upstairs."

Abbott said nothing.

Remembering Dee's advice, Olivia left him to his grievances and climbed the spiral staircase alone.

Seconds later she was back inside, rubbing the goose bumps on her bare arms. It was football weather, much too cold and windy for short sleeves. She'd have to change, but to what? She'd just taken her active winter wardrobe to the cleaner. There'd be nothing warm in her closet except clothes that didn't fit.

Muttering against the iron rule that decorators must at all times appear infallibly chic, Olivia tried on and rejected a half-dozen outfits before concluding that her gray suit would have to do. Wool crepe wasn't heavy enough to cause trouble if the wind dropped and the day turned warm, and the skirt had belt loops. She'd just bunch the extra waistband at her back, no one the wiser.

She was rummaging through her belts when the doorbell rang. Sally, right on time.

"Can you get that?" she called to Abbott. "I need three more minutes."

"Should I run down and do my *manners?*"

"Please," she said, pretending his barb wasn't for her as well as his grandmother and every other smooth, lying, go-along-to-get-along adult in the known universe. For good measure, his sneakers pounded down the staircase, punishing the innocent carpet.

The way she found him, bent to the open window of Sally's car, Olivia was unable to see his expression. But there was no misunderstanding Sally's smile as they pulled away from the curb. "I do believe that grandson of mine is growing up," she said.

Better an oblique peace offering, thought Olivia, than none at all.

* * *

Handsome in her navy blue suit and matching straw skimmer, Sally gave Harvard Yard an encompassing salute. "Wonderful, isn't it? All this dear old brick? And these divine elms?"

Olivia murmured agreement, but her mind was still on the conversation they'd had on the way over. Sally, in characteristic reversal, was claiming perfect ease in regard to the Woodside contingent. Irritated, Olivia said she wished she'd known earlier, in which case she'd have stayed home.

Sally reared back in alarm. "You weren't planning to come? Why on earth not? Jane's still got her furniture and so forth, doesn't she? Nothing's changed on that score, has it? Well then. Seems to me you'd want to keep your hand in."

"Isn't that a bit crass?" Olivia asked.

"What do you mean?"

"Going to a memorial service for profit."

"Oh for heaven's sake, Olivia. Wait till you've gone to as many as Flip and I. If business friends didn't rally round, the churches would be half empty."

Olivia had to ask. "Why didn't Flip come today?"

"Poor lamb, he's got wall-to-wall meetings all day long. Anyway, just between you and I, he and Jonny pretty much drifted apart after the divorce. Our sympathies were with Isabel, of course, but you don't want to hear all that ancient history, do you?"

"Yes."

"Yes what?"

"Yes, I'd like to hear about Isabel." And anything else, Olivia could add, you'd rather not discuss. Enough of this vanilla chitter-chatter. Dish me some dirt!

"This is hardly the time or place, darling."

Sally's most laserlike reproof. "Fine," Olivia said. "We can get back to it later."

7

At Memorial Chapel, Olivia and Sally cut through the jostling minicams and identified themselves to an usher, a man subsequently identified by Sally as a "top cardiologist." Learning from him that no one from Woodside had arrived yet, the Chapmans settled into their designated pew.

The chapel was filling rapidly, pinstripes and academic tweeds mixed with saris, turbans, and kufi hats. The conversational hum competed with the organ, which was offering "Michael, Row the Boat Ashore." According to the nicely printed program, this was part of a collection of folk songs. There would be two talks, separated by the Charles River Chorus singing the "Libera me" from Fauré's *Requiem*, Benjamin Griscom conducting. At conclusion, the congregation would sing "Swing Low, Sweet Chariot." Olivia, these days, hadn't much enthusiasm for folk songs, but she loved the Fauré, which she'd sung in college.

"Was Jonny religious?" she asked Sally.

"I really don't know, darling."

Reproof again. Nice people don't talk about religion? "I asked because this," she pointed to the Fauré selection, "is about eternal fire and divine judgment."

Looking pained, Sally found distraction. "There's Ben, down there on the left. My *word* but he looks like his father. That woman he's kissing . . . good heavens, it's Isabel. His mother. She's so blond I didn't recognize her. But I don't see Clayton."

Olivia asked who Clayton was.

"Clayton Hollingshead. Isabel's husband."

The incestuous nature of her in-laws' social set used to shock Olivia, but repeated exposure had hardened her. Now she found it funny, especially Sally's bland assumption that a current husband would rally round to mourn a former. "Maybe Clayton's running late."

"He might not come at all. He hasn't been well, you know. For quite some time now."

"And Jonny's second wife? Have you spotted her yet?"

Sally gave her daughter-in-law a look. "Bonita is dead. She was hit by a subway train."

"How awful. An accident?"

"That's what they called it. She was full of some kind of pills, so who knows. A thoroughly unhappy young woman."

"Are some of the kids hers?"

"Gordon and Anne. Gordon's all right—he has his food store—but Anne, from what one hears, still isn't over it. We never *knew* Bonita, you know. It's funny—Flip took one look and predicted she'd never stay the course. When she died everyone said how tragic, but the fact of the matter is that she broke up a perfectly happy home and then discovered Jonny was more fun to chase than to live with."

"Difficult, was he?"

"I didn't say that. But he'd won the Nobel by then, and famous people, well, you know."

"And Jane? When did she come into the picture?"

"Just in time. We were all quite worried. Chess—she's the eldest—went so far as to ask her father's old friends to stop him from turning into a complete playboy. Up until then Jonny could do no wrong in her eyes. She worshipped the ground he walked on. Well. He *was* a charmer. I'm sure you saw that yourself."

"Oh yes." Olivia thought of a snake charmer piping his tune, confident she'd rise from her basket and dance.

Sally smiled as if at some coquettish memory of her own.

Tip O'Neill came lumbering down the aisle, his fine head of hair looking Barbie-doll fake. He was seated next to the mayors of Cambridge and Boston. Not all the notables were in politics. Olivia had spotted numerous academic biggies—John Kenneth Galbraith, Alan Dershowitz, Derek and Sissela Bok. No one from the arts, though. Curious. You'd expect the Bob Geldoff types at least.

The air was suddenly dense with scent—one of those tobacco-tinged perfumes that always gave Olivia back her smoking days, the delicious pungency of a new pack of Luckies. A large, black woman in tight, black satin and matching turban stood at their pew. "Mrs. Murfin," the usher said.

Arnette Murfin settled herself next to Olivia. Sally leaned past Olivia to smile and make introductions. Arnette acknowledged the Chapmans with an agreeable murmur but no answering smile. Olivia felt her own smile turn over-wide, excessively toothy. The organ swelled, then abruptly ceased. So did the conversational hum. The first eulogist, Marshall Kohler, was at the podium.

Dr. Kohler, now at Stanford, began by telling them, in a graceful, self-effacing way, that he had worked under Griscom to isolate and code the genetically instigated Schiller's leukemia virus. Not long after those exciting days, he said, he had accepted his Stanford post, a move that had been professionally inescapable and personally excruciating, "as hard on Jonny, he gave me ample reason to believe, as it was for myself." Hardly a single week since then had passed without significant communication between him and his old boss. "If E-mail didn't exist," he added in a jocose aside, "our phone bills would have mandated its invention."

Kohler then reached the meat of his remarks, a description of the day the great man learned he had been awarded the Nobel.

"Many people brought champagne to the lab along with their congratulations. I'm sure you won't be surprised to hear that Jonny poured with a generous hand to one and all, himself included. I doubt that those old walls had ever witnessed so much laughter, such an outpouring of warmth and affection. Late in the day—it was dark outside, I remember—the phone rang for what seemed like the millionth time. Jonny happened to be standing next to it, so he picked it up. After he'd listened for a while, tears started rolling down his face. When he hung up, he was so overcome he couldn't speak. He left soon afterwards, and I didn't learn until the next day that the caller had been a man whose first child had died from Schiller's. His wife since that tragic time had borne two more children, healthy, beautiful children, with donor sperm. Jonny had broken down because here, in the midst of triumph, was what had driven his long hours of research—the terrible poignancy of this disease, its cruelly rapid onset and certain fatality.

"Since then, as most of you know, screening techniques have been perfected and their costs lowered. Schiller's leukemia has become rare. A moment ago I called it a cruel disease. It is also cruel, incomprehensibly cruel, that Jonny, this rare scientist and rare human being we were privileged to know, has been taken from us. We will miss him sorely. But we should not, I think, be so sad that we fail to remember how joyously he *gave*—to his family, his many, many friends, his colleagues, and the countless beneficiaries of his science."

Kohler sat down. The Charles River Chorus filed forward and formed three rows across the transept. Benjamin Griscom strode to his place. Oddly, he faced the audience rather than his singers. For one weird instant, Olivia wondered if he wanted to emphasize his physical resemblance to the dead man. But then he began to sing, with great beauty and conviction, the baritone solo that begins the piece. When he turned to direct the chorus, they, too, were impressive, their tone focused, their dynamics clean and moving.

Olivia gave herself to the music, but when it was over and the second eulogist was approaching the podium, she became thought-ful. Choruses, especially amateur ones, won't sing as well as this one had unless the director is fully with them, alert to every nuance of the score, every cue, every place where one or another section might go wrong. Benjamin Griscom, clearly, was a thor-oughgoing professional. But wasn't he also a bereaved son? How had he managed such absolute control over his emotions?

If one of Philip's sons, when the time came, could summon that much aplomb in the face of his father's death, she'd fear for him. And fear to be around him, too.

The woman speaking now was Catherine Alexander, an earnest, clean-cut doctor who was part of Griscom's current research team. She was about Benjamin's age. Her voice, in conspicuous contrast, wobbled occasionally as she read from her prepared pages.

"My first encounter with Jonny was a job interview. I came prepared to talk about the usual, my dissertation and post-doc work. But he had a very different agenda. How, he wanted to know, did I define *good?* I fumbled around, produced some kind of re-sponse. But he had more questions: What do you think is the greatest good? What is truth? A moral act? How do you think you should act?

"I see many of you smiling. You're probably remembering how many times you stayed up half the night with Jonny, talking and arguing and laughing. Maybe you're also remembering the excite-ment of discovering the values you truly believed in, as opposed to those promulgated by mainstream culture.

"I want to talk specifically about something that happened five years ago. It was winter—February tenth, to be exact. On top of the demands of my job and my first child—he was six months old—my husband's company announced a major retrenchment and guess who got one of the first pink slips? My solution to all these problems was to come down with a world-class case of flu. As soon as I could, I dragged myself back to work. Somehow Jonny found out what had happened to us, because he called me into his office and handed me a check. What's this for? I asked, not really looking at it. Whatever you like, he said, but my advice is, hire a sitter and go off alone with your husband. Someplace hot and sunny, for at least a week. But that'll cost a fortune, I said. Life is short, he said, and love is fragile. Then I looked at the check and saw how many zeros were on it. I can't take this from you, I told him. You have to, Cath, he said, didn't you just hear me say that love is fragile?

"We went to Saint Croix and it was perfect. One of the best days was in the rain forest. We were walking around under this huge canopy of giant trees, swinging from vines, having a great old time, when we came upon a tree that had recently fallen. There was a huge hole where it had been standing. A giant patch of blue sky."

Describing the moment, her voice had gone tight, with frequent pauses to swallow back tears. Now she stopped altogether to wipe her eyes and blow her nose. So did many of her listeners, including Sally. Arnette Murfin and Olivia hung cool, Olivia recalling her first visit to Harding Hill, the disciples she'd imagined heaped around at Griscom's feet.

"I'm sorry," Dr. Alexander said. "I was hoping that wouldn't happen." She cleared her throat, gave a sad smile.

"When Jonny fell," she continued, "I thought of that tree. Even though the space it left was so big, my husband and I knew it wouldn't be long before other trees would move in to fill the gap. Jonny leaves a different kind of space. Everyone who knew him and his work will understand why it cannot ever be filled. Dr. Kohler said it was our privilege to have known Jonny. It is also our privilege to understand the extent and permanence of our loss."

She smiled again. "Jane Griscom has asked me to invite you to stand and sing one of Jonny's favorite songs, 'Swing Low, Sweet Chariot.' "

Among the chorus there was confusion. Some started forward as if to lead the singing, others, seeing Ben immobile, stayed put. As the organ finished the introduction, all were back in their places.

Despite this distracting shuffle, the spiritual's nearly universal familiarity had the congregation in full voice by the time they reached Jordan and the band of angels. Olivia was singing a conventional harmony until Arnette Murfin's resonant soprano encouraged experimentation. As if inspired, Arnette, in the final refrain, took off on a soaring descant, her notes bound only, it seemed, by the vault of the nave.

When the spiritual was over, Olivia wanted to embrace the woman. "That was wonderful," she said.

Arnette accepted the praise with a stately nod. "I do love to sing."

People around them, alerted by the music they'd made together, were watching and listening. Hell with them, Olivia thought, I'll say what I want. — "It's like it's still floating around up there," she said, gesturing. "Like some gorgeous silk banner."

Arnette nodded again. "The doctor's boy, he have hisself a fine voice too."

"Excuse me, Mrs. Murfin," Sally said. "Jane Griscom wanted me to tell you she hopes you will come to the house for lunch. We'll be glad to drive you."

"I can't do that," said Arnette. "A neighbor lady's keeping my grandson. She be wondering where I'm at."

"Couldn't you give her a call? Jane especially wanted you to come. No? Sure? All right, fine, I understand. Let's push through this mob, then. You'd like a word with Jane before she leaves, wouldn't you?"

Arnette's consent was regal. I don't think I like you, Olivia thought.

The meeting between the great man's widow and his much-discussed Woodside friend was brief and intense. Jane hardly acknowledged Sally in her eagerness to make contact. "Thank you so much for coming today," she said, grasping both of Arnette's hands. "And thank you for everything you were to my husband."

"Dr. Griscom, he *good,*" Arnette replied. "Jesus call the good to His side."

Jane hung there as if waiting for more. There was no more.

Intervention came from a young woman in a beautifully cut black suit, her blond hair pulled into a smooth chignon. "We really should start for the house, Jane."

"Oh Chess. Have you met Mrs. Murfin? Chess is Jonny's daughter, Mrs. Murfin."

Jane then launched into a major dither with Arnette about lunch. Chess let her talk but kept nudging the two women steadily toward the door.

Outside, Jane accepted the finality of Arnette's refusal by giving her an impulsive hug. The waiting photographers grabbed their reward: thin, pale Jane and large, dark Arnette, the shine of tears and black satin, the ecumenical pathos. The AP man outdid himself; his version appeared in publications all over the world. This meant that Olivia's face, in the near background, also appeared all over the world. She'd been caught just as she'd decided that the least Arnette Murfin could do for Jane was hug the poor pathetic creature *back.*

"No one," Dee assured her, "will notice you."

But of course they would. She knew they would. "Look at my *mouth,*" she wailed. "Where else have you seen a white face with lips curled like that? In Selma, Alabama, that's where. In *Southie,* for God's sake."

Dee dropped into his Father O'Malley routine. "Is it yer Confession yer makin', me child? Are ye callin' yerself a closet racist?"

"It's what I *look* like that's the issue. Not what I *am.*"

Prophetic words, if she only knew it.

8

The Griscom meadow, in the nine days since murder thwarted Olivia's first appraisal visit, had become freckled with bright dandelions. Someone (deft, fastidious Chess?) had thought to pick up the beer cans and other trash.

Olivia and Sally joined the group moving slowly up the walkway and front steps. A pair of uniformed policemen stood on either side of the open door, Cambridge cops with alert eyes. The wind was still gusty, the sky full of fast, puffy clouds. Olivia was glad of her suit jacket.

"There's dear Billy," Sally said, meaning the governor of the state. "Talking to those awful Kennedys. Oh, and there's Michael Dukakis. Isn't it extraordinary to think he ran for president?"

Olivia never discussed politics with her in-laws. "I'm glad to see cops on duty."

"So am I. Obviously Jane's thrown her doors open to every Tom, Dick, and Harry. So easy for someone to pocket one of her aunt's little treasures."

"It was Jane's welfare I was thinking about," Olivia said.

"Why, darling?"

"If no one knows why a husband has been murdered, who's to say the wife is safe?"

"Really, Olivia. So dramatic."

It occurred to Olivia that Sally had yet to comment on the manner of Griscom's death. He might have had a heart attack. "Why do you think he was shot?" she asked, keeping it mild.

"He went where he had no business going and got caught in one of those fights they're always having. Isn't that what everyone thinks?"

"I don't know."

"Well of course I don't *know* either. But it's what I hear on my talk shows."

Sally suffered from insomnia. Between three and five most mornings she popped on her earphones and tuned in to the voice of the people, whose consensus, apparently, was that stray bullets, in Woodside, are no big deal, as routine and predictable as rats and roaches. *Wall the whole place up, finish themselves off quicker that way.*

Inside the door stood Chess Griscom, chief welcomer, and, possibly, backup security. Sally introduced herself and Olivia.

"Mrs. Chapman. Of course! It's so good of you to come. Darn, though—if my mother knew you were going to be here, she'd certainly have made time. Nice to meet you, Lavinia. Sorry, Olivia. Thank you both for coming. Oh! Olivia! You're the one Jane called about the appraisal. Sorry again. My mind's a sieve. You'll find lunch out on the terrace. Gordon—you remember my half brother don't you, Mrs. Chapman?—Gordon's packed these terrific little boxes, everything a hundred percent organic and whole-grain." Smiling to speed them on their way, she turned to the next arrival. "Hello, I'm Chess Griscom, so good of you to come . . ."

Grace under fire, Olivia decided, must be a specialty of the Griscom kids. Musical grace for Ben, social for Chess, culinary for Gordon. And what about Anne, the youngest? What was her specialty? Olivia couldn't wait to find out.

"There's Jane," Sally said, plunging into the crush. Olivia kept close behind. A handful of mourners, The Duke included, stood waiting their turn with the widow; the groups crowding around the Kennedys and the present governor were, Olivia noted, both larger and more aggressive.

The living room had been cleared; sofas, pillows, and hassocks were shoved against the walls. The doors that had led to Aunt Martha's treasures had been pushed wide open, but the treasures themselves were gone. In their place were tables and chairs, people tearing zestfully into Gordon's box lunches.

Olivia stared, not wanting to believe. Someone had snatched her job away from her, beaten her time. Her finder's fee—four percent of hammer, thousands and thousands of dollars—was up in smoke.

Sally waved a slighting hand at the duct tape, the stained carpet. "You'd never know what a lovely room this used to be. Isabel has marvelous taste."

Get a grip on, Olivia told herself. It's only money. *Twenty thousand? Forty?* "It was Isabel's house?"

"Of course. If the decision had been Jonny's, Lord knows where they'd have ended up."

"Probably right here. Jonny stayed on, didn't he?"

"Why, yes, so he did. Funny, I never— Jane darling. Oh Jane."

The two women embraced. Jane then turned to Olivia with a watery smile. "You were there that awful day. I can't tell you how many times I've been just about to call you when something interrupted."

"Of course. I understand completely."

"Chess kept worrying about Aunt Martha's things. Of course she was right to, with only me in the house."

"Please don't trouble yourself about it now."

"I simply didn't know what else to do. This seemed simplest."

"I'm sure you made the right choice."

"Really? You aren't concerned about the glue?"

"Glue?"

"Chess's auction people—Southey's?"

"Sotheby's."

"Why can't I get that name straight? Sotheby's said old glue is so delicate that three moves are as bad as a fire."

"I've heard that too, but surely distance is a factor. Where has it been moved to?"

"Oh dear, I'm not sure. Aunt Martha's people have a Duxbury office, but their warehouse might be someplace else. At any rate, whenever you're ready to look at it, they'll be expecting you."

Olivia clamped her teeth together. Relief, coming fast like this, always made her burst out laughing.

But Jane was frowning. "The trouble is, I've started thinking I don't want everything to go. It's selfish of me, and I hate to think what Jonny would say but Aunt Martha was the last . . . she was my only . . . oh dear."

Tears. Sally offered Kleenex and her open arms. The real thing, Olivia saw. Sally could be maddening, but she was a far cry from Iceface Murfin.

"There now, Olivia," said Sally after they'd left Jane with her next sympathizers. "If I hadn't insisted you come today, Chess would have gotten her sticky little paws right back on that furniture."

"She's something, Chess."

"Isn't she? Ever since she was a tiny girl. Oh thank God."

A waiter had appeared with a tray of Bloody Marys.

The tables on the terrace, set for four or six, had clever little clamps to hold their cloths in place. The wind, even in this protected location, felt chilly. The sandaled feet of two Indian women looked ashy and cold under the gold-bordered hems of their saris.

Gordon Griscom, overseeing his stacks of box lunches, seemed at first glance to be wearing an exotic costume, his conventional dark suit at odds with his burly form and laid-back manner. "These are vegetarian," he said to people as they came up, "and those are chicken." When Sally broke in to remind him who she was and offer her sympathy, he took her hand in both of his and bent over it as if in prayer.

Gordon had a helper, a strong-featured woman with a mop of dark hair. Her immaculate, white chef's coat and long apron gave her, too, a burly form. The way she was looking at Gordon, she had to be nuts about him, head over heels in love.

As if fearing to affront vegetarian sensibilities, Sally pretended she couldn't decide which lunch to choose. "How is the chicken done?"

"Broiled, with a little sesame oil and some almonds for crunch," Gordon's helper said. "It's been a real good seller."

"Seller?" Sally, astonished, touched the clasp of her purse.

"At Leaves* of Life," Gordon said. "Darla invented the recipe. Meet Mrs. Chapman, Darla. She's known me all my life."

"And this is Olivia," said Sally. "Pip's wife."

"We've met. Good to see you again, Olivia." Gordon gave his head a weighty shaking. "Old Pip," he murmured.

"We keep our hopes high," Sally chirped. "That's the main thing, hope."

"Pip was so great," Gordon said. "Never once did he treat me like the little pest I was. I wish I'd stayed in touch with him. He was a real hero to me. Right up there with my dad."

Bullshit, Olivia thought.

Darla moved close, tucked her hand into his.

"I met your father just once," Olivia told Gordon. "I liked him very much. It's easy to see why he'd be your hero."

"Thank you, Olivia." He gave her shoulder a light caress. "Thank you so much for sharing that with me."

Duty was calling. Hungry people, members of Benjamin's chorus among them, were lined up four deep. Food is love, Olivia concluded, watching him hand out boxes. The lunches were Gordon's tribute, to the admiration and love Dr. Jonny apparently had inspired wherever he turned.

Just as Olivia was going to ask Sally if she'd like to try one of the terrace tables, a gray-haired couple came charging up. Old friends at last. Sally must join them, they cried. They'd staked out a nice quiet corner inside—the Rogers, the Mayburys, Paula Channing—yes, *isn't* it a shame, especially when it's been so hot, God knows *what* August will be like, but at least it's not raining, *so* depressing, rain at a memorial service.

Sally turned to Olivia. "Shall we?"

"You go ahead," Olivia said. "I'm happy out here."

"Really darling?"

Buffeted as she'd been by Tom, Dick, and Harry, Sally sorely needed a tribal fix. If Olivia tagged along she'd only dilute its comforting powers. "Really," she said.

You don't have to run, Olivia would love to yell after them. I won't change my mind.

Where to sit, though? The only other solitary was a man at a table for four. He looked old enough to be her father and was either naturally melancholic or unafraid of letting his sorrow show. After a morning of social smiling, either possibility appealed. Also, he looked Jewish. Olivia was predisposed to like Jews, mostly for their own predisposition to stay apart from the white-bread mainstream. Dee, another kind of outsider, had accused her of rabid pro-Semitism.

The bottle of wine standing on his table had been scarcely touched. "Are you saving these places?" she asked.

He shook his head, said, "Sit, sit," shooing her toward a chair with an impatient gesture. Don't fuss, his grimace said, you're entitled.

Entitled. Entitled because human. A concept alien to the house Olivia had grown up in, where everything was muddled by God, goodness, and the dour Methodism Marion Ryland had turned to when her husband re-enlisted.

In Marion's house, you were God's child, worthy and good in His eyes—providing you behaved. Olivia and her brothers often misbehaved, proving themselves neither worthy nor good. Worse, goodness, unlike badness, was slippery. You could not, for instance, judge yourself good enough and leave it at that. You had to keep striving toward a finer, purer, more generous, and selfless goodness. You couldn't be perfect, of course. Only God was perfect. But neither could you slack off. You had to keep trying and praying to do better. If that didn't work, it was because you weren't trying and praying hard enough.

"Entitled," against this murk, was a blast of alpine air. Olivia introduced herself.

"The appraiser. I saw you before, in the chapel. Morton Thaler."

"Nice to meet you. How's the food?"

"Not bad. Gordon's girl is quite a cook. Have some wine."

She passed her glass and Thaler poured briefly. "Splash at a time, keep it cold," he explained.

Olivia thanked him and ate some of Darla's delicious chicken. "Have you known the Griscoms long?"

"You could say that. I've known Jonny since we were boys at Boston Latin. I was two years ahead, so we didn't really get together until Harvard. Do you like coincidences? All right, I'll give you one. My sophomore year, when I first got to Leverett House, the senior who lived next door took charge of me. Showed me the ropes. By the time I was a senior I had his old room, and who do you think they assigned to my old room next door?"

"Whereupon you took charge of him?"

Thaler gave her a look. "You didn't know him too well, huh?"

"No."

"The only person who ever took charge of Jonny was Jonny. Isabel tried and look where it got her."

"Where?"

"Dumped."

"I see." And houseless besides. Jonny must have had an extremely good lawyer.

"In some ways he was a very demanding man. Demanding sounds bad, but, my own experience, he knew what he wanted and how to get it. One thing I can tell you, we never had a fight. Twenty-seven years I knew him, and never once did we fight." Thaler indulged in a brief laugh. "I'd only lose, so why bother?"

"You saw a lot of each other? After Harvard?"

"I'm his lawyer. That's the correct tense, not a slip of the tongue. I had some heart trouble a few years ago and had to cut way back on my client list. But Jonny I kept."

Makes sense, Olivia thought. Lawyers protect property. Griscom, unfettered by goods and chattels, wouldn't make many demands on a man trying to cut his work load. She wanted to ask if he'd masterminded the divorce but didn't dare. "Are you involved in setting up the foundation?"

"And how. Paper work you wouldn't believe."

"Yo Mortsie."

"Annie! How's my Annie? Sit with us. You know Olivia Chapman? Sit, Annie. Did you eat?"

Eating, Olivia couldn't help thinking, might be Anne Griscom's specialty. She was, in the current phrase, a woman of size. She had a pretty, if sulky, face and the same thick, curly hair as her brother Gordon. Her black dress was a tight, elongated tee that emphasized the mass of her hips and breasts.

She sat down, nodded in response to Olivia's words of sympathy and poured herself a brimming glass of wine, splashing some on the tablecloth.

"You need a lunch, Annie. Sit tight and I'll get you one."

"I'm not hungry. Especially for Gordon's slop."

"The chicken was damn good. Olivia? You liked the chicken?"

"Loved it," said Olivia.

Anne turned to her in sudden recognition. *"You're* the one. Boy, is Chess pissed!"

"Why?"

"What do you mean, 'why?' You aced her on Jane's auction. Laid a big, itchy hair smack across her ass. I'm delighted to meet you, thrilled. Specially after I'd gone and nailed you for one of Dad's popsicles."

The pouches under Thaler's eyes sagged and deepened. Anne's specialty, obviously, was brattiness.

"One of Dad's *many* popsicles," Anne amplified. She threw back her head, groaned loudly. "Lordy me, what a day. One more speech shoveling it on like that and we'd all need hip boots. And what about the mix-up at the end there, Ben's poor little songbirds milling around, no idea what to do. You can't blame them. It's an all-time historic first, Benjamin Griscom, Conductor, passing up an opportunity to conduct." She laughed. *"Zero de Conduite."*

"Annie, Annie."

"Don't scold, Mortsie. I'm only recounting the witness of my eyeballs. Lawyers're deeply into eyewitness truth, aren't they? And don't tell me you haven't noticed Ben and the sainted Barb didn't make lunch. OK, forget those bores. What I really want to know is, when can I start spending like an heiress?"

"Soon. I still have to pull some figures together."

"Oh dear. Dad left a mess. Bad Dad. Come on, Morts. Give your blood pressure a break and admit the terrible truth. Despite your endless labors on Dad's behalf, he—wait, let me get this right—*he left his affairs in a dreadful muddle."*

Anne's imitation of a horrorstruck patrician was so exact Olivia almost burst out laughing. But Thaler was looking wounded, and he was too nice to mock. Also, her role as appraiser put her firmly on the side of rectitude, in league not with the family brat but the trusted family counselor.

"Aw, Morts. I didn't mean to upset you. It wasn't *your* fault. Dad was a great man. A giant tree! Giant trees don't futz around with details. I just hope his greatness and giantness—giganticness?—didn't keep him from noticing how much you did for him. And maybe even thanking you every decade or so."

If this was bait, Thaler passed it up. "Tell me, Annie, how's the new job?"

"Ex."

"I thought you liked it there."

"What's to like? My sexist-pig boss? My dipshit salary? My crummy little vacation? Think about it, Mortsie. They quote-unquote *give* you two weeks, two days of which are weekend and yours anyway. Ten big days out of three hundred and sixty four. What's wrong with this country? In France, even street cleaners get an entire month, plus *years* of maternity leave, plus housing allowances, plus, plus, plus. Universal hospitalization, you name it. Two weeks vacation is a joke. A total fraud. Like the fifty-minute shrinkage hour."

"Or the ten-speed bicycle," Olivia said. She'd finished her lunch, helped Anne finish the wine, and been a listener long enough. "Only eight are operational."

"Is that right?" said Thaler. "I never knew that. My last bike was a one-speed. For my paper route."

Anne liking none of this, Olivia felt impelled to give her a tweak. "Did the two of you admire the Fauré as much as I did? I thought your brother was superb, Anne."

"He's only a half brother."

"Latin, wasn't it?" said Thaler. "I caught a few words. *Morte aeterna;* eternal death. *Judicare* something *per ignem.* Judgment by fire?"

"Exactly," said Olivia. "Final reckonings, fear and dread. Heaven and earth shaking on the Day of Judgment. And, of course, a prayer for deliverance—*libera me, Domine;* free me, Lord."

"I hate stuff like that," said Anne.

"Was your father religious?" No reason not to fly this winner by again.

"Him? Never. Did you say punishment?"

"Fauré did."

"Whatever. Ben and Dad haven't talked for years, you know. No one'll tell me why. Mortsie won't, will you, Mortsie?"

"I know nothing about it."

"Sure, sure. But look how Ben had the last word. Called punishment down on bad Dad's head, right in front of everybody. Huh. Little Ben. Amazing he had the balls. Unless . . . Mortsie! Did Dad cut Ben out of his will?"

"Don't ask me things like that, Annie. You know better."

"Because if he did . . . Oh my God. This is fantastic! *Who's got the last laugh now?*"

Anne wasn't bad with a tune either. Must be genetic, Olivia thought.

9

For her younger son's homecoming dinner Friday night, Olivia had bought the loin lamb chops he relished (madness, trying to fill a growing boy at three dollars a pop) and made a special curried couscous. When Ryland hadn't shown by nine, she and Abbott sat down without him. In an atmosphere of vexed tension they ate, cleared, did the dishes. Abbott then escaped to the relief of his own room.

Alone, Olivia oscillated wildly between fear and anger. Ryland had been born three weeks overdue and run late ever since, odd man out in a family infallibly punctual. The three normal Chapmans would collect in the family car, all set to leave the ski slopes. They'd be shivering because they'd worked up a sweat and needed hot showers, but where was Ryland? "Why don't we just take off?" Abbott at length would say. "Let the fucker find his own way home." "Language," Philip would chide, no heart in it. "We can't," Olivia would say, because Ry could be up there on the mountain with a broken leg, and then what?

Olivia and Philip continually lost perspective. Of course they did. That's it, they'd fume. Never again, they'd swear. Family fun, solidarity, is a doomed dream.

Hope springs eternal, though, and sooner or later yet another family outing would be planned. How many beginnings of movies, first acts of plays, had Ryland caused them to miss? How many times had he wandered off in museums, nowhere to be found at the time they'd all agreed to leave? Watches were synchronized, promises exacted, penalties well advertised in advance, all to no avail. One January day, he arrived at the airport fifteen minutes late, four APEX tickets to St. Bart's down the drain if not for a chance flight delay. Because you couldn't go off and leave the fucker to fend for himself. The fucker was only ten, twelve, fourteen. Leave a kid that young alone, you'd drive yourself crazy worrying.

They consulted a psychologist, learned about passive-aggressive behavior. The psychologist said that Ryland, as he matured, would probably wise up. "Don't quit on him. Keep expecting him to do better, and try to help him find more appropriate ways of dealing with his anger."

Philip's eyebrows climbed. "What's he got to be so angry about?"

"Not being as smart as Abbott," Olivia said.

"Or life in general," the psychologist said. "Some kids take it harder than others. It's good that he has confidence in you, that he trusts you to act responsibly even if he can't or won't. Otherwise, he'd never risk testing you the way he does."

This year, finally, some improvement. Ryland had begun to wear his watch more consistently, carry phone change and use it if he couldn't be on time. In a voice childlike with discovery, he had revealed to Olivia the amazing truth that calling ahead saves trouble. "And not just for other people, Mom. For yourself, too."

The upshot of this improvement? Olivia, tonight, was not simply braced to hear the latest feeble excuse of an erring, much-loved son. No. Tonight she was awaiting the phone call that would confirm disaster. Given Ryland's new awareness, what other explanation sufficed?

The minutes dragged. She gave up trying to read a new collection of Alice Munro stories that would thoroughly absorb in normal circumstances and switched on the TV. Cops and crime, danger and mayhem, everywhere she clicked.

Should she *call* the cops? The school? At eleven, she'd decide.

At ten thirty, she heard footsteps on the stairs, Ryland's voice greeting his brother as if nothing were wrong.

From Abbott, total disgust. "Where the hell have you been? Mom's climbing the walls."

"She around?"

"Upstairs."

"Come on up, Jill."

Jill?

"Hi, Mom."

For more than two hours her imagination had served up Ryland bloodied and unconscious on a highway shoulder or hospital gurney. Against this, the two robust sixteen-year-olds standing before her seemed fake. As unreal as a pair of Young Pioneers on an old-time Soviet propaganda poster. "There's no way this is going to be good, Ryland."

"I'm sorry. We missed the bus."

"Are the phone lines out between here and Connecticut?"

"It was a whole bunch of us. I'm sorry. We went to get something to eat and started fooling around—you know."

"The only thing I know is that I'm extremely angry."

The girl, Jill, took a half step closer. Her dark eyes were wide and earnest beneath her ragged bangs. She had beautiful hair, blue-black, slippery straight, shining with health. Thick eyelashes tangled the bangs. "It's really my fault, Mrs. Chapman. I was the hungry one."

"It's not your fault Ryland didn't call me. After he introduces us, I'll tell you why."

"Jill, Mom, Mom, Jill. She's going to be a J.C. at Treetops."

Treetops was the sister camp of Moosehead Lake where Ryland, if he survived Olivia's wrath this night, would spend the summer as a J.C., junior counselor, attached to the waterfront area. They loved him at Moosehead. They considered him a responsible human being, someone to be trusted with the safety and welfare of helpless little kids, many of them nonswimmers. "At your house, Jill, if you come home with a guest, do your parents lay off on you?"

Jill, cute to begin with, became more so with a confessional grin. "Yeah. I guess they do."

"This house isn't like that. I hope Ryland warned you. The reason I blame Ryland, not you, is because the last time Ryland was late he convinced me he understood why he has to call."

"I do understand, Mom. Really."

"No you don't."

"Unless I call, you have no way of knowing that I'm not in serious trouble. But Mom! How could I be? I mean, school just got *out.* Like, there wasn't *time.*"

"How much time does it take to . . . Oh, forget it. I don't want to talk to you anymore tonight. Or look at you, for that matter. I'm too angry."

"OK. Can Jill stay over? Her parents won't be home from Europe until Sunday."

The boys had always been free to bring friends home for dinner or to spend the night. Until now, all the friends had been other boys. And another thing: what if she said no? What kind of parents did this Jill have, consigning their kid so blithely to the kindness of strangers?

What kind of parent am I, producing a kid who so blithely consigns me to my worst fears?

"You're welcome to stay, Jill. Don't take that as a sign of forgiveness, Ryland. I have no idea when I'll manage to forgive you, but it sure isn't now. Get some sheets and make up the sofa bed."

"In your office? How come?"

Olivia deliberately misunderstood. "Because Dee lives in our guest rooms."

Ryland looked about to say something. To point out, probably, that he had a perfectly good twin bed in his room, much easier than messing up her whole office to undo the sofa bed. And besides, guys at Cheshire are always sneaking in and out of the girls' dorms, no big deal.

"Don't push your luck," she said.

Hearing challenge, his fists and jaw clenched, but Jill slid her hand under his belt and yanked him out of range. Before long, Olivia heard them banging around in her office, then muffled shrieks and laughter.

Abbott's door slammed.

Family fun.

"On the other hand," she observed to Dee the following week, when the boys had left for the summer, "they both claim—Jill too—to be too terrified to sniff coke even once. And smoking's out—smoking anything—because it totally zaps your wind. Thank God for sports. And competition."

"Ryland pass all his courses?"

"Yes. He also went out to see Philip. Unprompted by me, you'll be interested to hear."

"Did Abbott go?"

"No. But Jill did. I didn't like that, much."

"Why not?"

"I guess because she never knew Philip before."

"Fair enough."

"What were you thinking, I was doing some heavy proprietary number? I want my son all to myself?"

"Not exactly an unprecedented dynamic."

"Huh. The sooner Ryland's out on his own, the better. I'm tired. Jill's welcome to him." Olivia laughed. "You know what? After he did Jill's sheets, I found a rubber in the washing machine. So much for separate sleeping quarters. And you know what else? I think Ryland's ensuing mellowness is why the boys didn't have their usual fight—which is sort of the point you were making before, but not exactly." She laughed again. "Lovely to have them here, lovely to have them gone. And lovely that Ryland uses rubbers. As Philip used to say, it's a great life if you don't weaken."

Dee smacked his forehead. "What time is it?"

"Ten of."

"Good. I want to watch the news. Big story breaking. I caught some of it in the 7-Eleven. Griscom was about to get an NIH grant to develop something that'll handle crack addiction the way methadone handles heroin. It's a new kind of blocker—a spin-off from Griscom's work with hyperactive kids. Existing blockers damp down the pleasure sense to the point that no one wants to take them. Griscom's is different. Subcutaneous implants, slow release."

"What's NIH?"

"National Institutes of Health. Major bucks."

"So now Griscom's research team will do the job?"

"No. The grant's been cancelled."

"That's crazy."

"Budgetary constraints, they said. The citizenry isn't supposed to know any of this. It was leaked."

Dee turned on his TV. Griscom's cancelled grant was the lead story. After the anchor restated what Dee had just told Olivia, an NIH official read a prepared statement. "At this moment in time, no substance exists that can safely control crack-cocaine addiction without incurring probable secondary addiction. Our projected grant would have been awarded on the basis of hope alone. This is not the usual policy of our agency but a departure prompted by, *a*, the acute and escalating social costs of crack-cocaine addiction, *b*, by Dr. Griscom's track record, and *c*, by Dr. Griscom's work on a related therapeutic, a slow-release dopamine blocker. The grant was awarded, in short, to Dr. Griscom. Without him, and in cognizance of budgetary constraints, we regrettably have no choice but to cancel and wait for the emergence of concrete research out-comes and research personnel who are not as yet known to us."

"Gummint sure talk funny," said Dee.

Next came a segment showing a hospital nurse trying to estab-lish contact with a newborn strung out on crack. The voice-over said this was just one example of the acute and escalating social costs referred to by the NIH.

Finally, the mayor of Boston. Ever since Griscom's shooting, his face on the tube had looked increasingly tired, stunned around the eyes. Not now. Now he had a fierce glitter, a warrior's alertness. "The wanton murder of Dr. Griscom," he said, in a new, hard voice, "originally appeared to be an act of senseless violence. This news changes everything. This news infers that powerful entities, covert business enterprises with tremendous financial resources, had their own warped reasons to want this man of science removed from his laboratory."

Microphones waved. A reporter asked if there'd be a new tacti-cal response from the police. "I can't answer that," the mayor said. "We are up against very powerful, very determined adversaries. I don't want to show our hand."

Commercials. Dee killed the sound. "How am I supposed to lead America's young to wisdom if men in high places say *infer* when they mean *imply?*"

"Did any of that make sense?" Olivia asked.

"Sure."

"Oh please. How did these powerful, determined adversaries find out about Griscom's research?"

"Someone blabbed. An accidental leak. Or, if you're into para-noia, a deliberate leak. Why not? Aren't Farrakhan and those other agitprop brothers always saying crack's a genocidal plot hatched by the man? OK, say there's a white supremacist at the NIH. Or at the medical school. A real skinhead. He's convinced genocide's the way to go. He blabs, word gets out, some drug lord says whoa, there goes my market, and the rest is history."

"If Griscom was the real target, why'd that other guy go into hiding? Jamal something."

"Jamal Sutton. They still haven't found him?"

"If they have, they're keeping it secret."

"That's paranoia for you. Give it an inch and it's everywhere. The oil spill of the emotions."

10

The appraisal went briskly. Aunt Martha's notes, written in perfect Palmer Method script, almost terrified Olivia with their completeness and accuracy. Some pieces, among them, thrillingly, the bonnet-topped desk, also had the uncontestable documentation of the maker's signature.

Olivia had been given a large room at Morgan and Company. She'd chosen this auction house partly because she and Christopher Morgan, the clever young president, were long-standing friends. Very privately, she'd chosen Boston over New York because of the murder's publicity value. Stomach-turning as this might be, there was no escaping its logic—especially now, with the uproar surrounding the cancelled crack-blocker grant.

The auction would be limited to the Early Americana that constituted the bulk of the collection. The later pieces that had been in Aunt Martha's bedroom, the (signed) Tiffany lamp with its intricate tesserae and bronze base, the inlaid table with its secret compartments, the Gothic Revival settee and its two accompanying chairs, had already been shipped back to Harding Hill. So had a pair of English carved chairs and the Sheraton camelback settee, also English.

Olivia's decision to exclude these items had been prompted by Jane's breakdown after the memorial service. At first Jane wouldn't hear of it. "I can't possibly take anything for myself. Not with so many people needing the foundation's help."

"You and your aunt loved each other," Olivia said. "You should have some keepsakes."

"If only . . . it's Jonny, you see. He'd be so disappointed in me." Her dithering continued even as the movers were carrying the things into her house. Not until the little room off the living room was arranged to Olivia's satisfaction, the lamp switched on to show the glory of its green and gold leaves, its purple, red, and blue grapes, did Jane finally shut up and, tremulously, lay claim.

Olivia also had to talk Christopher around to accepting the subtraction. He had a fit over what he called her high-handedness. "The whole *point* here," he insisted, "is *freshness*. A long-lost treasure trove has—ta-dah!—miraculously come to light. It gets out you've sneaked away a single candlestick, the dealers will start passing the word. Forget the Griscom auction, they'll say. The owners siphoned off all the cream."

"And left a Thomas Affleck desk? Come on."

"You know the game. Anything to keep the amateurs home. You're playing right into their hands. I can't let you do it to me."

"Nonsense," Olivia had serenely countered. "We're auctioning an important collection of Americana, in all its fresh and miraculous entirety. The rest is incidental. A distraction."

Christopher, of course, was after the Tiffany lamp, sure to bring in upwards of two hundred grand. Olivia thought he'd calm down when he saw the full scope of what was left.

Her work took her three days. Late in the final afternoon, every object described and valued to her satisfaction, Olivia gave the crowded shelves and tables a final review. There were toys— Indian braves made of jointed sheet tin, various Uncle Sams, some whirligigs, several dozen mechanical banks. Bought for pennies in the twenties and thirties, they would fetch hundreds now. There were flocks of hand-carved birds and waterfowl, most of them bearing the coveted rectangular stamp of A. E. Crowell. And quantities of fire screens, fire buckets, oil lamps, stoneware crocks with historically significant cobalt markings, blue and white Staffordshire ware, red and blue Sandwich glass. Dozens of quilts in excellent condition, some with trapunto detailing so fine your eyes watered in sympathy.

The desk glimpsed that first day had been bought by Aunt Martha in 1935, the depths of the Great Depression, for $175. As a teacher, she'd had work, a steady salary. The Mayflower-rooted Duxbury family who'd been forced to sell the desk had neither work nor income, only some cranberry bogs no one wanted to buy.

Gracefully proportioned, with almost all its original hardware, the desk might reach, even surpass, an auction record. Olivia couldn't study the wood up close without getting a lump in her throat. Trees yielding mahogany like this had not grown anywhere on earth since the late eighteenth century.

And then there were the two surprises she'd set up for Christopher.

Altogether, 254 lots. Concentrating so intently had drained her, and the ride home would feel good. Morgan and Company was on Commonwealth Avenue, just west of B.U. She'd cut through the campus to the river, get a workout by riding up to Watertown.

There was a tap on the door—Christopher. "Oh *my*. Oh Olivia."

What had caught his attention was the first surprise, arranged on one of the worktables. Its centerpiece was a portrait of Mary Eliza Marsh, painted in 1838, when she was three. In the corner was Erasmus Salisbury Field's high-shouldered signature. Mary Eliza wore a high-waisted blue dress with a lace collar that Field had given his finicky all to. Her auburn hair, smooth on top, was parted in the middle and fell in short ringlets over her ears. Around her sweet little neck was a double strand of coral beads. She was sitting on a carpet striped in blues, reds, and oranges, one leg bent, the other sticking straight out. One chubby hand held a miniature china teapot. Next to her was a miniature chest, one of its drawers opened to show a stack of plates in the same pattern as the teapot. In front of the chest was a doll-sized table and two chairs.

"The frame's either original or exact period," Olivia pointed out.

"Of course. But the *rest.*"

It was the rest that was going to enrich the foundation. Slowly and, as her notes indicated, suspensefully, Aunt Martha had found an age-documented duplicate of every object in the painting. A length of heavy linen carpet with the same stripes and colors formed the basis of Olivia's tableau. There was a toy tea set with the same rosebud pattern, a double strand of the coral beads that were supposed to fend off illness, a little, round table and two chairs with the same Windsor detailing. Best of all was the three-drawer chest which was undeniably the original of the one in the portrait. Built of light-colored mahogany, it had knobs and keyhole plates carved from whalebone. On the top, in a darker variety of mahogany, was inlaid a three-masted sailing ship. Below it was inlaid Mary Eliza's name.

"Her father was a whaling captain," Olivia explained. "Bet anything one of his sailors made the chest for her."

"It's wonderful. Astonishing. The kid's even cute. They're going to kill for it."

"And for our encore," said Olivia, turning with a flourish to the second surprise. The portrait, in this grouping, was of Mrs. Stephan Brainard, painted by John S. Blunt. Mrs. Brainard was in her parlor, seated on a yellow chair with bamboo-turned legs and pineapple detailing across the back. One of her arms rested on a sponge-painted green table. On the wall, which was stenciled in a charming blue-green leaf pattern, was a mirror with an urn and pediment design at the top.

"Blunt died young," Olivia said, "before he really got going as a portrait painter. This is an early one—1830. He died at sea. I wonder if he knew Mary Eliza's daddy."

Christopher wasn't listening. She didn't blame him. Next to the portrait she had set an exact duplicate of the yellow chair, nicked and worn but wearing its original decoration and solid as a rock. The green table, its finish no less distressed but fully recognizable, stood alongside.

Olivia handed him a flashlight. "Look under the table."

When Christopher recovered from seeing the signature scratched into the wood—like other portraitists of that period, Blunt had started out by decorating small objects and furniture— Olivia gave him more. "The mirror's over there on that shelf."

"All right, that does it. I'm calling the Getty. Rumors are flying they're about to plunge big into Americana."

"If the buyer wants to copy the stenciled walls, I've got just the man. He's not cheap, but he's the best. Being as it's a good cause, I'll toss in his name for free. You think Blunt did the table on one circuit and came back the next year for the portrait? Or did he do both at once?"

"I think Aunt Martha was a genius, is what I think. A genius who's going to make us all rich."

"Without Tiffany," Olivia had to say.

"I suppose."

Olivia laughed. "You do your usual good job on the auction, and if Jane decides to sell the lamp she'll doubtless contact you directly. In which case, no percentage to Chapman Interiors. Can I use your phone?"

If Jane was home, Olivia might as well drop by. Under the guise of reporting that the estimates were finished and that things looked splendid for the foundation, she would set her hook. The instant Jane decided to redo Aunt Martha's upholstery, if only to get rid of the dog smell, Olivia wanted Chapman Interiors to flash across her mind—in urgent red neon.

Jane seemed pleased to see Olivia but refused the wily decorator's tempting hooks. Not that she was resisting; resistance requires will.

Jane, perched on the edge of the Gothic Revival settee, was passive. Out of it. Her eyes and the tip of her nose were red. When she sneezed, Olivia asked if she'd caught cold.

"Just these ridiculous allergies," Jane said.

They were drinking sherry. The sherry bottle and a bowl of stale peanuts stood on a carved chest, Aunt Martha's sole foray into China Trade, that served as a coffee table. Olivia was sitting opposite, on the other settee which, had it turned out to be American Sheraton instead of English, would still be with Christopher Morgan. A real *fritto misto,* this room, especially without the unification of intentional color. Given a free hand, Olivia would pull her colors from the glorious lamp and the worn Tabriz that had been in Aunt Martha's dining room. She'd use the Sheraton someplace else and add an ordinary Lawson sofa and a pair of easy chairs for comfort. To Jane, though, she breathed not a word of this. Jane would either become confused beyond recovery or want to bring in the duct-taped beauties from next door.

Most of the pillows and hassocks had been given away. "They were all presents to begin with," Jane explained. "That's why there were so many different kinds, from all over the world."

A tiny mystery solved. "I wondered about the pillows the first day I met you," Olivia said. "Neither of you seemed like collectors."

Jane's mouth twisted. Not a smile. "Jonny collected people."

Who, gathering round and finding the floor at his feet hard, had introduced pillows. Olivia murmured something to hide her uncharitable thought.

A silence grew. Olivia checked her watch, said she'd best be off.

"Oh don't go yet. Please. Have some more sherry. Or something else. People have brought no end of bottles. I could open a bar."

"Sherry's fine. Just a touch. Whoa—I've got to ride home."

Jane froze, bottle in midair. Then she set it down with a decisive bang. "The way you just said that? Home? This house isn't my home. Not really. The neighbors—I used to think they were unfriendly because Jonny didn't care about the yard and so forth. Now I know it's me they're watching. They're waiting for me to fall to pieces like poor Bonita."

They. Right after Philip's accident, Olivia had been convinced that people, virtual strangers, were watching her with malicious expectancy. Her tragedy was their juicy story. They could hardly wait for the next plot development. Later, when she was calmer, she knew most of this was her own imagination. Not all, though. People could be shits.

And Jane was that much more vulnerable. Her husband's death unmitigated by any clear-cut explanation or motive, she could believe the worst. Especially in the middle of the night. Waking, unable to fall back asleep, the questions would come without mercy. Had Jonny really been killed to halt the crack research? Or had he been punished for some secret offense? And might her name be next on the hit list?

Reluctant to enter into this murk with someone more client than friend, Olivia played it safe. "Have you thought about where you'd rather live?"

"Yes. Woodside." Jane smiled shyly. "You're the first to hear."

Oy. "You might not have much in common with your neighbors," Olivia said, smiling to keep things easy. "The Woodsiders I saw on TV sounded like they'd rather live anyplace but."

"That's because they've been *condemned* to Woodside. I won't have that problem."

"Right. Not that one."

"I'm not afraid of problems, Olivia. I want to set up a preschool there. The kind of thing I did in East Cambridge."

"Are you talking about Aunt Jane's Place? You were Aunt Jane?" Olivia was astonished. Multiracial, mixed-income, the school had won dozens of awards. There were stories of parents enrolling their children at conception in order to assure a place for them. "Philip and I had hoped to send our sons there, but you were full. Good for you, Jane. Congratulations."

94

"Thank you. Those were happy years. I visited Arnette Murfin yesterday, and all of a sudden I knew what I wanted to do. Woodside needs a good preschool as much as I need to be working with children again. I never should have let Jonny talk me into . . . well, what's past is past. And you know what else? Arnette's three-decker is exactly like the one I lived in when I was Aunt Jane. I was climbing her stairs, and it came back to me as if it was yesterday. I'd come home at night and I could smell my neighbors' dinners cooking, see light under their doors. You don't feel so alone, living like that."

"Did you try this plan on Mrs. Murfin?"

"No. I said, you're the first."

Smile. Keep it simple. "Are you trying it on me?"

Jane laughed a little. "I must be. How does it sound?"

Familiar ground for the decorator. What about you? Even the most confident clients inevitably needed to ask. Do *you* like it?

This wasn't about taste, though. This was serious, with serious consequences. "I'd say go slow. A decision this big—give yourself plenty of time. You've sustained a tremendous shock. And how about trying your ideas on some other people? Gordon, for instance."

The decorator knew what that balky look meant. "I'm not saying take Gordon's *advice,*" she hastened to add. "Or anyone else's, for that matter. But the back and forth is useful, I think. Whenever I have to explain my position to other people, I end up understanding it better myself."

"Really?"

Olivia heard, in that one word, a lifetime of misplaced confidence, disappointed trust. She stood, wanting this over and done with. Jane needed a friend, but she, Olivia, wasn't an applicant. Couldn't be. Too much on her plate. Unkind to pretend otherwise. "Every time," she said, piling on the firm conviction.

At the front door, she paused to offer the trifle that was honestly hers to give. "If you do go for a three-decker, Aunt Martha's Victorian things will love you for it."

"They will?"

"Sure. Good high ceilings, the right windows and moldings. Much better than here."

"Oh." A bleak little smile. "Maybe that proves this is all, I don't know, sort of *meant*. As if it's all been laid out somehow and we're just starting to see patterns."

Olivia had to say something. She said what would get her out fastest: "Maybe."

11

The following morning Olivia had a phone call from Chess Griscom, who got right down to it, no sociable chitchat. "This is short notice, but are you free for lunch today?"

"I am if it's early," Olivia said. "I have to be back here for a one-thirty appointment." With, as it happened, a potential client—someone brand-new.

"Where's 'here'?"

"Joy Street—top of Beacon Hill."

There was a pause at the other end, as if Chess were rearranging her own schedule. "How about twelve sharp, at Maison Robert?"

"Perfect," said Olivia, and they hung up.

Now what? It had to be about Jane's Woodside plans, or, close second, the auction. That Chess was redecorating—and Chapman Interiors would get two new clients on the same day—was highly unlikely.

Chess had booked an outdoor table. Arriving a minute early herself, Olivia found her sitting right under Ben Franklin's round, bronze belly. She was wearing wraparound sunglasses and a crisp linen dress whose pale yellow worked nicely with the terrace's striped umbrellas.

That Chess had been better than prompt was a good beginning. And at Maison Robert, the food would be good too.

The restaurant was housed in Boston's Old City Hall, an imposing Second Empire structure that was a pioneering example of renovation in preference to wrecking. ("Adaptive re-use," Olivia remembered, had been the clumsy term back then, not even the most ardent preservationist dreaming of the mixed blessing that lay ahead: ficus groves and Gaps in abandoned warehouses, mills, and railroad stations from sea to shining sea.)

The terrace, shaded by ancient trees, would be more pleasant if not for School Street's eternal traffic snarls. "We should have gone inside," Chess said when they'd finished ordering.

"This is fine," said Olivia. "Such a pretty day."

A tour trolley dawdled by, its amplified patter overwhelmed by honking from the impatient cars behind. "They should outlaw those damned things," said Chess.

"Not the tourists, though," said Olivia. "I like it that they come from all over the world to see what's right outside my door. Makes me feel prosperous."

Chess's laugh was short. "You're an optimist."

"Aren't you? Starting new companies, don't you have to be?"

"In general, yes. But too much blue-sky thinking can backfire. We're hung out pretty far right now. A deal we'd had big hopes for just crashed, and losing Daddy's crack blocker was no picnic either."

"Is it lost altogether? The rest of the team can't keep on?"

"Not unless they find someone as rich as Uncle Sam. But let's not waste time on my problems. I called you because I'm worried about Jane—this idea of hers to live in Woodside. She says you're all for it."

The waiter set down their goblets of mineral water. Olivia drank before answering. " 'All for it'? Were those her words?"

"So I understand. She called Gordon, and Gordon called me. Jane and I aren't close. Gordon and I aren't exactly close either, but we recognize that the family's divided into people who make sense and people who don't."

"Jane doesn't?"

"Hardly."

"I'm curious—who else doesn't?"

"Ben and Anne, of course. And their mothers."

"Did you say mothers, plural? Yours and Bonita?"

Chess gave Olivia a look. "Don't tell me you think a little thing like death changes the way a family functions."

"Good point."

"So what do you know about Woodside that I don't?"

"First, what I said to Jane was that anyone who's had a shock like hers should wait awhile before making major changes. I also suggested she talk it over with some other people. It occurred to me afterwards that she might have to move, that the house might have to be sold for some reason."

"Of course not. She's just trying to get back at us."

" 'Us'?"

"The four of us. Daddy's children."

Jane as wicked stepmother? Olivia let her skepticism show.

Chess looked gratified. "You don't believe me. You can't imagine plain Jane, world-class, long-suffering, sad sack, plotting revenge. Well, wait till you've known her as long as I have." Chess stretched her neck to make the cords show and mimicked Jane's plaintive smile. " 'I just don't *understand*. Chess used to *love* me.' "

"Did you?"

Chess shrugged. "She was terrific with Jonno and Susan. My kids. I'm not good with children, particularly—I'm too impatient. I suppose I did love her for that. God knows I was grateful."

A light dawned. Olivia asked to make certain. "Your kids went to Aunt Jane's Place?"

"Of course. How else would a woman like Jane ever come in contact with a man like my father?"

Good enough to mind the kids, not good enough to marry into

the family. Olivia smiled nicely. "It's always interesting, the things that bring people together."

"I brought it on myself. It happened during that awful period after Bonita. Daddy was devastated, of course. He wouldn't accept help, so I made him think I was counting on him to help me. He picked up Jonno and Susan every Tuesday and Thursday, which meant that week after week he was seeing Jane at her best. I don't blame him. Gordon and Anne needed someone at home, and Jane certainly filled the bill. Or seemed to. The way Anne turned out, you have to wonder."

Their food arrived and they started to eat. Olivia wanted to hear more. Chess seemed intent on exonerating her father at Jane's expense. But was she a besotted daughter? Or a gypped one casting about for a scapegoat, someone safer to blame than the man who done her wrong? Sally had indicated Griscom had dumped his first children along with his first wife. And Ben had sung passionately of the eternal torment awaiting the sinner.

"When my own kids were little," Olivia said, "I tried to get them into Aunt Jane's. I didn't realize you had to apply years in advance. Why did she ever give it up, do you know?"

"No idea. Daddy's sabbatical, maybe. They were traveling around together, researching *Lost Children*. I suppose she was helpful to him."

"Ah," said Olivia. She had read a *New Yorker* excerpt of this book and forgotten, if she'd ever registered it in the first place, that Griscom was its author. He had interviewed children in a dozen different countries whose lives had been maimed by large political forces like poverty, war, and famine. The book had created a brief stir. The children's artless accounts of the adult behavior that threatened to destroy them were moving and troubling. But the book never achieved the fame or durability of *Leaves* of Life*. Which figured. *Leaves* of Life* offered painless solutions as close as the shelves of your local natural-foods store. *Lost Children* offered yet another dump of hopeless grief, intractable woe, man's in-humanity to man.

Had Jane been given credit for her contribution? Olivia didn't remember.

"But to get back to why I asked you to meet with me today," Chess said, "Jane likes you. Trusts you. Stubborn as she is, I think she'll listen to you. Gordon and I would be very grateful if you'll do what you can to talk her out of this Woodside lunacy." She stopped talking because Olivia was smiling. "Did I say something funny?"

"She *didn't* listen to me. Not if she believes she heard me promoting Woodside as a great place to live."

Chess waved an impatient hand. "Gordon must have gotten it wrong. Skip that part. The main thing is, you have a lot of influ-ence over her. Look how she packed up all her treasures and put them back in storage. Don't tell me you weren't behind that one. And I know for a fact you talked her into keeping the Tiffany lamp and those other mementos, so-called."

Olivia felt the hot breath of yesterday's it's-all-meant mysticism. "Wait a second. You and Gordon aren't opposed to the preschool idea, are you?"

"Not per se. But not, never, in Woodside."

"Why?"

"It's preposterous. Can't you see the headlines?"

"Sure, but so what? The cause is as good as they come. From what I know about your father, he'd welcome headlines."

Chess was taken aback. "What on earth makes you say that?"

"Years of talk shows and op ed pieces. The sack-of-trash exer-cise."

Chess carefully buttered, then abandoned, a piece of her roll. "The situation's entirely different," she then said. "There's really no comparison."

Maybe not, but her surprise had created a strange little moment.

"Just before," Chess went on, "I was complaining about business difficulties. I don't want to give you the wrong impression. I've certainly had my winners, and I've got more in the pipeline. The way venture capital works, when I make money, the entrepreneur I've backed is really rolling in it. I don't know what your image of an entrepreneur is, but mine tend to be heavy-duty techies. Nerds without the foggiest notion of how to spend their new millions. They want a big new house, of course, and they're sitting ducks for whatever slick talker comes along. I've seen some of your work, and I'd have no hesitation recommending you. Not only would you keep them from blowing their wads foolishly, you'd be able to teach them something about taste."

Her bribe proffered, Chess eased off, smiling and shaking her head. "I'm thinking of one house in particular. Everything was white and sort of *tufted.* In the garage, three white cars, a Rolls, a Jag, and a Cherokee equipped with every bell and whistle known to man. I can't tell you what a relief it would be to go to one of these housewarmings and not have to fake the compliments. Do you have time for coffee? Or dessert?"

Olivia said she didn't, and Chess signaled the waiter. "Shall I tell Gordon we can count on you?"

Olivia didn't answer immediately. The funny thing was that she'd probably have said yes without a second thought if Chess had built her case solely on the basis of Jane's physical safety. Even the simplest explanation of Griscom's murder—he'd caught a bullet intended for the other man, Jared, no, Jamal Sutton—lessened the menace of Woodside's mean streets very little.

Why, then, hadn't Chess and Gordon argued safety? What could have blinded them to the merits of an argument so indisputable?

Chess was waiting for her answer.

"You can count on me to say again what I've already said."

Chess smiled. "Better spell it out so I'm sure what it is."

"Woodside needs you but Woodside's got problems. Take some time before you make any big moves. Talk to other people to help clarify your own thinking."

Chess scanned the bill and laid some money on it. "That's all? You won't talk her out of it?"

"She's a grown woman. She's great with kids. Woodside would be lucky to have her."

"I'm disappointed. Very."

"If it helps, I think you've inflated my influence."

"Oh? I'm usually right about these things. I have not, for instance, 'inflated' my influence on my eager new millionaires."

"Thanks for lunch," Olivia said.

Instead of answering, Chess glanced at her watch and jumped to her feet. "I was due at my broker's ages ago," she said in a rude, blaming voice.

Olivia had to hustle too. In a few minutes she'd be meeting Steven Dunbar, who had just purchased three thousand square feet of duplex, with penthouse, on the water side of Beacon. Upwards of seven hundred grand, he had to have paid. "The first thing we gotta settle," he'd said this morning on the phone, "is the penthouse. I'm torn between a monster Jacuzzi and an exercise pool—you know, you swim into jets. Ever tried one? They're not bad."

He'd sounded young. If he'd inherited his money it was the new kind; Olivia hadn't found him listed in the Social Register. The new kind was sometimes the drug kind.

The closest Olivia had knowingly come to drug money was a trial lawyer who lived on Boston's waterfront and maintained a shockingly lucrative practice in Miami. She had deposited his checks no differently from anyone else's.

Suppose high-roller Dunbar wasn't in the wings. And suppose she didn't have such exciting expectations for the auction. Might she, with her stack of overdue bills, the Hamricks filing for divorce, and no new business in sight, have taken Chess's bribe?

Would Jane have listened to her, allowed herself to be sold out? Probably. Definitely, if Olivia came on like a friend. Here was an irony: it was this very malleability of Jane's, her timorous, doormat quality, that made it hard to imagine her as a friend.

Another obstacle to friendship was the simplicity of Jane's goodness. She seemed to see only virtue in people and their deeds, a view that left her unburdened by ambiguities, flip sides, general human crappiness. So for Jane, too, Dunbar was a lucky break. Without him, would Olivia have mustered sufficient goodness to turn Chess down? It was, general human crappiness obliged her to admit, an open question.

12

Up by the Prudential Center, the unlovely, windswept, fifties "Pru," Boylston Street seems to attenuate, to prefigure the strip development of the suburbs ahead. And, as in a suburban strip, eateries are easily found, but good food is remarkably scarce.

Keith Somers, waiting this noon in J. C. Hillary's, was too new to Boston to approach the menu with proper wariness. Besides, he had too much on his mind to worry about food. Any attention he could spare from worrying about his great project was claimed by the awesome decor of the place and the mob of slick, young executive types that crowded it, talking at the confident top of their lungs.

It had been Deb's pick, J. C. Hillary's—probably to impress him. Keith was new to Deb, too, but he doubted she was in the habit of coming here on her own. Prices like these, your clientele isn't going to be hospital clericals.

Before this spring, Keith had hardly stepped foot out of Hampton Bays, Long Island, New York. Now here he was, settled in and starting to feel at home in this truly, truly amazing city. The new life he'd come up here to find would begin in earnest this September, when classes started at Harvard. (Pressed, he'd admit he was enrolling in the Extension School, Harvard's open-admissions program.) Until very recently, he had divided himself between work—"I'm in sales"—and a self-designed reading program. Occasionally he'd gone out with people from work—to the movies or a concert—but he didn't consider them friends any more than he considered sales his destined career. The friends he aspired to he would find at Harvard, in the process of forging his new life.

Slightly built and delicately handsome, Keith was older than he looked. "Late twenties, max," people guessed. He didn't correct them. Starting a new life, the younger the better.

His eyes, with their "to die for" lashes, found themselves in the massively ornate mirror over the bar. Pretty Buns, his last girl friend, Janice, had called him. He liked to hear her say *pretty*, liked the exciting reminder of her greedy grip on his ass, pulling him deep inside herself. But only in privacy. This strict rule Janice, in her enthusiasm, often ignored. He gave this carelessness as his reason for breaking up with her when he decided to leave Hampton Bays, begin his new life.

She'd taken it badly. In J. C. Hillary's mirror his face swam into hers, blotchy with rage, streaked with furious tears. You're dumping me for *saying* something? Well fuck you, shithead. You're a lousy fuck anyway, and wait'll I say *that* in front of the guys.

To erase her, he closed his eyes. His prettiest look, girls had told him, the thick, dark length of his lashes set off by his fine-grained, pale skin. (When open, his small eyes, pale blue, often bloodshot, were not his best feature.)

Janice would have tagged right along to Boston. Or, one fine day, shown up on his doorstep, about as compatible with his new life as a turd in a goldfish bowl. But: a lousy fuck? Was he? No one had ever complained before, but did that actually prove anything? With females? Because who could figure them?

"I ran all the way from the T stop," a breathless voice announced, breaking into his thoughts. "The old bag wouldn't let me leave."

The old bag was Deb's supervisor and the main obstacle to Keith's ambitions here. In the last few days he had heard a great deal about her hawkeyed dictatorial ways.

"Deb," he said, going instantly to sales mode. "I was starting to worry."

"Yeah?" A pleased smile improved Deb McCaffrey's face, flat and plain as an Irish bog. "How come?"

"Because we hardly know each other," he said, honey warm. "You were right on time Saturday, but that coulda been a fluke. Down deep you coulda been one to make dates and not keep them."

A backfire, he saw at once. Face like hers, a nothing bod, she'd be the one stood up. Dumb to go and remind her. "They said twenty minutes for a table, but we can eat at the bar right now."

"Whatever. She kept me late, she'll see me when she sees me. Right?"

"Right." The bartender was approaching. "Care for a drink?"

"Vodka collins."

"I'll finish this," Keith told the bartender, keeping a firm grip on the mug his draft had come in. Alertness was at stake as much as cost.

When Deb's drink arrived, she took a dainty pull on the straw, grimacing slightly before she swallowed.

Not a drinker, Keith guessed. Doesn't like the taste, even with a sweet mix. So why not order Pepsi and save me some bucks?

He smiled. She sucked again, then smiled back. "As far as *knowing*," she then said, "I know something you don't know."

His heart banged. She'd done it. "Like?"

"You weighed seven and a half pounds."

"Wow. That's big, isn't it?"

Deb considered judiciously. "Above average, anyway."

"What else?"

"You're an Aquarius."

"I knew it. No way I could possibly be a Pisces."

107

She opened her bag, fished out a note card. "Here's the exact date. See that? Crittenton-Hastings House? Anyone has their baby there, it's top, top, *top* secret. Sealed in blood. You'd never ever have found it out on your own."

She tossed the precious thing carelessly over to him. He grabbed, caught it just before it fell to the floor. She was a little mad at him, and he knew why. Asking so much of her, he'd had to hit her with every bit of his salesman's finesse. He'd had to touch her heart without coming on to her—or at least not blatantly, not in any way she could hold against him afterwards. Careful as he'd been, her downturned mouth told him she'd gotten ideas. Lucky he'd thought to tell her, right off the bat, that he had an insanely jealous girl friend who watched his every move and had already swallowed a bottle of sleeping pills over nothing whatsoever.

He gave her arm a little sock, light and brotherly. "You think I don't know sealed in blood, Deb? This many weeks beating my head against the bureaucrats, you think I don't know?"

"Yeah, but that's not *me*. I mean, don't lay that on *me*."

"My God, Deb, what're you saying? It's thanks to you all that bad stuff's over and done with. I mean, listen! You know? This is the absolute and total best thing that's ever happened to me. I mean, my whole life, you know? Like, I've been waiting for this one single thing my whole entire life. Like, until now my whole basic identity's been up for *grabs.*"

Overwhelmed by the tremendous truth of it, he slumped forward, forehead propped on fists, and stared into the dregs of his beer.

She touched his shoulder. "You OK?"

He raised his head, cleared it with a shake, blew out air. Then he swung around to face her, his eyebrows two sharp peaks, his smile wide. "OK? Deb! For the first time in my life, I am one hundred percent OK! And, wow, all of a sudden hungry beyond belief. Let's have something special. Lobster? Could you go for lobster? Hey, come on! It's like it's my birthday. My first real birthday!"

They settled on lobster salad plate, to be eaten at the bar. Arm and a leg, but who cared? Keith was floating. It was done. Safely done. Deb didn't even seem mad anymore. And she only had two questions for him, both easy. Was he going to tell his grandmother he knew? And what about his real mother?

He went back to honey warm. "My grandma's so old, I have to really weigh it. Plus, I'd definitely have to tell her face to face, which I can't because I'm not in a position to travel right now. But it's weird, what just happened. You said 'real mother' and I went, hey, my grandma's my real mother. Account of she raised me and all."

"Yeah, you said. But what about, you know, *her.*"

Not daring to use the name, even with him. Keith covered his satisfaction with a helpless little laugh. "I don't know, Deb. I just don't know. Weird, huh? All this effort and I'm like oh boy, what now? I hafta put myself in her place, I guess. Think about her, what she's been through and all."

"I'll tell you one thing, you surely do look like her. That picture in the paper, you could be twins."

"Well, like I said. Half of why I came to Boston was for Harvard, and half because Boston was all I knew, that I'd been born here, I mean. But I hadn't gotten down to it, you know, started my search, until I saw the picture. It still amazes me. The coincidence and all. Or maybe . . . sometimes I think there's this huge, you know, *web* connecting every human on earth. You can't see it with your naked eye but"—Keith brought his thumb and forefinger together to yank an invisible filament—"things like this happen and everyone goes wow, what an amazing coincidence."

"I look like my mom too," said Deb. "People say we could be sisters."

Keith grabbed this opening and kept her talking about her large, quarrelsome family until they'd finished eating and he'd paid the bill.

Now he wanted to run, get away from her fast, never lay eyes on her again. The girl broke into sealed records, he had to remind himself. She risked getting fired in this mother of a job market. Take some pains saying goodbye; do it nice.

What she wanted, he knew, was his promise to call, get together soon. She wasn't the type to ask outright, but it was written all over her plain, hangdog face.

He'd found her last Friday, at the hospital records desk. Saturday they'd met in the Public Garden, near the swan boats, to talk. She'd said she couldn't commit yet, she had to sleep on it. "I'll call you tomorrow," he said. "When's a good time?" "No," she said. "I'll call you." "My number's unlisted," he said. "You might lose it and then what?" "I won't lose it," she said. "I never lose things, that's why the old bag trusts me."

In the end, he'd had to give her the number. Now, anytime she got in a mood, she could phone him. Two in the morning, if she wanted. Get loaded, rant in his ear. Or whine and beg.

Out on the sidewalk it was like one of those dreams where you're glued to the ground and can't run away from the monster. They were the same height, but she must outweigh him by twenty pounds. "Deb," he said, giving her major eye contact, "Deb. I'm so happy. It's great what you did, just great. Please—let's shake."

Caught her by surprise, that one. Her hand was hot, damp, boneless.

"Thanks, Deb. Thanks a million, million times."

"No problem." Hangdog.

He saw a cab and signaled.

"Wait."

The cab pulled over. "I gotta split, Deb. I'm really, really late." *"Wait."*

She could make big trouble for him. He opened the door, but he waited.

"Let me know, OK? What she says when you tell her?"

He got in the cab, slammed the door. The window was open. "I surely will," he promised. "And you have a great day, OK?"

13

It was June. Normally Boston welcomes June, real summer, but not this year. Muggy, freakish May had been summer enough, and who knew what punishments were still to come?

Olivia, wearing white duck sneakers, a navy-and-white striped T-shirt and cropped, wide-legged white pants, was wheeling her bike out the front door as Dee, whom she hadn't seen in days, was coming in. "Nautical and *very* nice," he said. "Look, I'm finally dug out. I'll put the check under your door."

What check, she almost said, then remembered Dee had asked for an extension on his rent. Her new client, Steven Dunbar, had given her such a fat retainer she hadn't noticed the hole in her checkbook balance—leeway that Dee, underpaid and underpublished, hardly needed to hear about.

She said fine, thanks, and he said, too elaborately, that the thanks were entirely his. She wished he could sell more stories, that money wasn't such a chronic difficulty for him. She also wished she'd never agreed to his latest economizing scheme. Rather than pay his share of the new tax hike, he'd taken over the halls, staircase, and front entry from the housecleaning service she'd been using. He did a good job, better than the service, but whenever she heard him running the vacuum she had to fight her inclination to drop what she was doing and pitch in. Meaning she was not only a wimp but a sexist pig; if the situation were reversed, she'd never expect the same of him.

"Let's get together soon," she said. "I'm off to Jane Griscom's right now. She wants to talk upholstery, if you can believe it."

"You're working nights?"

Olivia buckled on her helmet. "A decorator's gotta do what a decorator's gotta do. Anyway, I'm a Griscom junkie. Can't say no to a fresh fix."

"I've peaked," said Dee. "Entire hours pass without my giving this case and its endlessly fascinating puzzles a single thought."

Olivia grinned. "It's different when you're up close and personal."

"Doubtless. Ride safely. Got your light?"

Olivia patted her handlebar pack. "Right in here with my swatches."

Nice to have a send-off, she thought as she turned the corner onto Pinckney. To have someone making sure you remembered your light.

"Olivia! Come in, come in."

Olivia blinked. Jane was transformed, radiant. "You look wonderful, Jane."

"Do I? I feel wonderful. Oh, Olivia! I have to make a confession. We'll talk about the furniture, but mostly I brought you here to meet someone."

A clone, was Olivia's first thought. Male version.

He had the same pale, bloodshot eyes, the same slatty, awkward-looking body. The same smile in the same face, though his teeth weren't as perfect. His red hair, buzzed on top, long at the nape, had none of Jane's gray. He was too young for gray.

Jane beamed. "This is Keith, Olivia. Thirty years ago I gave birth to a baby I never even saw—that's how they handled newborn adoptions then. Keith is my son. My baby boy, all grown up."

Nonplussed, Olivia grabbed for formula. "Jane! For heaven's sake! What a wonderful surprise!"

"Keith Somers, Olivia Chapman," said Jane.

They shook hands. Keith had a decent, if clammy, grip. He was wearing snug, black slacks with a knife crease and a short-sleeved white-on-white shirt, cut close to the body. The top buttons were undone; a heavy gold chain lay on his hairless chest. His shoes were shiny black slip-ons. Not loafers, slip-ons. Jane, too, was cheaply dressed—T-shirt, Indian-print jumper, and her invariable rubber thongs—but Keith's was the other kind of cheap, flashy rather than ecological. Wait, though. Jane must have gotten pregnant in high school. Had she been a flashy kid too? A sexpot teen?

They sat on the duct-tape beauties, Mother and son together, Olivia opposite. Everyone was smiling. The doors to the other room were closed. "We can't use the new sitting room," Jane said. "Keith's allergic to dog dander."

"Just like Mom," said Keith. "Though she'll never admit it."

Jane laughed like a girl. "I will so too admit it. My eyes always itched in there, I just didn't know why. Jonny wasn't much help with allergies. He didn't really believe in them. All in the mind, he used to say."

Keith's look showed what he thought of this. Then he moved to happier ground. "Do you think Mom and I look alike?"

"Of course," said Olivia, fighting a surge of giddiness. "Everyone must."

"Oh they do," said Jane.

"Chess—you know Chess? She thought Mom was my sister. Which she could be, accounta she was only seventeen when I was born."

Olivia hated the way he said "Mom," his lips slack, as if closing around a spoonful of soft, sweet food. Nursery food.

Knock it off, she told herself. And knock it off on the gold chain, too. "How in the world did you find each other?"

"It's an amazing story," said Jane. "You tell, Keith."

"Part of why I moved to Boston was to begin my search, you know, find my real mom. But with work and all, I hadn't started yet. Maybe I was putting it off, who knows. Then I saw her on TV. You know, at the memorial service. Instantly I was like, hey, there she is, there's my mom. The more I'd go, this is crazy, things don't happen like this in the real world, the more I'd think it's her, I found her. Then the next day? At work? Totally wild. People had their papers, that picture on the front page, you know, Mom hugging her friend. Everyone's going, hey, Keith, what is she, a relative or something? The more I looked at the picture, the stronger my gut feeling got. I told myself to wait three weeks, give it the test of time. Don't ask me why I picked three weeks, this whole thing has been totally on instinct. Automatic pilot."

Jane had to cut in. "The letter Keith sent me was brilliant, Olivia. All he put down was his birth date, saying we hadn't seen each other since then, but if I'd like to get together, please call. So of course I called right away, and here we are."

"It's a standard search letter," Keith told Olivia modestly. "I got it out of a book."

"Keith's a real reader, Olivia."

"Books are great. If I didn't have to work, I'd read all day long."

"What kind of work do you do, Keith?"

"I'm in sales."

"They call it telemarketing," Jane amplified. "Stocks and bonds."

Keith gave an apologetic laugh. "Phone pest, right? It's not the best. People scream insults and hang up on you. But I'm pretty good at it, and it pays the bills."

A short silence followed this. Olivia had a million questions, but she didn't want to grill the kid. Kid? Yes. Something unformed about him, thirty or no.

Jane jumped up, crying that Olivia had not yet been offered a drink.

White bullet in hand—she had ended up pouring her own, Jane unsure how much vodka to offer—Olivia raised her glass to the happy pair. (What did natty, barbered Keith make of the duct tape? The stained shag carpeting?) "To your life together," she said. They raised their own glasses, smiled, and thanked her. Olivia smiled back. Mother and son looked expectant. Olivia returned to their main, possibly only, subject, asking Keith if he'd grown up knowing he was adopted.

"Not for sure, though I sensed something. Especially after my dad was killed in Nam and my mom married again. My stepfather and I didn't get along, to put it mildly, so, right after my eighth birthday, I got sent to live with my grandma—my dad's mom. The next thing I know, my mom's disappeared out west someplace. Not a peep until I was almost fourteen. Totally out of the blue, she calls from Denver, Colorado. She's sick in the hospital—the big C. Died before we could get out there. Yeah. But hey, it coulda been worse. I mean, I had my grandma, right? And us two were like this." Keith showed two fingers pressed together. "Really tight. She used to own this little motel out on Long Island—Hampton Bays?—so that was my job until she had her stroke. A real shame. Some of the time she was great, sharp as a tack. Then blam, she'd be totally out of it.

"Right before she checked into the nursing home, she sat me down and told me I was adopted. Half of me's like, right, I knew it all along, but it was kinda tough too. I mean, how could a mom skip without telling a kid who he really was? My grandma's like, No whingeing now, you've got to get out and make something of your life. Go to college, whatever. Oh, and she was totally adamant about hanging around the island for her sake. You do that, she goes, and I'll refuse to let you visit me."

He shook his head over the memory.

"Remarkable woman," said Olivia, wishing she didn't feel so cued. Hampton Bays. She and Philip had occasionally visited friends who summered in the Hamptons. The locals, she remembered, had Keith's distinctive *i*. Long Oiland. Make something of your loife. Almost cockney, it sounded.

"I'm so grateful to her," Jane said, blinking back tears. "So very grateful. But don't ask me to understand your mother."

Keith seemed gratified. "Like I told you, Mom, it was the war, my dad getting killed and all. So anyways, back to my grandma. I'm like, college, Grandma? What college takes guys my age? Get off your butt and find out, she goes. What a pistol, huh? Then she tells me she knows two things about my real mom. One, she had red hair, and two, I was born in Boston. So here I am, and in the fall I'm going to Harvard."

Harvard?

"The Extension is wonderful," Jane said.

Olivia admired her tact. Kids get grandiose and mothers have to bail them out. Do it right—Jane had done it right—and the kids learn something.

"Extension students," Jane went on, "have the same professors as the other undergraduates, but they're with people their own age. People with more life experience."

A buzzer sounded from the kitchen.

"Keith?"

"Oh. Right."

They'd arranged it, Olivia saw. She and Jane were to have a private chat. Keith, enjoying his star turn, had briefly mislaid his part.

When they were alone, Jane's smile turned anxious. "Has this made you uncomfortable, Olivia? Wait, don't answer yet. I want you to know that I have no idea what became of the boy who made me pregnant. He was older; he'd been out of high school for years. I hardly knew him. We only went out that one time. These days they'd call it date rape. Aunt Martha took care of everything; she got me to Boston and paid all my bills. You must have heard of Florence Crittenton—Crittenton-Hastings, it was by that time. The staff there was wonderful. They did everything they could to keep you from feeling like a bad girl. A sinner. But if you're upset or embarrassed, I understand."

"I'm not any of those things. I'm happy for you. And very sorry you had to go through a painful time when you were so young."

"Oh but once I was in Boston I was fine. Really. All of us in the house felt certain our babies were going to make some lucky young couple very happy. And Keith seems to feel that his adoptive parents *were* happy, at least for the short time they had together."

"And now you can claim your own happiness."

"Yes! Oh thank you, Olivia. It's so beautiful that you understand. And you know, in a little corner of my heart I've always imagined this. I'd open the door one day and there he'd be." Jane laughed, delighted by the fulfillment of her dream, its miraculous newness. Then she became sober and urgent. "Keith is terrified of Woodside, Olivia. We drove over to visit Arnette the other day and he could hardly force himself out of the car."

"Hampton Bays is pretty small-town. Not to mention white."

"He likes it *here*, Olivia."

Now Olivia understood Jane's urgency. She wanted Keith to come and live with her. To fill the emptiness left by her husband's death, to make up for the years lost by the adoption. "He likes this house, you mean?"

"He says he's always wanted to live in a neighborhood exactly like this one. He wants to fix it up. He's good at painting and so forth—from his work at the motel."

"How's that sit with you?"

"I've thought and thought, but I can't shake my funny little dream of a three-decker like Arnette's. It would be perfect, Olivia. Keith could have the top floor, me the middle, and the preschool could be on the first."

Olivia didn't know what to say. Keith's obvious respect and affection for his grandmother augured well for Jane's hopes. A simple segue from Grandma to Mom.

On the other hand, blood tie notwithstanding, he was a stranger.

And wasn't there an aimlessness about him? He'd clung to his childhood home, Grandma's contented odd jobber. He'd be there still if she hadn't kicked him out. Was this worrisome? Common among adoptees? (Was that the word, *adoptee?* The entire subject was a blank to her. Lately, it seemed, adoption had been much in the news—yet another set of human rights and plights to wring your hands over. She hadn't read the stories. You had to pick and choose or drown in overload.)

When you don't know what to say, questions are best. "How does sharing a three-decker sound to Keith?"

"I don't know."

In the kindest possible way, Olivia suggested she find out.

When Jane responded, her voice was so low Olivia could barely hear. "I'm afraid to ask him. I want it too much, and I'm afraid he'll turn me down. So naturally he's assumed I'm staying on here. Oh, it's so complicated! Because of course Jonny's children won't hear of my moving to Woodside either."

"No? Why?" Olivia was careful to keep her voice level.

"I suppose it's understandable. They're angry at Woodside. Very angry. Gordon told me my willingness to turn the other cheek was an insult to his father's memory."

"Let's hope he calms down soon. Keith mentioned Chess—has he met the other three?"

"Oh yes. Anne's between jobs, so she's been in and out a fair amount, and the others came last weekend. Chess and Gordon first, then Ben and Barb. Seeing me happy with my son was hard on Barb. They can't afford children because Ben's music comes first. The minute Mort Thaler finishes untangling Jonny's estate— we're still completely in the dark, you know, even on his bequests—I'm going to try to help Barb. Ben is a true artist and I respect that. But a woman who wants a child as much as Barb . . . it's just not fair."

Something new was going on. Olivia had never before heard Jane criticize anyone, especially a stepchild. And look how wry she'd been about Jonny and allergies. Was this Keith's influence? Better stick to housing matters, though. What decorators are for. "So if you go ahead and move, you'll be bucking quite a crowd." She counted on her fingers. "Eight to one."

"It's really nine to one. Mort says Keith's offer to work on the place is a godsend. He says the improvements will boost the price whenever I sell." Jane sighed. "I suppose he's right. He kept talking about cost-effective cosmetics. Can you imagine what Jonny would say to that?"

"Still, if Keith's willing . . ."

"But Olivia! Every stroke of work he does will only make him more involved in this house. More emotionally attached. How can I allow that? You know how I feel about Harding Hill. It would be terribly wrong of me to encourage him. Wrong and dishonest. Even with him at my side, I'll never belong here, never. And of course he's not at my side, not really. He has his own life to live, as I have mine. And my life is in Woodside." She lifted her chin. "Nothing's changed about that, you know."

No question, this was a new woman. Olivia chose her words carefully. "Your *work* may very well be in Woodside. But what I hear you saying is that your *life*, if it's to include Keith, may have to be someplace else."

"Oh it's such a mess. I can't think straight anymore."

"It's not such a mess. You're scared of Harding Hill, he's scared of Woodside. So find a three-decker someplace neutral—not as rich as here, not as poor as Woodside. You commute to work, he commutes to the Extension."

The hopefulness that flooded Jane's face told Olivia that this entirely ordinary compromise was, to her, a brand-new possibility. But was that so surprising? Jane's advisors were dead set against her moving at all. They'd be an unlikely source of ideas for compromising.

Keith called out that dinner was on the table.

119

Good timing, Olivia thought. He might have been listening behind the door.

Reinforcing this suspicion was that there had been very little noise from the kitchen while Keith was absent. Also, their supper, which had come straight from Darla's kitchen at Leaves* of Life, had hardly needed as much time as Keith had taken. Still, if his intent had been to thwart exploration of Olivia's compromise, wouldn't he have followed up at the table by proclaiming the joys of Harding Hill?

Instead, he talked about Aunt Martha's furniture. He loved it. It was so classic. And that lamp—to die. Like something in a museum. If he didn't have to work, he'd love to come along when they went shopping for the new upholstery.

"Shopping?" Jane broke in. "Why do we have to shop, Olivia? I thought you were bringing the fabrics tonight."

"Yes, but we're hardly limited to them. The Design Center has zillions of samples."

"Oh. I thought we'd just get what Aunt Martha had."

Keith let out a hoot of laughter. "Mom's great, isn't she? I mean, have you ever met anyone so totally unmaterialistic?"

"Never," said Olivia. *He's fond of her,* she realized, *he genuinely likes her.* She was surprised how good this made her feel.

"The only reason she's doing it at all is allergies," Keith teased.

"All right, you two." Again the girl's laugh. "Let's talk about something more interesting than me. Tell Olivia about your reading program, Keith."

He was happy to. "Every Sunday morning I go through the book review, you know, in the *Times,* and list everything that sounds good. Then I hit the bookstores, Harvard Square, mostly, they're the best, and work my way through the list. Some books, I read a couple of paragraphs and I know it's not for me. The ones I like I can get through a couple of chapters before they give me the hairy eyeball. Some weeks I have to read every night until I'm done with my list."

Olivia had to ask. "Wouldn't it be more comfortable to use a library?"

"Yeah, but the books wouldn't be just waiting for me like in a store. I'd get way behind, and how could I ever catch up?"

Jane beamed and beamed. How long, Olivia wondered, before she's buying books for him, five, ten a week? And anything else he asks for?

Knock that off. Don't you buy stuff for Abbott and Ryland? What's a mom for?

Interesting to watch, though. Would Keith embrace the less-is-more Griscom ethos? Or would he move from fixing up the house to fixing up himself? And Jane, too, if she'd let him.

Of course she'd let him. She was in love.

Jane in Talbots, trying on a tasteful little suit, pumps to match, a nice pearl necklace.

Horrible thought. Why, though? Hadn't she, the decorator, interfered as well, pushing hard for Tiffany over duct tape?

She and Keith, between them, were going to be good for the economy.

14

The night of the auction was so splendidly clear the sky showed stars when it was still lapis lazuli, the horizon a vivid apricot. The large hall at Morgan and Company filled rapidly, standees crowded three-deep around the edges.

The arts contingent missing from the memorial service was here in force. Olivia had spotted four movie stars, a best-selling doctor-novelist, dozens of well-known decorators and dealers. From Christopher Morgan's excited report she knew that all the relevant museums had sent agents or curators. There were also some Japanese in business suits and a scattering of the old guard, including Sally and Flip.

Tout le monde, except for Jane Griscom. "It's just not me," she'd told Olivia during their rather surreal prowl through the Design Center. Which forthrightness, being Jane, she instantly amended: "Not that I'm not looking forward to my nice new sitting room, Olivia, please don't think I don't appreciate all you've . . ."

Keith had come late and was standing in the back. Every time Olivia looked around, a dumpy, plain-faced young woman had his ear. Someone from work? He seemed less than happy with her company.

She saw no Griscoms besides Chess, who was waiting with Christopher at the front of the hall. Chess's look tonight was winsome—short, swingy dress, blond hair falling in loose, tousled curls.

Christopher approached the podium, repeated the word *welcome* until the din quieted, and introduced himself. Then he introduced Chess: "Co-chair, with her brother Gordon, of the Griscom Foundation."

Chess was brief and daughterly, the crisp executive who'd tried to bribe Olivia nowhere in sight. "Thank you so much for coming here this evening. Some people have described my father as a man martyred for his convictions. It's impossible for me to think of him in such gloomy terms. Much as he took human suffering, whether from disease or social injustice, very much to heart, his spirit was always light and full of joy. I know he would want you to have fun tonight. He would want you to take delight in every aspect of this evening—the exciting competition of the auction, the beautiful treasures you carry home from it, and, of course, your satisfaction in contributing to a deserving cause in memory of a wonderful man. Thank you again for coming."

Not a word about Jane's generosity, not even to milk the grieving widow angle—get out your handkerchiefs and your checkbooks, too.

Maybe Gordon, co-chair, was supposed to say that part. Where was Gordon? Olivia had run into him and Darla a week or so ago, all three of them cycling on the Esplanade. Hadn't he said then that he was looking forward to the auction?

It was a strange little encounter, flooded with that distinctive enthusiasm that affects chance meetings in unexpected places. All three had braked spontaneously, then, as if surprised at themselves, started chatting like long-lost friends. Darla's bike had an old-fashioned handlebar basket. Seeing that it held Leaves* of Life food containers, Olivia said, "Lucky you, such great takeout." "It's scraps," Darla said, "for my geese." "Yours, Fudge?" Gordon teased. "I think of them as mine," she said, a little defensive about it. Then she'd gone on to tell Olivia they were, mysteriously, white barnyard geese living in the wild. "They roost back where the river makes that wide bend. You can't see any sign of them from the bike path." Olivia knew just where she meant. "That wild grassy part," she said, "sort of a vest-pocket savanna." "Savanna," said Gordon, "I like that." "They were real small and thin when I found them," said Darla, "but you should see them now." "She's given them names," said Gordon, "Snowy, Bianca, *white* names. She says they know her voice." "They *do*," Darla said. She likes his attention, Olivia thought, but not the teasing. She'll take teasing if that's all there is, but she doesn't like it, at least not when the subject is geese.

That was about it. Some conjecture on the flock's origins— maybe a kid's Easter present had escaped and multiplied—and then Gordon said, "See you at the auction," and they'd ridden off in their opposite directions.

So why wasn't he here? He couldn't be hidden; he was too big to hide, and anyway, Christopher would have introduced him. He must have decided to give it a pass.

Not nice, the way he'd kept teasing Darla. Almost cruel.

Olivia's estimates had been too conservative. Lot after lot was hammered down beyond the top figure of the range printed in the catalog. Giddy glee swept the hall as the bids grew wilder. Curators tensely sparred; there were frequent clashes between the most famous movie star and the blockbuster novelist. The Getty was, indeed, plunging into Americana. It beat out Boston's Museum of Fine Arts and the Abby Aldrich Rockefeller bidder for Mary Eliza Marsh and all that went with her. The most famous movie star got Mrs. Brainard. A Japanese man, rumored to be an agent for someone at the very pinnacle of Mitsubishi, landed the Affleck desk for a million two.

Olivia entered the bidding just once, for a particularly beguiling

Crowell sandpiper—Philip had loved sandpipers. She never had a chance.

When it was over, the Griscom Foundation had cleared nearly two million dollars. Because so many lots had exceeded a thousand dollars, thus earning the gallery its maximum percentage, Christopher was quite cheerful about Olivia's share, four percent of hammer.

Quite cheerful about it herself, she pushed through the crowd to say hello to Sally and Flip. Flip seemed annoyed. "Weren't your prices way off the mark?" he asked. "That going to cause you any trouble down the road?"

"I hope not." Whole point of auctions, dummy.

"The Griscoms certainly did themselves proud," said Sally. "I wonder what they'll do with all the money."

"Probably whatever Chairperson Chess wants," Olivia said. "I wish she'd thought to thank Jane."

"Jane? Why, darling?"

"For donating the stuff."

"Oh. Well. Still, I doubt very much, don't you, Flip, that this mob turned out in behalf of poor Jane."

Olivia made an excuse to break away. She had caught Keith's eye; curiosity called more strongly than squabbling with her in-laws.

Up close, Keith looked hot, dazed. Olivia asked how he had liked his first auction.

"I don't know. I guess I didn't get it. Everything was so kinda crummy-looking. And the paintings? The kid was OK, her little beads and all, I could relate. But that woman? To me, she was just plain ugly. I wouldn't want her hanging on my wall. And fifteen thou for that dirty old table? Please."

Olivia laughed. For all the fuss over Mrs. Stephan Brainard, she was no less homely than Keith's friend, squeezing through the crush to claim his side.

Olivia had to introduce herself. "Oh," said Keith. "This is Deb McCaffrey."

"How did you like the auction, Deb?" Olivia asked.

A shrug. "It was OK."

It's him I want, her shrug said, not you. Have it your way, Olivia thought, turning her attention back to Keith. His unbuttoned shirt showed red, peeling skin, no gold chain. Even his hair seemed sunburned, though that might be the gallery's bright lighting. The long fringe at his nape had been trimmed short and the top allowed to grow. He looked more ordinary this way, also older. "How've you been, Keith?"

"Not too bad. Real busy. I quit my job, you know, to work on Mom's house. You should see it. I raked up in front and seeded in some clover. It's still a meadow, just not so ratty. And I scraped and painted the whole front. Next week I start on the sides. Oh, and to get ready for the new furniture? We trashed the carpeting."

"Good."

"Mom hated doing it, accounta the landfill and all. But Mom, I'd go, it's a health hazard!"

His grin wasn't sneery, Olivia decided. An edge of complicity, maybe, but no disparagement. "Bare floors are nice for summer," the decorator said. "When it gets cold again, if you want a rug, I'll be glad to help. Another oriental would be good. Oversize orientals can be quite cheap at auctions."

Keith showed consternation.

"Has tonight turned you off on auctions?" she asked.

"It's not that. Mom's so . . . it's like she can't focus on anything but Woodside. It's kinda hard, because otherwise we get along great."

"Keith?" said Deb. "Let's go. I'm really hungry."

"Just a sec," Keith said. "There's gonna be a big article on Mom in the *Globe* tomorrow. Pictures and all."

"Because of the auction?"

"I guess. And Woodside. The reporter kept asking about Wood-side."

"Keith." Deb plucked at his sleeve. "Come *on,* Keith."

"Wait, OK? Will you just *wait?* Jeezies." To Olivia: "She skips dinner, it's my fault? Anyways, basically, you think it's a bad idea, Mom living in Woodside, right? Basically? So anything you can do or say, believe me, I'd appreciate it. Accounta I'm *with* her, you know? I'm totally sympathetic and supportive. But I'm not gonna lie to you, the place scares me."

Christopher was beckoning, trying to catch her eye. Next to him stood one of the museum curators. A cutie.

"Go feed Deb," she said to Keith, giving that graceless creature a smile she didn't deserve. "Call me at home if you want to talk some more—Jane has my number. And be sure to tell her the auction was a wonderful success."

The cutie, Olivia, and Christopher closed down the Ritz Bar, laughing all the way.

Next morning, headachy from champagne, Olivia picked up a *Globe* at the corner store. After so much silliness and giggling, getting into the article, into earnest good works, took real determination.

There was a picture of Jane at home, and another of her and Arnette Murfin standing on the steps of the burned-out house on Wardell Street. "Mrs. Griscom aims to purchase this property," the article said, "as soon as negotiations are completed with the real-estate trust that currently holds it."

Jane's plans for the building were described in some detail. The drug dealers' side of the house, the side where the family had perished, would be demolished to create an outdoor play area. The other side, rehabbed, would house the preschool and some of its staff.

Staff, Olivia thought, did not exclude the director—if Keith ever managed to conquer his fears.

The construction crew would be "drawn from the community." Arnette Murfin, Jane was quoted as saying, had advised her on hiring. "Mrs. Murfin has been with me throughout the planning process. I recommend her without reservation to anyone who is considering restoring one of Woodside's many good solid houses. She has the skills and abilities of an experienced subcontractor."

Was this forthright diction more of the new Jane or the result of editing?

The next paragraph was about the auction and the Griscom Foundation. It must have been slid in right before press time because "a stunning success" was claimed. But Jane seemed at pains to differentiate between the preschool, which she would personally endow, and the work of the foundation. "The foundation is new, so its goals are still general. But of course my husband's concern with Woodside makes projects in this neighborhood natural candidates for funding."

Take that, you angry Griscom kids!

The article concluded with a brief rehash of the still scanty facts on the murder: time of day, dark American-made car, weapon yet to be found, and the wounding of Jamal Sutton, still at large, his relationship to the Nobel laureate unknown.

Just before lunch that day, her head finally clear of champagne, Olivia had a call from Gerry Rothfarb, Philip's doctor. "I've just seen him, and there are some signs of incipient blood clotting. What we're likely to get, maybe pretty soon, is a pulmonary embolism—a clot in the pulmonary artery. I wanted to let you know before I ordered heparin treatment."

Olivia had no idea what heparin treatment was, but the essence was unmistakable. Her heart lurched. "Gerry. Are you saying what I think you are?"

"Want to drop by my office? Better than the phone, huh?"

He was saying it. Heparin treatment, in contrast to the coffee milk-shake stuff decreed by law to flow perpetually through Philip's feeding tube, could be withheld. And, should it be withheld, Philip would probably die. Soon.

"Just tell me, Gerry—could he suffer?"

"No. Definitely not."

In a sense, Olivia had already decided: no heparin. But nothing should happen until certain procedures and ceremonies were honored. The doctor must talk, seriously and carefully, to the wife and help her devise some means, Olivia prayed, to keep Flip and Sally completely out of this. After this talk, she would go immediately to Philip's bedside. With awe and humility she would articulate and confirm her decision. Finally, she would lie down next to him, hold him, kiss him, and whisper a new kind of good-bye that held a new and terrible hope.

Gerry's office was right down the street at Mass. General. "I'll be there in fifteen minutes," she said.

Fran Concannon, heart-of-gold Fran, who had kept Philip clean and, please God, comfortable these two long years, was waiting in the hall for Olivia to finish her visit. Silently, her lips hardly moving, she was using the time to say as many Hail Marys as she could—for Philip, certainly, but mostly for Olivia and the boys. Blessed Mother knew their sorrows and would intercede for their release.

At last Olivia came out, shutting the door gently behind her. Fran approached. "Did you come on the T, Olivia? Well then, would you take a ride from me? I've got an errand on the way to your house, and I could use a hand."

The woman's kindness brought fresh tears to Olivia's eyes. A simple welling, this, of gratitude rather than anguish. "Thanks, Fran," she said when she'd wiped her eyes and blown her nose. "I'd love a ride."

Fran's errand turned out to be at Leaves* of Life, where the party food she'd ordered for her daughter-in-law's baby shower was waiting. "Even if you don't believe everything they say about these additives, you have to admit they fix a lovely platter," she said as she pulled into the parking lot. "They garnish with fresh berries and grapes, none of that foolish parsley no one ever touches."

Bearing a cheese platter like a ceremonial offering, a sack of high-fiber, low-fat, low-sodium crackers dangling from one arm, Olivia followed Fran's sturdy form through the crowded aisles to the express register. There was Dr. Jonny's book, right up by the register. And there was Gordon Griscom, busily replenishing the impulse shelves with granola bars.

Olivia greeted him with the same friendliness of their Esplanade meeting.

Stoneface. He must not recognize her. "Olivia Chapman, Gordon."

"I have nothing to say to you. Nothing!"

With that he barreled past her, knocking the platter to the floor.

She gaped after him as he strode to the rear of the store. Then, collecting herself, she stopped to retrieve the platter. It had been wrapped securely with plastic film so no damage was done, aside from some squashed strawberries. But Olivia hadn't been the only customer jostled, and agitated sounds of protest rippled down the line.

"Who's the jerk?" asked Fran.

"Gordon Griscom," a woman jumped in. "The owner, if you can stand it. He practically broke my eggs."

"Would you like Deli to make up a new platter?" the checker asked. "I'm sure they wouldn't mind."

"We don't have the time," said Fran. "Give me five bucks off and we're square. What's his problem, anyway?"

"He's been under a strain," the checker said. "His father and all."

The elderly man in line ahead of the egg woman wasn't having any of this. "Yeah, well, what's my life, roses? Do I go around shoving people?"

130

"Exactly," said the egg woman. "I mean, where's he get off?"

"I'll need authorization for the five dollars," the checker said.

"Jesus, Mary, and Joseph!" cried Fran.

The ground swell of support from the rest of the line had attracted a curious crowd. The checker decided to authorize herself.

At home, up on the deck and into her second white bullet, Olivia stopped thinking about Philip and moved to Gordon's peculiar behavior. What had possessed the man? And did his nonappearance last night fit in somewhere?

Maybe. Keith had known about Jane's big splash of ink in advance of publication, presumably Gordon had too. Maybe he was furious that she'd broken out of her identity as the great man's widow to show herself freestanding, a woman taking positive steps toward meeting one of Woodside's more urgent needs.

The father Gordon loved so dearly had *talked* in Woodside; Jane was hands-on, bricks-and-mortar commitment.

Your willingness to turn the other cheek, Gordon had told Jane, *is an insult to my father's memory.* The article's implied contrast between philanthropic styles might have struck Gordon as a further insult. Next thing he knows, the woman he considers Jane's partner in crime appears in his store. Still smarting over the rest of it, he gives her a whack, too.

What was certain was that Gordon's business success rested, in no small part, on the personality he projected. To the world at large, he, like his father, personified all the good words: *warm, caring, nurturing, open, sincere, together.* When such a man declares his food pesticide-free you trust him. Lulled by that trust, you become a loyal customer who willingly pays premium prices.

In light of this dynamic, his treatment of Olivia had been not only rude but self-destructive. A cracked facade always makes a juicy story, and there'd been plenty of witnesses.

131

Wait, though. Was it healthy to have a guy the size of Gordon mad at you?

But that was silly. By now he probably realized how badly he'd overreacted. He might already be wondering how to make amends. She wished he'd call. Just send me one of those party platters, she'd say, heavy on the smoked salmon. Nice thin slices, OK?

Her mouth filled with saliva. She was longing for dinner, more hungry than she'd been for ages.

Since before the accident. Was it Philip's gift, this hunger? His way of letting her know she'd chosen right on the heparin?

As soon as she finished her drink she'd call the boys. And Dee would have to be told. For his sake—he'd known Philip longest of all—and hers too. There'd be times when she'd need to talk.

15

Camp Moosehead had a single phone link to the outside world. Ryland, reached after much delay, resisted understanding the import of his mother's call. "But I always tell Dad good-bye," he said. "Whenever I see him."

Olivia tried again. "Without the heparin treatment, a blood clot may reach his heart quite soon."

"Oh," Ryland then said. "You mean like this is it?"

"Probably," she said.

"So isn't that good? I mean, compared to . . . you know."

"Yes. But that's my decision, Ry. We're talking about yours— whether or not you want to see your father one last time."

In Maine, a silence. Olivia had to fight herself to allow Ryland to end it.

"I guess, you know, like I said, I tell him good-bye every time I visit. And the water pageant's next week—I've got all these practices scheduled." Another silence. "But Mom? If you want me there, I'll come."

Did she want him? Certainly she had wanted him to offer. "How about this," she said. "I'll call again if I need you."

"OK," said Ryland, sounding relieved. "Love you, Mom."

"Love you, Ry."

Abbott, with the time difference, was just finishing his lunch break. He, too, didn't take in easily what she was telling him. When he understood, he said he'd be there as soon as he could set up the flights.

"Fine," said Olivia. "You've got the Visa card? Want me to meet you at the airport?"

"That's OK. I'll take the T."

He wanted to be alone with it. "Fine. I love you, Abbott."

"Me too, Mom."

When normal life returned, she'd have to remember to tell him that when somebody, your mother included, says "I love you," almost any reply is better than "Me too."

It was curious, she thought, that neither brother had asked if the other was going to be there. But then, she'd never counted much on her own brothers either. Had her parents, her mother, at least, ever expected the three of them to be close, beneficially dependent, "a family?" Such a hope, even in that emotionally parched household, wasn't farfetched, impossibly romantic, or wishful. And the upshot? One son settled in Minnesota, the other in San Francisco, and the daughter in Boston. They would meet infrequently, nothing much to say when they did.

Come to think, very few of her friends were genuinely part of "a family"—an extended organism whose members lived in the same general area, played and worked and celebrated happily together. Cleaved to each other in prosperity or need, sickness or health.

Much more common were families like the Griscoms, whose proximity seemed to facilitate jealous rivalries more than anything positive and supportive. Was this whole "family" number an invention? A marketing device dreamed up by the perpetrators of sentimental fiction, TV sitcoms, and Hallmark greeting cards?

Whatever, if proximity had produced the sniping Griscoms, she and her brothers had been smart to scatter, run away.

Abbott stayed overnight, the maximum absence, he said, his boss would allow. He'd gone straight from the airport to Arlington House, arriving at the crest of Joy with red, puffy eyes. From the way he hugged her, Olivia didn't think this was simply due to the night flight and lack of sleep.

During dinner, she invited him, with careful tact, to speak of his feelings. He changed the subject. She spoke, again carefully, of her own feelings. He grew expressionless, then erupted into huge yawns.

Olivia remembered those yawns from girlhood. She shut up and offered strawberry shortcake instead. "If you want to hit the hay early," she said, "I wouldn't blame you a bit."

The following evening, Olivia and Dee were up on the deck being good to themselves. Dee needed distraction too. He'd made his own farewell visit to Philip, and he was in the midst of teaching a particularly demanding workshop at Northeastern.

It had grown dark. Their only light, a hurricane candle, stood next to a nearly empty pitcher of margaritas. There was more frozen mix downstairs and Mexican takeout waiting in the microwave.

On the whole, Olivia felt pretty good. She had started a new ritual by ending the workday with a hard, fast ride over the eighteen miles of river pathways. Tonight, after a quick shower, she had put on a long, loose dress, white cotton with a brightly embroidered yoke. It was nice, getting slowly, peacefully zonked up here in the dark. Dee having unloaded a couple of workshop stories, she launched into Jane Griscom's visit to the Design Center.

"We penetrate the first showroom—Greeff, I think, doesn't matter. The samples, hundreds of them, are ranged along the walls—imagine pages in a giant book. I give Jane the usual pitch—just leaf through until you find something you like, don't bother about why you like it, or what it goes with, or price, we'll deal with that stuff later. She starts leafing along, awkward as hell. A virgin shopper. She's trying so hard, I have to love her. All of a sudden she stops. She's found something she likes. Remember that chintz sample?"

"The vines?" Dee mimed strangulation.

"Yup. Not quite, but close enough. I write down the number and hustle her off to Clarendon House. Page, page, page, then, last rack, bingo."

"Vines."

"Shockingly expensive ones. Handprinted—I still can't get my head around it—in Italy. Italy! I write down the number and she says, What about you, Olivia? Do you like it too? I do, I say, drawling it out *molto* dubioso, but let's look just a bit more.

"Three guesses what she finds at Brunschwig. The decorator gives up. Two minutes later I've set her in front of the safe little Aunt Martha damasks. Look, Jane, I say, flipping along, pretending I'm knocked out, *look*. I pause for a genteel sneer at the Italian vines writhing in my tote bag. Nice as far as they go, I say, but the scale, the *feeling* is off. I wish I'd listened to you in the first place, Jane. You and Aunt Martha. These damasks are *right*. No, not another word. I was wrong.

"So that's that—except for the silver lining. There's been a cancellation of some sort. The handprinted vines are immediately available. I call Mrs. Madden, I messenger the sample. She's sold, delighted. Doesn't care if it costs three times more. I call my upholsterer, bribe him with the Dunbar job—you remember Steven Dunbar, my workaholic fat cat?—and get the Maddens back into the head of the line. By five that night, everything's settled."

"And a bigger markup for the decorator?"

"But of course, dollink."

"Is that fair?"

"You think I should shave my markup? Why? The stuff's a

rip-off. Mrs. M. could have demanded a fresh start, but she hung in. Client wants ugly that bad, why shouldn't she pay for it?"

The buzzer sounded. Intruder at the front door, miles and miles away.

"Nobody home," Olivia announced to the night.

"OK if I get that? Jeanmarie Crowley, my best student, said she might drop off a new story."

Olivia waved an airy hand. "You don't mind Jeanmarie seeing you shitfaced, go right ahead."

But the voice that came through the intercom identified itself as the police, a Detective McGuire. "Mrs. Chapman handy?" he asked. "I need to talk to her in reference to the Griscom case."

Up on the deck, instant paranoia. Hide the stash! Open the windows!

"Christ," Olivia said in disgust. "We're only drunk. Alcohol's legal. Tell him I'm on the fifth floor and moving slowly."

Enunciating carefully, Dee passed the message on. Then he caught himself. "Remember the art thieves who ripped off the gardner? Disguised as uniformed cops? We better verify this guy."

"How?"

"Ask for his badge number and call 911."

"He said detective. Do detectives have badges?"

"They must. Some kind of ID."

"You ask him. I'm too drunk."

"I'll post myself inside your office. You check his ID through the window before you open up. I hear anything fishy, I'll dial 911."

"What if he's armed?"

"Armed is normal. Check him out through the window. Anything bothers you, leave him there and run like hell back up the stairs."

Olivia had to giggle. "This is nutsy, Dee. Paranoid. Friendly Officer Muldoon?"

But Dee was dead serious. "McGuire. Better safe than sorry."

Feeling like an idiot, Olivia asked for, and tried to examine,

McGuire's ID card. It showed a heavy, tired-looking map, as she phrased it to herself, like the face of Ireland. A match for the man standing on her stoop. Now she noticed the cruiser parked across the street, gumballs going madly. Creating a scandal, she thought, swallowing giggles.

She opened the door. "Sorry to fuss," she said.

"No problem, Mrs. Chapman. I'm here about Mrs. Griscom."

"Jane? What about her?"

"She was shot about an hour ago."

"No." Olivia shook her head so hard the floor tilted.

"She was at home, getting into her car. They took her to Mount Auburn Hospital."

She was still alive, then. And she hadn't been shot in Woodside. Olivia grabbed for the bannister and dropped like a dishrag onto the bottom step. McGuire sat too, on the scuffed bench that lined one wall of the small vestibule.

She risked the central question. "How is she?"

"Not good. The doctors aren't optimistic. But she was conscious in the ambulance—just for a few minutes. She mentioned your name. Cambridge and us are cooperating on this, Dr. Griscom being our jurisdiction. That's OK, Mrs. Chapman, I'm no stranger to crying. Here."

He was offering her a pack of Kleenex, half-empty and crushed from his pants pocket. Who had needed Kleenex before her, she wondered wildly. Keith?

"Was Keith there? Her son?"

"Well, that's one of our problems, Mrs. Chapman. No one seems to know where Keith is. Maybe you can help."

"He likes to read in bookstores. You could try Harvard Square."

"That's what Miss Griscom suggested. Anne. She's out in a squad car right now, looking for him. No one's got a picture of Keith, you see."

What Olivia saw was something that froze her blood. "Are you saying Keith was involved in the shooting?"

"What makes you think that, Mrs. Chapman?"

"I don't think anything. I asked what you thought."

"Excuse me, Mrs. Chapman. You're the one who said Keith's name in that context."

Before Olivia could answer, Dee came into the vestibule. "You wouldn't be bullying, would you, Detective McGuire?"

McGuire stayed friendly. "Who's this now?"

"Diego Quintero." Make something of it, Dee was inviting. Call me a spic. Take issue with my earring.

Confrontation on top of crisis, thought Olivia, just what we need. "Mr. Quintero," she primly told McGuire, "is a family friend. He's also our tenant. We were just sitting down to dinner."

"Quintero, Quintero. Where've I heard that name recently?"

There'd been a big drug bust in Miami yesterday, a Quintero part of the Fed's bag. Olivia decided that McGuire could recall this on his own. "You said Mrs. Griscom mentioned me in the ambulance. What did she say?"

The detective opened his notebook. "The Cambridge officer took down her exact words. 'Get Olivia help Keith money money Olivia help.'"

"That's it?"

"Yes. Anne Griscom said she didn't know any other Olivia, so here I am."

McGuire was holding out the page on which he'd written Jane's words in neat block letters. "Take a look, Mrs. Chapman. Ring any bells?"

Focusing, Olivia could hear Jane's struggle to articulate her message. For a moment it was as if Philip, too, were fighting unconsciousness, trying to tell her something, and Olivia shuddered with pity and fear. "I don't think Keith has much money of his own," she said. "His financial survival would be a concern to Jane. He'd come into her life just a few weeks ago, you know. Morton Thaler can probably tell you more about her finances. He's the family lawyer."

McGuire made a note. "Could she be asking you to take care of Keith financially?"

"Doubt it. I'm not in that bracket."

"See, she says 'Olivia help' twice. Olivia. Not the lawyer. Not Anne, or any of Dr. Griscom's other kids."

"We'd become friendly in the course of some decorating I helped her with. Clients sometimes invest their decorators with special powers. And of course I was involved in the auction."

McGuire seemed to know about the auction. "She must've had a lot of confidence in you, dropping everything to run out and see that house."

"What? What house?"

"The one you called about. Where Mrs. Griscom was headed when she was shot."

Olivia's jaw dropped.

"I've been with Mrs. Chapman all evening," Dee said. "She's neither made nor received any phone calls."

McGuire kept his attention on Olivia. "Cambridge talked to Anne Griscom right away. Her name was in Mrs. Griscom's date book, for dinner tonight. According to Anne, Mrs. Griscom called to cancel a little before seven o'clock. Anne said she was surprised—her stepmother had never canceled a date before—but Mrs. Griscom told her you'd found a house for her that was too perfect to last long on the market. If she wanted a chance at it, she told Anne, she had to move fast. She was going to pick you up in Harvard Square at seven-thirty sharp so the two of you could have a look at it."

"Someone's lying," Olivia said. "I haven't spoken to Jane for days, on the phone or otherwise."

McGuire was deadpan. "Anne's lying?"

"Someone."

Dee got to it first. "The same person who shot Mrs. Griscom, betcha."

140

McGuire made no direct response to this. "You two got together when, Mr. Quintero?"

Dee shrugged. "Before eight. Quarter of, maybe. I wasn't paying that much attention."

Olivia thought fast. When Dee came home, his bike pannier full of takeout hot from Casa Azteca, she had glanced, no particular reason, at the clock. It was a digital clock, in the process of scrolling from 8:13 to 8:14. The step-sitters and dog-walkers of Joy Street would have seen him. Seen her, too, hot and breathing hard from her workout, arriving some fifteen minutes earlier.

Jane would have allowed at least ten minutes to get to the square. She'd been shot, then, around 7:20—neighbors hearing the shot had probably already verified this. From Harding Hill to the crest of Joy, with tonight's tail wind, was less than forty minutes. Meaning that Olivia could have shot her.

"I looked at the clock when you knocked, Dee. It was 8:14."

McGuire turned his notebook to a fresh page. "So just for the record, Mrs. Chapman, where were you between, let's say, 6:30 and 8:14?"

"That's quitting time, 6:30. I locked up my office, went upstairs. Changed, got my bike out, rode around the river paths, got back here around eight. Took a shower and got dressed. By then Dee, Mr. Quintero, was home and we mixed up some margaritas."

"See anyone you know while you were out riding?"

"That's jock rush hour, Detective McGuire. You don't recognize people out there, you dodge them. And I didn't stop at a pay phone to call Jane Griscom either. Which leaves three possibilities. Anne is lying, Jane lied to Anne, or someone managed to impersonate me. Which wouldn't be too hard to do. I've spoken to Jane maybe five, six times on the phone. I still have to identify myself; she doesn't know my voice right off the bat. The impersonator gets me a little wrong, no big deal. I've got a cold. Or hay fever. Jane's allergic herself. She'd buy it without a thought."

Olivia stopped, fatally certain she had protested too much. Ev-

141

erything in her was clamoring for reassurance. *You believe me, don't you? Please say you believe me!*

Dee had a thought. "Are reporters going to be pestering Mrs. Chapman about this fake phone call?"

"Fake's for us to discover, Mr. Quintero, not for you to say. But I made it clear to the Griscoms to keep quiet on it—for the sake of this investigation as well as their father's. So if you two don't talk either, we'll be fine. Let's drop the call for a minute, Mrs. Chapman. You know Mrs. Griscom pretty well, Anne says. Any idea who might have it in for her?"

"Jane Griscom is harmless to the bone. It's very hard for me to believe she's made an enemy at all, much less one angry enough to kill her." *Angry.* "Wait. Was it a shot to kill?"

"Who knows? It's a head wound—a bad one. Why?"

Again Olivia had to think fast. She wasn't yet ready to imagine a stepchild angry enough to kill, but what about angry enough to maim? Or frighten?

Was it her civic duty to bring up Gordon's certainty that Jane was insulting his father's memory? Mention his derailment in *Leaves* of Life*? And then there was Chess. Having failed at bribery, might Chess have opted for terrorism?

Two angry people. Neither, presumably, used to guns. A shot meant for the shoulder could have gone high and wide.

Civic duty or not, she couldn't stomach it. Couldn't inflict the nightmare of false accusation on another human being.

The detective's next question seemed to read her mind. "Mrs. Griscom get along OK with her stepchildren? All four of them?"

"She hasn't said otherwise." A truth, if not the whole truth.

McGuire sighed, closed his notebook, and dropped it into the sagging pocket of his suit jacket. From the other pocket he extracted a pack of business cards bound by an elderly rubber band. "Call me, OK? Something occurs to you, or you hear something?"

A bolt of pure relief shot through Olivia. He was leaving. And leaving her here instead of taking her downtown for more questions on that phone call. She was a free woman.

Freedom emboldens, allowing recognitions formerly clouded by fear. "Wait a sec, Detective McGuire," Olivia asked. "Is Woodside involved in this?"

Wariness tightened the man's tired features. "We're not commenting on that, Mrs. Chapman."

"Speaking as a voter and taxpayer, I want to say very clearly that I hope no one's planning another house-to-house search. Jane Griscom was trying to help Woodside. So was her husband. This ransacking through innocent people's houses, it's just plain wrong."

"I couldn't agree more," said Dee. "Speaking as a voter and taxpayer."

"These are tough times. Only way to stay on top of it, the good guys hafta be tough, too. You call me, huh? That number there works day or night."

"Sounds like you do think Woodside's involved," Dee said.

"No comment. I'll tell you something, though. Homicide, we look for the wallet or the bedroom—or a combination of the two. Ninety-nine times out of a hundred, that's what it boils down to. Call me. Any time."

When he was gone, Dee collapsed onto the step next to Olivia. They sat there awhile, as inert and stupid as two sacks of wet sand.

"Wanna eat?" Dee finally asked.

"I think what I want is a talk with Anne Griscom."

"She's out looking for Keith. Anyway . . ."

"What?"

" 'The wallet or the bedroom.' Maybe Jane was trysting, using you to cover her tracks."

"*Jane?*"

"Still waters run deep. Sleep on it, see how it looks in the morning. If Anne was lying, she'll have a bad night."

"She will? I don't assume normal human behavior from any of those kids. Jane's nothing to them. An embarrassment their father saddled them with. No, that's unfair. Chess thinks that way. I don't know about the others."

"You think one of them shot her?"

"I hate to, but it's possible. I guess anything's possible. For awhile there I was on the verge of suspecting Keith. Which is looney. For one thing, he really likes Jane. Seems to, anyway. But even if he's faking, he's smart enough to bide his time. Make sure he's in her will at least. Except where the hell is he?"

Dee checked his watch. "It's only nine-thirty. With Jane booked for dinner, wouldn't he have made his own plans? Seen friends, taken in a movie? He'll show before long."

"I suppose."

"Come on. Let's make another batch of margaritas. We've got to keep our strength up. Then we'll eat, and by the time we're finished, the news'll be on."

16

Claims she didn't make the call," Detective McGuire told F. X. Cromarty, the uniform driving him tonight.

"You believe her?"

"Not sure. She had opportunity." McGuire's sigh was heavy with frustration. "She's worried we'll toss Woodside again."

"That's two of us."

"No way he's not gonna take it personal." McGuire was referring to the mayor's reaction to the new shooting. "Like the evils're giving him the finger. He hasn't been this paranoid since busing."

"We had it good back then," Cromarty said. "No guns to speak of."

The Griscoms and their lawyer being outside their jurisdiction, McGuire and Cromarty were heading for what was left, Wardell Street. Night, inland, felt hot as day, Beacon Hill's faint breezes a memory.

McGuire left Cromarty in the cruiser and climbed the stairs to Arnette Murfin's apartment. She was sorry to see him at the door instead of Kimi and Kinesha. "They got strick orders they gotta be home by dark," she declared with the regal indignation that so frequently set Wardell Street's teeth on edge. "What do I do? Chain'm up?"

A new-looking window unit was keeping Arnette's front room downright chilly. McGuire walked over to admire it, shoot his pits a refreshing blast. "Little thing really puts out."

"I need it accounta my work with Mrs. Griscom." Arnette didn't add that Jane had paid for the air conditioner and was covering the extra electricity besides. "Summers, this here town, nobody work at all they ain't got ice."

A large TV stood dark. "TV been off all night, Mrs. Murfin?"

"Sure has. I'm a working woman. No time for foolishness."

"Then I guess you didn't hear the news. About Jane Griscom."

No one understands better than a woman in poverty what kind of news gets delivered by policemen. Arnette went rigid. McGuire took a deep breath and said his piece.

She blew. Monumentally and totally. All his years on the force, McGuire had never seen the like. Before long, her enraged grief woke little Talton and brought him peering wide-eyed around the door. His grandmother held out her arms to him, wailing even louder. Moments later—it seemed hours to McGuire—Kimi and Kinesha burst in, panicked over the cruiser parked below. Only when they were all crying and hugging each other did McGuire dare to get the hell out of there. He almost forgot to drop his card on the doily-topped TV.

Back in the cruiser, he told Cromarty to ease slowly down to the vacant lot where Cyrus Grier and his pals were arranged on their milk crates, winding up yet another day of commentary and witness.

Drunks have been known to let things slip. Maybe this time McGuire would get lucky.

The three kids finally in bed, Arnette dared to face the full import of life without Jane. No more job, no more of the respect and security she'd pined for—deserved!—all these weary livelong years. Snatched away before she'd even finished tasting them, much less eaten her fill. And in their place what? Nothing. No future, no brighter day, just more of the same old same. Or worse. Lamentation and woe beyond anything yet known or imagined.

With stupendous temerity she faced what she must do, dragged it free from the clutch of her quaking heart. Lord, she began, Heavenly Father, precious Jesus. Let Jane live, and I will root out the ungodly. I will find them, and, yea, will I name them. Unto the powers of righteousness.

Start with the doctor. With what she seen from her front window, directly the gunfire was done with. Been wanting to tell all along, specially with them cops rampaging night and day. But she been too scared. Them killers take revenge on her, who gon be left for her grandbabies?

(Them girls gon be wild as they mama. Out so long, who they with? Doing what? Shoulda licked them, then and there. First thing tomorrow morning, God my witness.)

Tired as she was, aching in every joint, Arnette sank heavily to her knees. Lord, she prayed, precious Lord Jesus, you *know* my pain and sorrow. You *know* I need this work. Help me now, sweet Jesus. Help this poor old nigger save her children.

She was still scared of revenge. Crazy if she wasn't. But how could she turn back after coming so far? A little more paperwork— that Mr. Thaler a paperwork *fool*—and everything gon fall in place. Just like Jane say.

Baby Jane, Arnette called her in her head. The kids plain loved her. Arnette never seen the like. Kinesha, though, *she* notice all right: "She *clueless,* Gramma."

Even so, Arnette steadied herself, even so. Ain't Jesus hisself say a little child shall lead them?

The law of the street was hump your back, take your beating, shut your mouth, hide. Even so, even so. Lie down and quit, this close to glory, that be death too.

Help me, Lord, she prayed. Come down to this valley of pain and desolation and *help* me.

* * *

The ringing of the phone reached Olivia in the depths of a complicated dream set in Media, Pennsylvania, her childhood home but
populated by the mayor of Boston and his public relations staff.
Everyone was lying, glibly proclaiming Boston's freedom from
drug addiction, violent crime, homelessness. Olivia was supposed
to applaud, tell them how great they were, but the fraudulent
words wouldn't come. Instead she mutely cowered, unable to flee,
her throat aching from suppressed outrage.

It hurt to say hello.

"Olivia? This is Keith. Keith Somers."

In the background she heard loud talk, laughter, a heavy metal
beat. Her bedside clock said 12:37. "Keith. Where are you?"

"Some bar, I don't know. Boston. A guy here just said . . . Do you
know what's happened to my mom, Olivia?"

"She's been shot, Keith. She was getting into her car and someone shot her."

"Oh my God. Is she . . . is it bad?"

"She's still alive, far as I know. But the doctors don't have much
hope."

"This is horrible. I can't believe it."

Olivia heard more fear than grief. "The police are looking for
you, Keith. You should be calling them, not me."

"Looking for me? What did I do?"

"You tell me." She was wide awake now, a boozy headache—
those margaritas—overtaking the dream pain in her throat.

It took awhile for Keith to mumble an answer. She let her
irritation show. "Can't hear you."

"I came home in time to see the cruisers. The ambulance and
all."

"Really. Then why didn't you run to your mother's side?"

Again he mumbled.

"You want me to stay on the line, talk so I can hear."

"I couldn't help it. Cops . . . I'm scared of cops. Ever since I was
a little kid. Is that a crime?"

Disgusted, Olivia let him have it. "If you'd gone to her, it might have given her the extra bit she needs to pull through."

From Boston, a snuffle that sounded authentic. "I know."

"Good. Jane was thinking of you, in the ambulance. Of you and me together, matter of fact. I'm to help you with finances."

"Oh God," Keith wailed, breaking down.

Olivia let him sob awhile. Then, speaking more gently, she told him to go home to Harding Hill.

"What if they're waiting for me? The cops?"

"You'll have to face them sooner or later. Sooner seems harder, but it really isn't. And Keith? Better level with them. You pretend you're surprised, it'll come across fishy."

"I can't tell them I ran away. They'll think I have something to hide."

"Cops aren't dumb. They want people to be scared of them. Otherwise the country would be in worse trouble than it is."

"You think? Really?"

"Plead your wayward youth. Father dead, mother disappeared, you acted out. Petty delinquencies, a run-in or two with the cops."

A pause, then: "OK. Thanks, Olivia. Did I wake you up?"

"If you're straightened out, it's worth it. Let's talk again tomorrow morning. I'll call the hospital now. Maybe there'll be some good news."

"I'll call too. Will they let me see her, do you think? Oh wait. Where is she?"

"Mount Auburn." Olivia had a thought. "I'm also calling the detective on the case—name's McGuire. He'll want to know you're on your way home."

"OK," said Keith, either unaware that she was covering her ass or indifferent to her reason for doing so: her every contact with this shooting, in McGuire's eyes, had to be a blameless open book. "Thanks again."

Olivia hung up, took two aspirins, peed, brushed the taste out of her mouth. Then she dialed the hospital.

Jane's status was communicated by Mount Auburn in virtually the same words Mass. General had used back when Olivia, sleepless, had suddenly required an update on Philip. "Unchanged," in those days, meant hope; if he hadn't changed for the worse, he might change for the better.

So might Jane, Olivia reminded herself.

17

When Olivia woke the next morning, McGuire's bombshell, Gordon Griscom's televised plea for "citizens having information on either of these wanton attacks to step forward," and Keith's tears all seemed part of that frightening dream she'd had, PR types trumpeting lies and forcing her to believe them. Under the shower, the two realms of bad separated, dumping on her the realization that her day, cleared for serious brainstorming on the Dunbar project, had been stolen by Anne Griscom's lie. If that's what it was.

Should she call Anne? Confront her?

Certainly she'd have to call Keith, if only to make sure he'd taken her advice, gone home to face whatever waited for him.

Assembling breakfast, she switched on the radio. Ads, weather, traffic report, another ad. When the news finally came on, the attack on Jane was the lead story. The reporter summarized what Olivia and Dee had seen last night on TV, including the inability of the police to provide a motive. Then: "WBX, in an exclusive interview with a source close to Mrs. Griscom, has learned that the injured woman received a phone call shortly before she was ambushed. The caller, according to the source, was Olivia Chapman, a Boston-based interior decorator. Police are declining comment, but WBX's source claims it was this call that prompted Mrs. Griscom to leave the house when she did. Mrs. Griscom's condition remains very guarded. In the Middle East this morning . . ."

Just like that. A name tossed to a public spooked by violence and hungry for answers. *Her* name. Strangers, people who would never meet her face to face, who cared nothing for her, could gossip freely, avidly, drawing whatever conclusions their prejudices and appetites required. Perfectly normal human pastime. She did it herself all the time.

A source close to Mrs. Griscom, the reporter had said. It didn't have to be Anne. Gordon had made his plea for information on Anne's front steps. In all probability, she'd told him about the phone call. Would Gordon break McGuire's injunction against talking? Didn't seem likely.

Why had Gordon snubbed her in Leaves* of Life?

Go after him? Corner him right in the store?

No. Anne first. Brats blurt. Having had time to repent his tantrum in the store, Gordon would be harder to crack.

She poured herself a mug of coffee and called Keith, who sounded as if she'd woken him. "I'm glad to find you home. Were the cops waiting for you?"

"Yeah. Two of them. They didn't yell or anything. They were kinda nice, in fact. I guess on accounta Mom and Dr. Jonny being, you know, important people. The worst was coming into the empty house. You know? There's all this yellow tape strung around. . . ."

"We have to talk, Keith. How about meeting me for lunch? You know Harvest? Twelve-thirty? Fine. See you then."

That settled, she thought she'd better call Morton Thaler, see what he had to say about Jane's words in the ambulance.

He picked up on the first ring. "I just heard them talking about you," he said. "On the radio."

"First, I didn't call Jane. Someone faked my voice or someone's lying. Second, Jane indicated she wants me to see that Keith's all right financially. I'd like your advice on how to proceed."

"I'm talking on my other line," Thaler said. "I'll get back to you." He hung up, cutting her off before she could say she'd be on the road and would rather call him.

Did he really have another call? Was he stalling for time? The person on the other line might have been a Griscom, howling over the breach of McGuire's orders.

Her phone rang. Since it was unlikely that Thaler had her personal number, she let the machine do its thing and broadcast. "Olivia? Are you there?"

Sally, fit to be tied. Might as well get it over with. "Hi, Sally."

"Oh thank God. It's awful—the radio said you lured Jane out last night and she's been shot. I'm in *shock*, Olivia. It's not true, is it?"

"It's true she's been shot. You didn't hear last night?"

"We came home late, and for once in my life I slept through. But Olivia! What about the rest?"

"I didn't call Jane last night. Someone's lying."

"Are you sure, darling?"

"Yes."

"Pip—you know how he clips things and squirrels them away—dug out that awful picture they took after Jonny's funeral. I've got it right here in front of me. You're looking *daggers*, Olivia. At poor Jane! What in the world is going *on?*"

"I can't talk now, Sally. When I have some answers, you'll be the first to hear."

"That won't *do*, Olivia. That won't do at *all*. What am I meant to *tell* people?"

"Back in May, when you first saw that picture, did you think I was looking daggers at Jane?"

"What?"

Olivia repeated the question.

153

"Well no. Actually I didn't even notice you, to tell the truth. But there you *are*, Olivia. Big as life."

Time for shock therapy. "This whole mistake is your doing, Sally. You're the one who roped me into that memorial service. I'm hanging up. I'll call when I can."

Olivia threw on her nautical rig, good for cycling. At her mirror, combing her hair, she almost threw it off again. What had cheery stripes to do with that taut, strained face, the thin, mean line of those lips?

Hell with it. If she struck the Griscoms as weird, scary, so much the better.

She was wheeling her bike out of her office when her business phone rang. Again she opted for broadcast. "This is Jerry Costello at *The Boston Herald*. I'd appreciate it if you'd give me a call at your—"

She slammed the door on him, but it wasn't over yet. Out on the sidewalk, blind with fury, heart hammering, she crashed into Steven Dunbar—or would have if he hadn't grabbed her handlebars and vaulted clear.

"The news, right?" he said. "Look, let's go back inside for a second. Here, I'll hold the bike so you can . . . Good. Just for a second."

They crowded into the vestibule, the bike between them. In his elevator shoes he came to the middle of her nose. His upturned face was knotted with concern.

"I hope this isn't presumptuous of me, Olivia. I saw the news and had to come right over. I wanted you to know I have no doubts about you, none whatsoever."

Is this happening? "Thank you, Steven."

"I told you how I made my dough, right? Junk bonds? When Boesky and Milken went down, everyone was, you know, hey, hey, hey, Dunbar, you next? Want us to bake a file in a cake? Chocolate or vanilla? And these were my friends, so-called. Know what I mean?"

Dazed, Olivia said she did.

"So, impulse—I'm an impulse guy, you must've noticed by now—I just said, hell with it, stop by on the way to work, deliver the message. She doesn't need it no harm done."

"I do need it. I'm glad you came."

"No problem. I gotta run, but you want help with this, you call me. Watch it, you're thinking, he's a client. Damn straight I'm a client. But you just remember this one thing: I've been there. Reporters can be scum. You need anything, I'm ready."

And with that he was gone. Funny, fierce little man, trotting down Joy fast as his little legs—

Stop that. He's not funny. And condescending on the basis of the man's height is no way to handle what he just gave you.

Which was what, precisely?

An offer of understanding. An act of human kindness. Prompted by—here's the rub—sexual attraction. His, not mine. And there's the *real* rub.

Would he so readily rush to her support otherwise?

Olivia found Anne Griscom's shabby clapboard house on a street of others much like it, each set on a narrow lot and built close to the sidewalk. Summer was the graceful season for streets like this, both sides deeply shaded by large maples and sycamores. This was townie Cambridge, with no discernable signs of gentrification. Students and other Harvard-oriented people might live here, but the ubiquitous chain link fences delineating each small property suggested they'd be temporary, renters. Harvardish owners can't abide chain link.

Locking up, Olivia was aware of the guy stretching on the small front porch of Anne's building. He'd been watching her, kept on watching—drawing a white circle around her face?—as she mounted the worn steps.

He didn't move out of her way, leaving his backwards-thrust Achilles tendon a low stile for her to step over. He had a nice taut ass.

When she was between him and the door he quit stretching and gave her a big, happy smile. "Hot out in the sun?"

He was naked except for Nikes, a bandanna around his forehead, and minimal running shorts. These were nicely filled in front too, her sunglasses allowed her to check. "Very hot. Should we be adapting by now, you think?"

"Nah. Too many inherent flaws. I say junk this version, retool from scratch. Do us all the same color this time, see if that helps any."

She laughed, partly from amusement, partly because to one man at least she wasn't the notorious decorator. "Is there a back door here? Or is this it?"

"This is it. You staking out Anne Griscom?"

"Shows, huh?"

"Had to be a stakeout or you'd have rung the bell by now. Didn't you guys get enough of her last night?"

"I couldn't make it last night."

"Amazing quantity of reporters in this town. Noisy bunch. Kept me from my studies. What are you, free lance?"

"How'd you guess?"

"The bike. Want a tip? Check out the rabbit. Bun. Terrific story peg, that rabbit. Has the run of the place, no cage or anything. He's much in demand for stud. I'm told—" a dirty grin, the nice kind— "that he and his mistress sleep in the same bed."

"You and Anne are friends?"

"Sorry. I want my fifteen minutes of fame arising from something more meaningful than a lease I happened to sign. Which doesn't mean you and I couldn't have a drink tonight. Or see a movie. You like movies?"

Olivia laughed. Two already, and the day still young?

"Was that a joke?"

"Different kind of laugh. Pleased."

"I'm Jeff Kirby."

"I'm married."

"So?"

"Happily married."

"Flux is truth, Heraclitus said. Something changes, you know where to find me. Jeff-with-a-*J* Kirby." He bounded lightly down the steps and swung into a fluent stride. Good body, long-waisted and spare, excellent definition in all visible muscle groups. Twenty-six or seven. That small, you had to throw them back, but still.

She settled herself next to the door, ready to move as soon as someone came out. Walk in as if she owned the place. Anne could still refuse to see her, of course. If she really believed she was involved in Jane's shooting she'd be too scared to see her. In that case, she'd conduct her business by shouting through the door. It would be much better if her stakeout produced Anne herself, right here on the porch. But that was unlikely. Unemployed people tended to rise late.

Minutes later, Jeff came loping back, covered with a light sheen of healthy-smelling sweat. He dug his keys out of the little pocket inside his waistband. "Third floor rear," he said, unlocking the front door. "You'll see the bunny stickers. Don't tell on me."

"Who let me in?"

"There's the directory, pick a name. Not Edie Burkholder, though. I happen to know she flew to New York first thing this morning."

"Thanks, Jeff."

He waved and was gone. All of a sudden she was scared. Of what, though? Anne Griscom, soft and slow, was no match for a woman who'd grown up brawling with two tough brothers.

It was stage fright, she realized. She was afraid she'd blow it, make a fool of herself.

Understanding this cleared a space in her head, and she saw

what she had to do. She scanned the house directory and rehearsed a sentence or two, her voice low so the neighbors wouldn't hear. Then she started up the stairs.

The stickers on Anne's door stopped her cold. There were rabbits in various costumes and poses, some Bugs Bunnys, many more Thornton Burgess and Beatrix Potter types. Ryland had gone through sticker mania too, his closet door as densely plastered as this one, his theme intergalactic.

Don't find this endearing, Olivia instructed herself. She's a troublemaker.

She pounded on the door, listened, pounded harder. Switched fists and pounded some more.

"Who's there?" Anne sounded cross and sleepy. "What's going on?"

"Hi, my name's Sally?" Olivia began in the down-home accents she'd just rehearsed. "I'm a friend of Edie Burkholder's? Downstairs? Look, I know this is a bad time for you, but I've got Mopsy here, my rabbit? I think she's got a tumor, looks like. Unless she's pregnant. Edie said you'd know for sure."

"Shit," Olivia heard Anne mutter. Then, louder, "I was asleep. I'm not dressed or anything."

"Oh gosh, I'm real sorry. But could you just take a quick look? I'm worried sick or I wouldn't push you like this. And of course I'll be glad to pay you for your trouble."

"You've got her with you?"

"Downstairs. I didn't want her upsetting your rabbit, Bun, Edie said his name was. Males can be real territorial."

"That's Bun all right. OK, hang on. Let me brush my teeth."

Olivia waited, listening hard, hearing nothing but plumbing noises. When the dead bolt clicked she moved aside in case there was a chain.

There was, but Anne slipped it without checking.

Olivia gave the door a quick push and was in, slamming it behind herself.

Anne's mouth formed a childish *O* of amazement. Then she blustered: "What are you doing here? You can't barge in like this. I'm calling the police."

"Touch that phone and I'll break your arm. Go ahead. After the trouble you caused me, I'd love hearing the bones snap."

Her garish muumuu was covered with stains and grease spots. The room was a mess, newspapers and fast-food wrappings everywhere. Bun was not in evidence, except for smell. Anne was a slob. A terrified slob.

Too terrified to be a liar? Convinced Olivia had set Jane up, gunned her down, and now it was her turn?

Furniture was a recliner and a sofa littered with trash. The recliner would be Anne's chair; it had the lamp and the phone. "Sit there," Olivia said, pointing to the end of the sofa farthest from the phone.

"Telling me where to sit in my own house?"

Olivia stood until she'd made herself a clearing and plopped down. Then she took the recliner.

"Which of my asshole neighbors let you in, anyway?"

"I don't know. A woman."

"Henna hair?"

"I didn't notice. Let's get to the point. Why did you tell the police I called Jane last night?"

"Why wouldn't I? She scratched our dinner to look at that house with you."

"There wasn't any house. I didn't call her."

This possibility, clearly, had never occurred to Anne. She narrowed her eyes and looked skeptical.

"Here's what we'll do," Olivia said, patient totalitarian dictator to inept functionary. "You tell me nothing but the truth and assume that I'm telling the truth too. I didn't call Jane. Did Jane call you? OK. Tell me exactly what she said. Her exact words, close as you can."

"She said that you called—"

"The exact words. Be her, talking."

"Be *Jane?* Sheesh. What if it's catching?"

Olivia waited for her to finish enjoying her wit.

"OK," Anne then said, "here we go." She cleared her throat. "Oh Anne," she fluted, "Oh good. I was afraid you might have left already. Olivia Chapman—you remember Olivia?—has found me the perfect house. It's so perfect we have to look at it right away or someone's sure to grab it. I have to meet her at seven-thirty, so you and I really can't . . . you understand, don't you, dear? Will you give me a rain check?"

Anne stopped, grimacing as if her performance had left a foul taste in her mouth. "How was that?"

"Perfect. You've imitated her before."

Anne snickered. "Me and Gordon used to do her hours on end. Before he got so high and pure."

"Was that the extent of the call?"

"Basically. I probably said hey, go for it, and she probably said, oh, thank you dear. Not much more—she was in a hurry to get off the phone. Get to her dream house."

"All right. I believe you. And I don't even blame you for not noticing that Jane never once said 'Olivia says.' "

"Huh?"

"What you just recreated was all secondhand. 'Olivia Chapman has found me the perfect house,' not 'Olivia just called to tell me.' You want to stick with that phrasing?"

Anne frowned. "It's not like I wrote it down or anything."

"Right. And it's not like I led you to say it that way, either. But the secondhand version solves the problem of how you and I can both be telling the truth. The caller could easily have told Jane that she, or he, for that matter, was my secretary. Or my answering service. When I was starting out, hungrier than I am now, I used to have a service that would relay calls like that. Expensive but very handy."

Anne still frowned.

"Did you seriously believe I went after Jane? For what purpose?"

"I didn't know what to think! It was a zoo here. Cops and reporters right in my face, Gordon doing his big hero routine. I never got a word in edgewise."

"I noticed."

Anne's face lit up. "You saw me on the news? Did you happen to tape it by any chance? Shit. I must've pushed the wrong button or something—all I got was a blank. Everyone else forgot. Even dopey Darla, the Camcorder Queen. She practically tapes Gordon's farts she's so nuts about him, but this time no. Probably because I was in it, too. She hates me, just like everybody else in this lovely family. Maybe dear Keith taped it. Like, you know, the murderer always returns to the scene of the crime. He ever show up last night?"

"Yes. He's home now. What do you mean, 'murderer'? Are you saying he shot Jane?"

"Maybe he did. What do we know about him, anyway? Aside from his delightful proletarian accent and taste in clothing."

"They told you what Jane said in the ambulance? Her worries about his finances? Doesn't that suggest Keith's not in her will yet? Pretty stupid to go to all the trouble of shooting someone before you're in her will."

Anne didn't like this. "People do stupid things."

"True. Did you mention to anyone besides the police that I supposedly called Jane?"

"They told me not to. Said it could hurt the investigation."

"Didn't you tell Gordon?"

"Sure. I told the whole family, but that's different. They're not going to blab about it."

"Why not?"

"Because of Dad, of course. Some of us, Ben for one, had our problems with Dad, but he was— Dad was great. A truly, truly great man. The animals who gunned him down— Listen, the cops

161

tell us jump, we jump. Whatever it takes. We want Dad's killers caught and punished."

"Fine. Unfortunately, I heard on WBX this morning that I called Jane."

"They named you and all? No kidding. Wow. I wonder if it'll be on TV tonight. Want me to tape it for you? Assuming I can make the thing work."

"No thanks. But aren't you concerned? Worried that the leaks will hurt the investigation?"

"Course I am! What, you think I'm not?"

"Sorry. Any idea who leaked? Ben?"

"Ask him."

"What was the trouble between him and your father?"

"Ask him."

Olivia picked up the gummy phone, set it in her lap, and started dialing.

"Don't tell Ben I sicced you on him," Anne squeaked, anguished. "Please!"

Olivia, who'd been calling McGuire, hung up. "Then tell me why he fought with your father."

"I don't *know*. Honest to God."

"Was Ben cut out of your father's will?"

"Wow. I never thought of that. Course, I'm the baby, no one expects me to . . . goo, goo, da, da. OK, OK, can't you take a joke? Let's see, what's our concept here? Gypped scion runs amok, shoots stepmom? Yeah. I like it. It's got legs. But the cops're the ones you have to sell. Hey! Here's Bun! Come over here, Bunsie. Come to Mama."

The rabbit, who had hopped in from the kitchen, checked out Olivia before obeying. Anne scooped him up and began to nuzzle and coo.

"You'll be inheriting, though, won't you? Getting your share?"

"It's little enough, considering what Schultzy takes out of my hide." Anne checked her watch, a massive multifunctional Rolex. "Shit. Late again. I *hate* how he changed me to mornings."

"I'll just use the phone while you dress. I want McGuire to know how you and I can both be telling the truth."

"Be my guest. Read my mail, help yourself to the fridge. Sheesh!"

She flounced out, Bun in her arms.

McGuire was at his desk. He listened to Olivia's account and thanked her for calling.

"So what now?" the detective's noncommittal response obliged her to ask. "Will you hold a press conference? How're you going to get me out of this thing?"

"It doesn't work that way, Mrs. Chapman. We do our job and the media does theirs."

"I've done some of your job for you, last night with Keith and now this. I'd say you owe me. Since I didn't make that call, who did? Anne says she spoke of it only within the family. Have you questioned them all about it?"

"I can't tell you that, Mrs. Chapman. I assure you we're working very hard to get to the bottom of things. Any assistance you or anyone else offer us, we appreciate it."

There Olivia had to quit. More back and forth would convey the dangerous impression that the police harbored doubts of her innocence, and Anne, malicious, talkative Anne, was almost certainly listening behind the door.

But what was her next move? Go home, trust McGuire's stated good intentions, try to get some work done? Or check out Gordon, see what he had to say about the mysterious call.

Anne might phone ahead, tip him off. The way to stay in charge here was to tell her to do so, see what happened. "You want to be nice to Gordon," she called through the door, "let him know I'm on my way."

"Nice to that one?" Anne shot back. "When he treats me like a retard?"

18

The door to Gordon's office was ajar. When Olivia entered, he rose from his desk, his expression contrite. Darla, sitting in one of the chairs facing the desk, stayed put. Her color was high, her posture tense.

Olivia took the chair next to Darla. No stage fright this time, not even the slightest hint.

"I was expecting you," Gordon said, sitting down. "Anne just called."

"Good. I asked her to. Are you the one who leaked my name?"

"Of course not. It's an outrage. You have every right to be angry and upset. I'm angry too, believe me."

"Who, then? Ben? Chess? Morton Thaler? Had to be one of you."

"Your name was all over that *Globe* article," Darla said. "Anyone could put two and two together."

"And produce the exact story Anne told the police? Be serious."

Darla shrugged. "Maybe it *was* the cops. They've done worse."

Olivia turned back to Gordon. "Did the police ask you where you were at the time of the shooting?"

"That's routine."

"I know. But since I was caught without an alibi, I'm curious how many others are in the same position. You, Chess, Ben, folks like that."

"I don't know about Ben. As usual, he's out of the loop. Chess and Boyd—that's her husband—were driving home from a late meeting out on one twenty-eight. There's no way they could have doglegged back to Harding Hill and reached Concord when they did."

"And we were home," Darla said. "With the phones off the hook, same as every other Tuesday."

Something—sexual pride?—tugged at the corners of her mouth.

Gordon, solemn, played it straight. "Tuesday's slow in the food business. Thursday to Monday we work our butts off, so it's really nice to kick back, pull up the drawbridge."

"We don't even let messages in," said Darla. "Which of course is why Anne couldn't reach us. Even later, when the police came around, we almost didn't answer the door."

Olivia decided she'd heard enough about one lucky couple's domestic bliss. "I'm glad to have this chance to compare notes, Gordon. After last week I wasn't sure what kind of reception I'd get."

Back to contrite. "I'm sorry I did that. Real sorry. I don't know what got into me."

"Some kind of spell? The phase of the moon?"

Gordon sighed. "Jane had been getting on my nerves—mine and everyone else's. Her Woodside thing . . . well. It's no secret I think it's a bad idea. I was scheduled to make a little speech at the auction, you know. Say nice things about Jane and all. I wrote it out, rehearsed a couple of times, and then this friend of mine on the paper called to read me that big publicity blast she gave herself, which I found totally outrageous. I mean, you've met Jane, right? Would anyone ever have heard of her except for my father? Anyway, the last minute there, I just couldn't motivate myself to make that speech. Kind of a system shutdown, I guess. I had to call in sick."

"And the next day you had to knock my cheese on the floor?"

"That's not fair!" cried Darla. "Jane's forever going on about you, Olivia this, Olivia that—like you walk on water. You can't blame Gordon for thinking you were behind all this stuff. I mean, Jane's no self-starter. *Someone* had to be pulling her strings."

Gordon gave Olivia a small, pleading smile. "The main thing is, I was way out of line, blowing up at you. And like I said, I'm really, really sorry. No hard feelings?"

"No hard feelings." Olivia didn't smile back. "One more thing—Jane's charge to me is to watch over Keith. I'm taking it seriously. I'm having lunch with him today, and it would help if I understood his legal position in relation to Jane's assets. I tried to reach Thaler this morning, but he was busy. How about you trying him for me?"

"Right now?"

"I don't mind waiting. Just tell him I'm one of the good guys, and he should give me five minutes."

Olivia could see Gordon weighing it. Then he picked up the phone and punched in a number he knew by heart.

"It's Gordon, Aunt Ruth. Uncle Mort there? Oh gosh, I'm sorry to hear . . . no, don't do that. It's only that Olivia Chapman's here, in my office . . . yes. She's meeting Keith for lunch, and she wants to ask Uncle Mort a couple of questions first. No, it's OK, I understand. Hold on a sec, OK?" He covered the mouthpiece. "He started feeling faint, and the doctor sent him to bed. Right now he's asleep. You want his wife to give him a message?"

"Keith needs to know how he stands legally. Specifically, can he count on an advance from Jane's estate in the form of an allowance, and can he stay in the house?"

Gordon passed this on, listened to a lengthy response, and hung up. "She'll tell him when he wakes up," he told Olivia. "She doesn't want to, but she will. He's pretty upset—his oldest friend gone, and now this."

Darla clucked her tongue, sighed.

"I wonder," Olivia said as if musing aloud, "why Jane asked her decorator to do lawyer work."

"I wondered that too."

Gordon's response, Olivia thought, had come a beat too fast. "Did she trust Thaler?"

"Of course she did. Why wouldn't she?"

"I don't know. But my guess is she didn't, any more than she trusted Dr. Jonny's children. Why else ask a relative stranger to watch over her son?"

Gordon went dark red. Darla bristled protectively. Neither spoke, and, after a long minute of silence, Olivia stood. "Thaler might be happier communicating with you than me," she said, offering Gordon her business card. "There's a machine if I'm out."

"Sure, fine," he said, all accommodation and helpfulness as he took her card from her hand and stuck it in his Rolodex.

Riding toward Harvard Square, Olivia summarized. Anne had fought her at every turn; Gordon, on the whole, had tried to placate. Simple personality differences? Could be. More conclusively, despite Jane's apparent loss of confidence in Thaler, Gordon's remained strong. Was this an indication of complicity? Were Thaler and the Griscom kids up to something that had made them untrustworthy in Jane's eyes? Up to something so big that Anne, no fan of Gordon's and running late besides, had second thoughts and made that warning call?

Complicity. Over what, though? Jane's "Woodside thing," to use Gordon's phrase? But had Anne even mentioned Woodside? Olivia didn't think so. In passing, maybe, but nothing more.

It was too hot for Harvest's outdoor terrace. After a stop in the bathroom to sluice cool water over her face and arms, Olivia asked for the most private table the dining room could supply and a San Pellegrino. Thirsty work, confrontation.

Keith was almost fifteen minutes late, the fault, he explained, of a *Herald* reporter who had cornered him as he was leaving the hospital.

"Guy named Costello?" Olivia asked.

"Hey. You know him?"

"Just the name."

The ceiling spot above Keith's chair lit him without flattery. He looked tired, distinctly older than he had at the auction, when everything had been going so well. "Bloody Mary," she told the waiter. "A double."

Keith said he'd have the same, and when the waiter had left, Olivia asked about Costello's line of questioning.

Keith rolled his eyes. "First he goes, how's it feel, finding your mom after all these years and then this terrible tragedy. I'm basically like, how do you think it feels, pinhead, so he starts on you. No kidding! He goes, what's the real reason Olivia Chapman called your mom last night? I'm like, whoa, what're you talking about, and he gives me this story about you calling Mom to look at a house. You didn't, did you?"

"No."

"I knew it. Creep wouldn't believe me."

"What made you so sure?"

"You woulda told me!"

Relief made Olivia laugh. Ingenuousness that pure had to be trusted. Whatever else Keith may have done, he had no part in setting up Jane.

She told him what she knew and heard out his amazement that Anne, and probably the other Griscoms, had presumed her capable of the crime. Then she asked the question that held her chief doubt about him. "How did the person doing the shooting know you wouldn't be there—either as a witness or getting in the way?"

"I guess because I go to the square every night."

"Who knows that?"

"Everyone my mom knows. She thinks it's great. Some nights?

When it's real hot? I'd just as soon couch out with the tube, but she won't let me. Specially not with college coming up."

"Might she have mentioned it to Arnette Murfin?"

"I guess. Yeah, accounta it's basically educational and education's their thing."

And Arnette could have told all Woodside. *This white boy? He don't go moping round, no money for books, he get hisself down the store and read for free.* "What time do you go out, as a rule?"

"Right after dinner—seven o'clock, seven-thirty. Last night was different, accounta Mom and Anne were having dinner together. I went out a little after six o'clock. I was going to read a coupla hours and then have a bite in the square. Basically that's the way I like to do it, but Mom likes to eat earlier. I guess I've, like, gotten in her habit, because I was real hungry by seven o'clock. And, you know, beat, accounta how hot it's been. I had a roast beef at Elsie's and walked straight home—until I saw the cruisers and all."

If you were so inclined, and Olivia was, you could conclude from this that the person who made the call had the Harding Hill household's habits and movements down pat. Knew details that Arnette Murfin, hence Woodside, probably didn't.

She asked about Jane.

"They only let me in for a coupla minutes. To be honest, I couldn'ta taken much more. It was a terrible thing, seeing her that way. It really hit me, you know? Right here." He banged his chest with his fist. "I mean, last night? When I left her? She was reading this book she's really high on, about a woman in Australia, no, New Zealand, who figured out all these ways to teach the native kids how to read. I hope that's what stays in my mind—Mom all excited, grabbing her yellow marker for something she wants to try in Woodside. That's how I want to remember her, you know? Not with the tubes and all."

Olivia nodded.

He was draining his glass when the thought struck him. "Oh

God, here I am yakking away and you've got your husband . . . I'm a jerk."

Jane, matter of course, would have filled him in on Philip—not the heparin part, nobody knew about that, just the old story. "Don't be sorry. It's OK." Because, she carefully didn't add, you can get used to anything when you're given no choice. "But listen, has Jane been conscious at all? Every time I call I get the same report—'very guarded.' "

"No one knows for sure what's going down. This one nurse? The one who was on most of the night? She picked up Mom's hand to fix the IV and Mom squeezed her fingers. But the doctor's basically like, don't get your hopes up."

His eyes were wide and bleak. Nothing to say, Olivia reached across the table to touch his arm.

"If only I'da stayed home, you know?"

Their waiter was in hover mode. "We should order," Olivia said.

"I guess," Keith gloomed. Then, having settled on a grilled pork chop with black beans and rice, he gave her an abashed smile. "Actually," he admitted, "I'm kinda hungry."

"Another round?" she asked, indicating their empty glasses. Nothing less appetizing than Bloody Mary sludge.

"I don't know. I can really feel that vodka."

"Whole point of vodka," she said, signaling the waiter.

She let him eat half of his chop before starting in. "How well do you know Morton Thaler?"

"I only met him once, coupla weeks ago. I was dropping Mom at his office."

"Have you spoken to him this morning?"

"No. Should I of?"

"Sure. I'm surprised he didn't call you."

"You are?"

"Come on, Keith. He's your mother's lawyer. He might have her

170

power of attorney. I've tried to reach him myself, but he hasn't gotten back to me."

Keith looked surprised. "You know Mr. Thaler?"

"We've met. I liked him."

Keith appeared to be weighing his response. "A situation like this, is Mr. Thaler working for my mom or the rest of the family?"

"Good question. Sounds like you think there's a conflict."

"No, not really."

"Oh? The Griscom kids care as much about you as your mother does?"

"I guess not, you put it that way."

"Better call him. Ask him where you stand. How long you can stay in the house, your chances of getting an allowance, things like that."

"Oh God. I couldn't. I mean, that's so, I don't know, pushy."

"You're not a little kid, Keith. You've got to be practical."

"I guess. But seeing Mom like that . . . it's hard."

Olivia stayed brisk. "You need to be able to plan. What if she's still the same when classes start this fall? See what I mean? If Thaler's hands are tied for some legal reason and he can't make you an allowance, you'll need to have a job lined up that won't interfere with your academic schedule."

"Yeah. God."

Misery again. Strike a constructive note. "How about calling your old boss?"

"I can't. I mean, I don't want to do that anymore. It's horrible work, being a phone pest. I don't know how I stood it so long."

"Still, if you did well there, they'll give you a nice recommendation. Which you'll have in hand, if and when you need it."

"I guess."

"Buck up, Keith. You're on the right track. Even if you have to scrounge, it's only until you get your degree. Not a life sentence."

"I know," he said, sounding far from convinced.

He turned down dessert and coffee, responding without spirit to every further attempt she made to draw him out.

Cut him loose, she told herself, before he drags you down with him. "Let's recap. I'll be in my office all afternoon. If you get Thaler first, let me know what he says, OK? And Keith? You'll get started on that recommendation, won't you? Where was it, again?"

"Huh?"

"The brokerage house where you—"

"I said! I'm not going back there!"

Well, well, Olivia thought, what have we here?

Leaving the restaurant, she was so ready to have done with Keith and her failed good intentions that she could hardly bear to look him in the eye. And thus almost missed a revelation that knocked her socks off.

19

At home, before she tackled her revelation, Olivia ran her messages. There was another plea from persistent Costello that she call him at the *Herald*—was the man hoping to get one of those true crime books out of this?—but the rest of the city's reporters seemed to have moved to fresher stories. Somehow the morning news had penetrated Dee's writing workshop: "I'm stuck on campus until ten tonight, but I wanted you to know I'm appalled. And rooting for you." Two other friends, women, their voices soft with concern, said, in various ways, if you want to talk, I'm here.

No word from Gordon or Morton Thaler. Dialing Thaler's number, she was told by a machine that he'd be out the rest of the day. Next she called Mary Jane Hughes, her own lawyer. Mary Jane had a profoundly linear mind, her perspectives not Olivia's own. The dissonance had often proved useful.

Ironically, Mary Jane had heard nothing and needed to be filled in from scratch. "I realize I'm mere supporting cast," Olivia finished, "and the real story is Dr. Griscom. Still . . ."

"It's a nasty business. I don't hear slander, though. And I don't recommend making a statement. The lower your profile, the sooner people will disconnect you from the Griscom loop."

"You know what really rankles? All but one of the Griscoms, Thaler too, have met me, talked to me enough to have a sense of what kind of woman I am. Even so, there's been no benefit of the doubt. Just this automatic assumption that I made the call, I'm part of the attack on Jane, I leaked the story."

"Forget them," was Mary Jane's advice. "Stuff them in the Bad Client file and slam the door hard."

When she'd hung up, Olivia was clearer on why she'd wanted to check in with her lawyer. She had needed to hear that none of society's orderly rules and patterns applied here. She could not, as her mother had always insisted she must, simply speak up and tell the truth. Not even the fundamental American recourse—*I'll sue ya!*—was an option. And as for relying on the police to silence rumor and speculation, why bother? It was she, not McGuire and his like, who was within grasp of a splendid secret truth.

Onto the revelation!

One of the friends who had offered a sympathetic ear was Nanda Lispenard, home on leave with her first baby. Like her husband Drew, Nanda was in venture capital, a good resource for the questions Olivia wanted to ask. Equally important, Olivia knew that nothing she said to Nanda would go any further. She'd probably tell Drew, but that was fine; Olivia and Philip had known Drew for years. They'd liked him. Not only was he attractive and charming, his mother had written a series of children's books they themselves and then Abbott and Ryland had been raised on. Still, he hadn't been a close friend until Nanda came into his life, love allowing him to shuck an exasperating playboy carapace. For this they readily forgave Nanda's relative youth, and the two couples had enjoyed one of those rare four-sided friendships; there'd been a memorable ski weekend, a week in the Caribbean. Trimmed to a threesome they sorely missed their old symmetry; the compensation, still emerging, was that Nanda and Olivia had drawn closer than before.

"How are you Nanda? How's Caroline?"

"Milky. Milk's our universe here. It's wonderful and amazing, and I'm very impressed with myself. The only problem is, I miss my real tits. I suppose that's not politically correct, so don't tell on me. But Olivia! How are you? I was listening to the radio and there's all this innuendo."

"Jane Griscom's my client, but I didn't make that call. Someone must have impersonated me or pretended to be my secretary. Listen, Nanda, I want to get together, talk at length, but right now I need some info. First, about Chess Griscom's business—does she depend on her father's position and relationships to find good investments?"

"You bet. It would be virtually impossible for a partnership of two to spread a net that big and potent without insider access. Even if Boyd Pierce were as smart as Chess, which he most definitely isn't. He's the capital—inherited, natch—and she's the venture. The brains and the contacts."

"So with the father dead, what happens?"

"Not much. Their network might even be stronger—the fallen hero, blah, blah. How I talk! I hope Caroline didn't hear that jaded note. But I'd say they're in good shape, Chess and Boyd. It's going to be a long time before the last generation of scientists Dr. Griscom personally touched hangs up their lab coats."

"Thanks. One more thing—do you know, off the top of your head, which Boston brokerage firms hire people to break the ice for their brokers? Initiate their cold calls?"

Only the biggest, Nanda said; her list was a short one. Olivia called them in alphabetical order. Four tries brought her to Norris, Pitney.

"Personnel."

"This is Sally Burkholder at Filene's. We've been given Norris, Pitney as an employment reference for Keith Somers . . . Thanks, I'll hold."

The woman came back on the phone to say yes, Keith Somers had worked in phone sales. She gave Olivia the dates he had started and terminated. "Anything else on him, you'll have to talk to his supervisor, Mr. Scanlon. Want me to transfer you?"

Olivia said yes, please, and Scanlon picked up. "Oh sure, I remember Keith well. A good kid, on the whole. Still wet behind the ears, but a real go-getter. Some of the kids here just put in their hours, but Keith was a tiger. The brokers loved him. I was about to send in his name for our on-job training program, so when he upped and quit like that I was real surprised. Kind of hurt, to tell you the truth."

"Maybe he got ticked off with someone? You know what they say about redheads and temper."

"Redheads? We talking about the same guy? Keith has brown hair."

"With red highlights?"

"Brown, I'm telling you. Light brown. I've got four kids with the exact same color."

"I think I need to go to the eye doctor," Olivia said. "One last thing. Did Keith have any face-to-face contact with the public?"

"To a degree. Bear in mind most customers deal with us by phone. But the office is set up so visitors pass right by the calling team. Personalizes things, right? They see flesh-and-blood results from their work, they can sell better."

"So how did Keith do, meeting people?"

"Fine, far as I know. Mostly he was on the phone, of course."

"Say he was coming back from a break and ran into a customer he knew. Was he the kind of guy who'd shake hands, chat a bit?"

"I can't cite chapter and verse, but sure, why not? He was a sociable guy."

"Thanks Mr. Scanlon. You've really helped me." She hung up and let out a whoop. Her perfect-pitch color sense had come through again. Keith's tired, faded look that had prompted her sympathy in the restaurant had become, out in the sunlight, something else—a dye job that was a barely perceptible fraction away from its normal intensity.

Hardly breathing, she flipped back through her datebook to the week that Personnel had said was Keith's next to last on the job. There, on Thursday's noon line, was what she'd been hoping to find: C. Griscom, Maison Robert.

The yellow and white umbrellas, Chess's nifty yellow dress. Chess complaining she was late for a meeting with her broker. Probably she hadn't laid out the deal to Keith then and there. She'd have been astonished at the resemblance and wondered if Jane's illegitimate son had come back to haunt them. Wait, though. According to Jane, the son was a deep dark secret.

Secrets will out, though; Jane could be mistaken. If Chess had pitched imposture to Keith, she had to be mistaken. And almost certainly Keith must have gone for the deal pretty fast, quitting his job soon after because he couldn't show up with his hair dyed red.

Olivia thought of one more duck to get in line before she could load and fire. Dialing Norris, Pitney, again, she asked for the executive in charge of brokers handling individual accounts. "I think you want Mr. Anderson," the operator said. "I'll ring."

Mr. Anderson, a different woman said, was in a meeting.

"Are you his secretary?" Olivia asked. "Wonderful. I'm sure you can help me. I'm Mrs. Burkholder, a good friend of Chess Griscom's. Francesca, she'd probably be listed as. She recommended her broker to me, but I lost the piece of paper I wrote his name on, and all I can remember is Norris, Pitney. She's out of town on a business trip, and you know how these things are. Today's the day I'm determined to get this money working for me."

"No problem," the secretary said. "Spell the name and I'll cross-reference it."

Olivia spelled, heard tapping keys. "Mr. Boardman has that account."

"Is he in a branch office or right downtown?"

"Downtown. I'll transfer you."

"Thanks a million," said Olivia and hung up.

Back in the saddle, back to Cambridge. With this adrenalin rush, she'd fly.

Climbing Harding Hill, Olivia made a distinction. There was gall and unmitigated gall. Keith's imposture had taken gall, but at least he had come into the sickening thing as a stranger, presumably for profit. Chess's indecency was miles worse. Chess had known exactly how eager and vulnerable, how much in need, Jane would be. And heartlessly counted on these qualities to insure the success of the fraud.

The yellow police tapes Keith had mentioned were gone. The glossy front door—Olivia had a sudden, horrible vision of Keith, conscientious son of the house, laying fresh paint over the surface he'd taken such pains to prepare—was closed and locked.

Olivia rang the bell, but no one came. He'd said he was going straight home. Was he in the backyard, scraping more paint? Fearful of finding a dark spot of blood on the driveway, she walked around on the other side, through Keith's recently sprouted clover.

He lay asleep on a new-looking chaise in the deep shade of an ancient sycamore. Other chairs, cheap aluminum ones with most of their webbing broken, were scattered around. A paperback of *The Stranger* had fallen to the weedy ground.

He wore only a pair of ancient Bermudas much too big for him—Dr. Jonny's? His chest was narrow and hairless, his legs skinny. His resemblance to Jane remained uncanny. Looking at him, Olivia felt disconcertingly close to what must have been Chess's initial impulse: *I can use this.*

Get Olivia help Keith money. The hoax unmasked, a different meaning emerged. What if Jane had suspected? Posed him some dithering questions? He'd evade, pretend he didn't understand. But he'd know she doubted him. He'd catch her looking at him in a certain way.

He had found, Olivia remembered, the form for his search letter in a book about adoption. Nothing would prevent him from spending his reading hours in the square with books on wills and inheritance, learning from them that the decedent's intent is often decisive in settling estates. Meaning that Jane dead without a will in his favor was a far better gamble than Jane alive and exposed to doubt's steady, corrosive drip. *Get Olivia to help,* Jane might have meant, *Keith's after my money.*

She felt a leap of fear. Who dares to fall asleep outside in a neighborhood where there's just been a shooting? Someone with firsthand knowledge about the shooting, that's who.

But wait. He'd convinced her at lunch that he knew nothing about the phone call. He was a good actor, good enough to carry off his fraud, but not that good. Anyway, he didn't have a gun right now.

"Keith. Keith! Yo! Wake up."

His eyes flew open. Panicked. Good.

Seeing it was only Olivia, he blinked, stretched, murmured about the vodka, the heat. He sat up, swung his legs over the side of the chaise. Then, afterthought, the wide panicky eyes again. "Is it my mom?"

"No. I've just been talking to Mr. Scanlon at Norris, Pitney."

"I told you, I don't want anything to do—"

"You're through, Keith. They blew you out of the water. You and Chess and your nasty fraud. Chess found you that Thursday and you quit because you couldn't show up with dyed hair. Then you pretended you were still working until you'd snowed Jane enough to set yourself up here. Mr. Scanlon thinks you're a born salesman. He's dead right. Shut *up*. You can carry on when I'm not around to listen."

Olivia, wobbly from relief because he'd started to cry instead of lunging for her throat, reached for the most intact chair. "The only thing I want to hear from you is Chess's game plan," she said, sitting down but keeping herself tall, fierce, ready to sprint if she had to. Or fight. Soaking wet, Keith couldn't weigh as much as her brother James back when she could still beat him up. "And don't try to lie. One whiff of fishy and I'm going straight to the cops."

"I didn't shoot her. I'm totally out of that."

"Yeah? Prove it. *Stop that blubbing.* All right. Begin with who you really are."

"I'm not adopted, that's the only difference. Everything else is the same—my folks, my grandma, the motel, everything. Which is how come Chess was sure it would work, accounta anyone checked, my grandma's really senile. Anyways, in Massachusetts, adoption records for people my age are sealed tight. Mom's real kid, if he's still out there, wouldn't know anything. I mean, he might know he was adopted, if his new folks told him, but never who his real mom was. And Mom wouldn't know who'd adopted him or what name they gave him. But basically Chess was like, no one's gonna think to check, accounta we look so much alike. Plus, don't forget I had the exact date."

"How? From Chess?"

"Who else? But you gotta understand, I didn't know Mom then! That's the whole thing! Now that I know her—listen, you think it's been easy? I *like* her. And she likes me. Lotsa guys I know, they're like, get me *outta* here on the subject of their moms. But Mom and me . . . you've seen us, right? We get *along.*"

"Sure. And every lie you've told her is for her own good."

"Like I said, you've seen her. Doesn't she look happy?"

"Yes, and that's enough of that. How did you come by the date?"

"When Bonita—Anne and Gordon's mom?—killed herself, Chess was like *it* for Dr. Griscom. Took over his finances and everything—accounta he was basically a basket case. Then he fell in love with Mom—I see you making that face, but what else should I call her? Anyways, somewhere in there Mom decided she'd hafta tell him about the baby, accounta it was what they call a life-defining event and also a major, major secret. Dr. Griscom shoulda respected her privacy. He was way outta line, telling Chess."

Keith mounting a moral high horse was a bit much. Olivia told him to get on with it.

"Even though she had the date, Chess wasn't taking any chances. She made me go through all the steps any regular adoptee would. Bureau of Records, all that."

"I thought you said the records were sealed."

"That's the state. The books I read said to try hospitals too. Remember that girl Deb? At the auction? She, uh, helped me out." He broke off, rolled his eyes meaningfully upwards. "I hadda tell her I had this insanely jealous girl friend. So she hangs out here, right here at the house, follows me for a coupla weeks. No kidding. Spies on me when I'm in the Square and all. So we have this major confrontation, accounta where's my girl friend, right? I go, we broke up, so a course Deb's ready to move right in, take her place. I'm like, no thanks nine million different ways to Sunday, and finally she gets it. Sorta gets it. You saw, right? At the auction?"

Olivia didn't want to be sidetracked by the hapless Deb. "Do the other Griscom kids know you're a fake?"

"Course not," He scowled. "They treat me like dirt. Mom thinks it's sibling rivalry."

"You don't?"

"I know a snob when I see one. Not Chess. She's all nicey-pie." Another scowl. "She has to be, right?"

Too bad, Olivia thought, she hadn't seen the four Griscoms interacting with their new stepbrother. Chess's uncharacteristic niceness—Olivia, too, knew a snob when she saw one—might have set off alarm bells.

"Jane said her real son was thirty. Don't tell me you are too."

"I'm thirty-two. No big deal. Hadda get a new driver's license, is all. I told them New York had screwed up way back when and I'd never bothered to fix it."

"What about your birth certificate?"

"If anyone asked, I'd just say I lost it. Which happens to be the God's honest truth, my mom disappearing and all. You don't

181

actually need a birth certificate in this world. Leastways I haven't had occasion to."

That's so, Olivia thought. She'd used hers exactly once, to get a passport.

"Weren't you afraid Jane would try to call you at work?"

"Not really. I told her we weren't allowed personal calls."

"And how did your neighbors react to your transformation into a redhead?"

"They didn't. I moved before I did it."

"OK, that's enough of Keith Somers, Master Criminal. Let's have the why—what this plan was supposed to accomplish."

"Basically I was supposed to keep Mom from going into Woodside."

"Come on."

"That was it, honest to God. Chess was like, she'll be so distracted by having a kid of her own, her real kid, she'll forget the place. Also, I could, you know, work on her. Basically Chess didn't want those people over there getting any good outta killing her father."

"And that was enough for you?"

"Hey. It wasn't my deal, was it? I went in to do a job and I did it to the best of my ability. Don't forget, it was me who got Mom off the idea of living in Woodside, which wasn't easy, believe me. Specially after I started liking her so much. OK, laugh, but it was hard. Actually, you helped."

"Oh? How?"

"You convinced her to keep her furniture, right? So how long before they'd break in, rob her blind?"

Right, Olivia thought, remembering the night she'd first met Keith. He had, indeed, been eavesdropping on her predinner conversation with Jane. That's why, returning, he had changed the subject to furniture—to emphasize its importance to Jane's happiness.

"Basically how I handled it," Keith went on, "I kept telling myself Woodside's dangerous. You like someone, you don't want them moving there. As far as the preschool, no human on earth coulda talked her outta that. Which Chess basically admitted. Once Mom agreed we'd look for a house someplace else—that was you, too—Chess kinda relaxed on the school issue. Widows need hobbies, she'd go, people expect it. Then the family had this big meeting with Mr. Thaler. Mom wanted me included too, but Chess told me to stay away, so I didn't push it.

"After the meeting, Mom comes home real quiet. That big article they did on her? I had it out waiting for her and she hardly looked at it. Yeah, weird. I'd go, hey, Mom, musta been some meeting, huh? But she'd just give me this sad little smile. Life's so complicated, she'd go, so unbelievably complicated. The only thing that seemed to cheer her up was visiting Arnette. She'd come home and be her old self again. Full of plans and ready to roll. For a coupla hours, anyways."

"What kind of plans?"

"The usual. Ways to get the parents involved with the school, stuff like that. I gotta admit, I didn't always listen too close when it came to Woodside. I don't exactly relate to the place."

"When was this meeting?"

"The morning after the auction."

The morning before Gordon snubbed her in Leaves* of Life.

"How much did Chess pay you?"

Keith looked embarrassed. I would too, Olivia thought, having to admit my price. "Two thou."

No point showing shock. Grotesque, though, that he held himself so cheap. "Mr. Scanlon said he'd been about to recommend you for some training program."

"He did?"

"You sound surprised. Didn't you think you were doing a good job?"

"No one ever said."

183

"What about the brokers? Mr. Scanlon said they loved you because you were such a tiger."

"Yeah, well, they kept it to themselves. The first person in Boston, Mass. who was ever really nice to me was Chess Griscom and the second was Mom. Now Chess won't even talk to me on the phone, and Mom will hate me too, soon as you tell her what I did."

"That won't be for awhile."

Too beaten for hope, Keith looked wary.

"Do you have any reason," Olivia went on, "to think Jane had any suspicion of your hoax? Think carefully. Any little hint or sign?"

Keith was very sure. "Not a one. Never."

"OK. Let's agree that the last thing Jane needs, assuming she regains consciousness, is to hear the truth on you—at least until she's fully recovered. So what's our main job?"

Keith had to think. "We gotta keep Chess from telling her?"

"Right. How about focusing on that for awhile? You've been a clever fraud. How clever can you be for the sake of decency and caring?"

"You gonna tell the cops on me?"

"Depends. Let's say you're on probation. You handle it right, I might not."

"You gonna tell Mom?"

"I have no idea."

This was the absolute truth. Admitting it, Olivia felt herself pushed a little further out on an extremely dubious limb. Keith, tears or no, was far from a reliable partner. Even though she was reasonably sure he'd played no direct role in the shooting, that hardly cancelled the rest of the scenario she'd devised earlier—the part about the decedent's intent. As easily as Chess, Keith could enter the hospital room alone, whisper the killer truth into Jane's ear. Could break her heart, snuff out her will to live.

"By the way," she thought to ask, "who do you think shot Jane?"

"I say it was drugs. A gunman hired by some drug kingpin. Some big importer who didn't want Dr. Griscom or anyone else working on that crack blocker of his. Because look: the doctor coulda told Mom something, right? Gotten her to memorize part of the formula for him."

Very dry, Olivia asked why the doctor would want his wife memorizing his formula.

"For security. You know, like the code in a spy story? And the Coca-Cola formula? Only three people know exactly what's in Coca-Cola. It's a known fact—only three people in the whole world. And even they only have their own special part of the secret formula. Accounta kidnappers and all. Industrial espionage. They could grab one and torture it out of him, but without the other two it's totally useless. That's what I think it was—something like that."

His unblushing pride in this idiotic theory made Olivia feel sorrier than ever for Jane. She reminded herself that love is blind; no news there. What was new, and surprising, was the strength of her own determination to protect Jane. Not from Keith's pretensions of quicksilver intellect—Jane was on her own there—but from the cruelty of his imposture, committed for a measly two thousand dollars.

20

Cycling back, Keith dealt with for the time being, Olivia started to feel light, bouncy, ready for anything. Though she was no closer to the phone call, a new puzzle stood vividly before her: the agenda of the secret meeting. At her drafting table, teasing out the solution to one design problem often revealed the means of solving another. If she could discover what had left Jane so muted and overwhelmed by life's complexity, she might be able to un-ravel the rest.

Her secret knowledge of Keith's imposture and Chess's master-minding role ought to be some kind of trump card. But how to play it and with whom? Not with Chess, obviously—at least not until Jane had completely recovered or there was no longer any hope for her. What about Gordon? "Wanna zap Chess, Gordon? Tell me what happened at the meeting and I'll give you all you need."

It didn't sound like much of a deal. Anne, though . . . Anne might jump at it. She'd love making Chess squirm. The trouble was it wouldn't stop there. Anne was far too much the brat, too hungry for public attention, to keep a secret so delicious to herself. One phone call from her, to WBX, say, and Jane's vulnerability would multiply beyond calculation. Ben? A blank. A blank who lived in

Framingham, some twenty miles to the west. You can't play your only trump by phone. A try at Ben would require the van, a long joust with the commuter traffic already clogging Storrow Drive. Which left the local blank: Morton Thaler.

As if by design, Olivia was approaching the B.U. bridge. Thaler's street, she knew, was a straight shot south, in the pleasant neighborhood that lies between the university and Beacon Street. Little to lose, she made the turn.

A few years ago she'd done a house around here, a capacious stucco pile wrapped with broad porches. A tower with a fanciful cloche roof had given her three round rooms to play with. Great house, lousy clients. The Wilcoxes. Rich scrimpers. Olivia's energetic pleas for restoration of the original ceramic roof tiles were answered with a smug we-know-what-we-like insistence on asphalt shingle. And they hadn't paid their bill until Mary Jane set a court date.

A low wrought-iron fence separated Thaler's yard from the sidewalk. The house was brick with casement windows and a slate roof. Score one for Mort, Olivia thought. Slate's as costly to preserve as tile. The shrubs of the foundation planting had been relentlessly shaved into mounds, cones, and cylinders, even the azaleas; geometric order, to this household, was more important than a full realization of spring bloom. No weeds or crabgrass blemished the carefully groomed lawn.

Olivia locked her bike up at the fence and stepped onto the walkway. The front door opened. The woman standing behind the screen door spoke. "I hope that bicycle isn't chipping my new paint job."

"I was very careful."

Olivia heard a click. Ruth Thaler, if that's who the woman was, had locked the screen door. She stood a shade over five feet tall. Strawberry blond with a salon set. A shade on the heavy side but, Olivia would bet, constantly on a diet. Too feisty to lie down and quit on fat or anything else. Olivia could imagine her view of Dr.

187

Jonny's environmental landscaping: It's a free country, he can do what he wants. But *my* house is going to look *nice.* "Mrs. Thaler?"

Who wants to know, her look said. "Yes?"

"I'm Olivia Chapman. Gordon Griscom spoke to you about me. I was in the neighborhood and—"

"My husband can't see anyone. Doctor's orders."

"I'm sorry to hear that."

"You're not the only one."

"Did you have a chance to pass on my questions about Keith?"

"The letter's in the mail. Chess wants the boy to have a weekly allowance. And he can stay in the house until they sell it. So stop with the calls, all right? He hears the phone, it gets him started. Have some pity."

Chess wants. The trump was looking better and better. "Thanks, Mrs. Thaler. I won't bother you again."

Ruth Thaler's grunt was skeptical, aggrieved. "Watch that paint," she said, then stood watchful herself, making sure Olivia obeyed.

A slight downgrade led to Beacon Street and a green light. Picking up speed as she approached the crossing, Olivia made a decision. If the light turned red before she could sail through, she'd call it a day. If not, she'd get out the van and have a go at the only Griscom left, the mysterious Ben.

The street where Ben and Barb lived had once been quite grand. Now it was a showcase of cheapo expediency—vinyl siding, aluminum awnings, crude asphalt approximations of brick or fieldstone. The spindly new trees at curbside were mostly dead. Cars were packed into driveways and along the street, indicating widespread conversion to multifamily use. At the Griscom house were four bells, no intercom.

The heavy door, scarred golden oak, had an oval window, an apt frame for the woman who answered Olivia's ring. A large white apron covered her highwaisted blue and white calico dress. Her brown hair was parted in the center and drawn into a long braid. She looked hot and exhausted.

Olivia fully expected to be told go away, we don't want any. But the woman managed a smile and opened the door. Olivia smiled back. "Is Ben home?" she asked.

"He's out Xeroxing something for the chorus. He'll be back soon—there's a rehearsal tonight and he still has to eat."

"You must be Barb. I'm Olivia Chapman."

Eyes widening, Barb reared back.

Olivia pushed into the foyer. "Don't worry," she said. "It wasn't me." Talking fast, she reviewed her visits to Anne and Gordon that morning. Then, encouraged by the way Barb was listening, she added something that had struck her on the drive out. "Over and above this name business, I'm responding to Jane's helplessness and isolation. The less the other Griscoms seem to be on her side, the more I feel her claims on me."

If Barb had asked why, she'd have tried to explain the rest. Having been banished to the same mysterious realm as Philip, Jane, too, deserved Olivia's care and concern. It might not make literal sense, she'd tell Barb, but it feels right. Satisfying.

But Barb only frowned, still wary. "That phone call—no offense, but why should I believe you?"

"Call Anne," Olivia invited. "Or Gordon. Or Detective McGuire. Who, don't forget, didn't arrest me last night—even though I had no alibi for the time of the shooting and couldn't begin to explain how Anne and I were both telling the truth."

" 'Anne' and 'truth' are two words I don't put together very easily. She's crooked as a corner, that one. But did I get you right? The person who called Jane is the same one who gave your name to the radio station?"

"Anne swears she mentioned my name only to family and the police. Got all huffy at the suggestion that she'd do anything to hurt the investigation of her father's death. Which narrows down pretty sharply who leaked. But as for the ambusher being family too, I don't know. Any ideas?"

Barb looked worried. "That detective—McGuire?—called us last night. He said not to talk about any of this stuff."

"Right. Just between the two of us, though, any idea who in the family wanted to get rid of Jane?"

"Except for Ben, the Griscoms are bad news. But that bad? I'd need to give it some thought."

"Can I come in while you think? And wait for Ben so I can ask him too?"

"I suppose. But he won't have much time for you. He had private students all afternoon, and he has to unwind or his stomach'll kick up."

The apartment was on the ground floor and, considering the size of the house, surprisingly cramped. A Bechstein concert grand—Bechstein!—nearly filled the first room they entered. "Here's where Ben teaches," Barb said as they edged through a clutter of music stands and battered folding chairs. "We've stayed on all these years because the landlady's a music freak. Someone complains about the noise, she says count your blessings, it's a free show."

From the adjoining kitchen came the smell of onions frying. Olivia sniffed. "Something burning?"

Barb swore and dashed to the ancient stove. While she was occupied with her skillet, picking out the blackest bits, Olivia sneaked a look around.

This must be where they spent time not claimed by music or sleep. There was a thrift shop dinette set and, standing on either side of a ponderously ugly floor lamp, two broken-down easy chairs. Near a wall phone hung a densely scribbled calendar. Yesterday's date said "6–8, soloists." The preceding Friday said "9 A.M. Thaler, Bkline."

"We're having westerns," Barb said. "If you're hungry, it's no trouble to break two more eggs."

190

If they were feeding her, they might not throw her out when her questions turned nasty. "I love westerns. You're nice to ask. What's the chorus singing?"

"Beethoven's Mass in C."

"Beautiful. I tried out for the alto solo in college. Didn't make it. One of the regrets of my life."

"You sing? You're so lucky. I've got a tin ear. The soloists were here last night, practicing. I thought they sounded fine but Ben's worried about the tenor."

Check. Barb and Ben didn't shoot Jane. "When is the performance?"

"Next week. That's why Ben's so busy. Conducting amateurs, you really work—much harder than with professionals. And not only because the raw material is, well, so raw. Ben's up to his ears selling tickets, finagling free publicity, raising money to pay the orchestra, you name it. The chorus members help, but it's on him to keep everything together."

"And I bet a lot of keeping him together falls on you."

"But that's my *privilege*. I love music. Ben says I don't hear it well enough to truly love it, so I suppose I should say I value it—what it does for people. To me it's miraculous that people can just open their mouths and have something beautiful come out. I'm praying hard our kids'll take after Ben, not me."

Her smile turned wide and real. "It's awful that Dr. Jonny had to die like that, but like they say, an ill wind can blow good. We're pregnant."

"That's wonderful! Congratulations."

"We're still pinching ourselves. Older mother, fibroids, you have to expect a long haul. But here we are, first try. Fertile turtle, Ben calls me, but my personal feeling is that the minute I knew we had enough money to try for a baby, everything in me relaxed and, you know, went for it."

"When are you due?"

"Late March." She giggled. "I'm all of five days gone. At the most. I got the kit on Sunday. I felt like a fool buying it so early but I just couldn't stand the suspense."

Five days ago was the meeting. Olivia could imagine Ben's arrival home, his arms thrown wide. *We're in the will! Dad didn't cut me out!* Whereupon Barb's tremulously waiting body, comprehending in an instant what her mind hadn't yet grasped, opened itself to him and his seed.

Ask Barb about the meeting? Olivia didn't want to spook her. Also, her unguarded reference to it indicated that she, like Keith, had been kept in the dark.

Better save the meeting question for Ben. And better change the subject—expectant mothers tend to get stuck on their central topic. "What's the exact date of the concert? Great. I'm going to be there. If the chorus always sings as beautifully as they did at Dr. Jonny's service, it should be quite an evening. Ben was superb, I thought. I wanted to tell him so, but I didn't see him at lunch."

"He skipped that part."

Olivia waited, continuing only when it was clear Barb wasn't going to say more. "My college chorus sang the Fauré too. I'm not religious, but that kind of music gives me the feeling of what belief must be like. Especially during Ben's solo. Eternal fire, divine judgment—listening to him, it seemed real. Not symbolic, *real.*"

Barb became very absorbed in spinning the salad greens.

"I have to admit," Olivia said in a much lighter voice, "the Griscom kids fascinate me."

Barb tore lettuce. "They don't fascinate *us.* We keep out of their way."

"Sure, but to an outsider—I hope this doesn't sound crass— that's fascinating too. I mean, here's Gordon, with his store resting on his father's funding and the fame of his father's book. And Chess's outfit gets first refusal on fancy medical technology invented by her father's pals. Anne—what's Anne get?"

A dry laugh. "Only total support since birth. The money she makes from her so-called jobs is gravy. She can blow it, do anything she wants with it. Dr. Jonny was big on carrot-and-stick persuasion. Hasn't exactly worked in Anne's case."

Barb turned, wiped her hands on her apron, and kicked the kitchen door shut. "You know a lot, so you must know how badly Ben's been treated." She dropped into the chair closest to Olivia. "Badly and cruelly. People in the arts expect unfairness from the world at large. Ben says America's motto should be Bombs not Bach. But when you're working yourself to the bone to make ends meet and your own father—"

Her voice had gone high and thin. She had to stop, swallow, collect herself. "My father makes about what Ben and I together do, but over the years he's given us what he can. You know, a nice check for birthdays and Christmas, dinner out, stuff like that. And Isabel? Ben's mother? In the early eighties, her second or third husband, I can't keep them straight, put most of her money into some oil fund that went belly up. Wait, it was her second husband. The one she has now is the tightwad. Even so, Isabel will pry something out of him if we're in crisis. And of course she bought Ben his Bechstein. But Dr. Jonny? The great humanitarian? From the time Ben decided to become a musician, he got nothing. Not a penny."

To keep Barb talking, Olivia was going to have to hold her nose; she was vehemently opposed to parental subsidies of able-bodied grown offspring. It seemed to her that corruption was inevitable, sparing neither giver nor receiver. The parents' root motive, admitted or not, was to undermine the kids' self-confidence, keep them bound, docile, dependent. Then the backfire: no docility. Instead, bitter, blaming resentment angry enough to last a lifetime—the lifetime of the younger hostage.

"I can't figure Dr. Jonny out," she temporized. "Wasn't it drummed into him to give to his children equally—love, money, treats, whatever?"

Barb had a teacher's answer. "He must have cut that lecture."

As if thinking aloud, Olivia pressed on. "The love part's a

dream, of course. Hopelessly idealistic. Kids can't be invariably lovable, parents can't be consistently capable of love. The rest, though, the rest stands. Parents disposed to give materially should give equally. Period."

"Of course they should!"

"The way you described the chorus, why wasn't it right up Dr. Jonny's alley?"

Barb's mouth twisted. "Five years ago Ben turned to his father for some money. The first and only time since he decided to become a musician. There was a movie theater downtown here, a little one, all gold carving and crystal chandeliers. Developers were about to tear it down. Ben had this beautiful vision of turning it into a performance center, not just for the chorus but for all kinds of amateur groups. He had to move fast, so he put all our savings down as a binder and went to his father for the rest. Dr. Jonny listened for five minutes and turned him down flat."

"The binder?"

"Lost. Ben never spoke to his father again."

"I can see why."

"I went crazy. Bombed right into the sacred laboratory, people in white coats standing around with their mouths open. How can you say no to this? I yell. All your talk about how American society erodes our capacity for communal action—what's a more viable community than a chorus? Up go the famous eyebrows. Viable? he asks. In what way? So I let him have it. Poured it out straight from the heart. The basic goals of a chorus, I told him, are unity, harmony, and beauty. To reach them, everyone has to rise above pettyness and ego tripping. If everyone sang in a chorus, I said, you and your crowd wouldn't have so much to criticize. And the world would be a better place." A wan smile. "I really put on a show."

"And made some excellent points. What did he say?"

"Same old shit. The arts are narcotic. They divert the citizenry from facing up to and reforming the pathetic charade they mistakenly call life. I'm a man of healing, a man of conscience. I can't in conscience support the arts any more than I can support TV, consumerism, military adventures, or organized religion. They're all diversions from the real blah, blah, blah."

She'd brought it all back down on herself. Her outrage was as fresh and disbelieving as if the encounter had been yesterday.

Olivia wanted to keep her going. "So that's why I didn't see anyone from the arts at the memorial service."

"Yes, and you know why we didn't go to lunch afterwards? Remember the talk by the woman in Dr. Jonny's research group? The one who needed a break because her husband had been fired and all? Well, it just so happens Dr. Jonny wrote that check for her the very day after I barged in to clean his clock. Damage control. Hiked himself back up on his pedestal. Thank God Chess is such a sexist she put the big shot Nobel guy at the beginning and the woman last. Ben's a pro, but that would've been too much for him. He wouldn't be able to sing a note. Thousands for an employee, zero for his own son. . . . There's the door, he's home. Don't tell what we've been talking about, OK?"

In shorts and T-shirt, Ben looked skinnier and less tall than Olivia remembered but enough like his father to remind her of the afternoon she'd fallen in lust. The same intensity, the same air of conviction. *Don't argue, don't think, just follow my lead, do my bidding. You'll love it, I promise.* No wonder his chorus could perform with such precise timing, such a sure sense of dynamics.

"This is Olivia Chapman, Ben. I invited her for supper so she could ask you about family stuff."

Alertness lifted his tired features. "The same Olivia Chapman who called Jane?"

Ignoring his weird glee, Olivia repeated what she'd told Barb of her visits to Anne and Gordon.

Ben had dropped into the chair opposite. "What's this got to do with me? My family's a toxic dump. I stay away from them."

"You consider Jane toxic?"

"Jane's not family. Not to me. I hardly know her."

195

It would be fruitless, Olivia saw, to plead her own kinship feelings for Jane. She tried a different tack. "What do you think of her plans for Woodside?"

Her question caught him by surprise, a reaction he immediately concealed. "What plans?"

"Her preschool."

He shrugged. "She picked one kind of rathole to pour water in, I picked another. Live and let live."

Barb swung around from the eggs she was whisking, her face puckered with concern. "Rathole? Music's a rathole?"

"Everything's a rathole. Or nothing is. Dealer's choice."

Barb flinched as if slapped, went back to her eggs without another word.

Pop the question, Olivia decided. The mood he's in, might not get another chance. "Barb said you'd need time to unwind," she said, giving it plenty of deferential concern, "so I'll get right to the point. I want to unhook myself from the attack on Jane. The best and quickest way to do that is to find out who really called her. Friday morning, all of you met with Mort Thaler. There's a connection between that meeting and what happened last night."

"Really. What kind of connection?"

"Causal. Jane learned something that caused her to react in a way that caused someone in the family to want her either scared past further action or crippled or dead."

Glee again. Less spontaneous, though. Might be an act.

"Wow. Even for the toxics, that's a lot. How'd you manage to concoct something so, what's the word? Baroque? Direful?"

Olivia smiled. "Easy. I've been with Griscoms all day."

Ben didn't glance at Barb. Olivia saw him being careful not to.

"None of your siblings," she continued with some truthfulness, "were ready to talk to me about the meeting. Thaler's been sent to bed by his doctor, so I couldn't ask him. Which left you. I ditched my bicycle, got out my van, braved the traffic, and dirtied the air burning gallons of irreplaceable fossil fuel. So, how about it? Who better than the family maverick to fill me in, see justice done?"

"Nope. Uncle Mort zipped my lips."

"McGuire—one of the detectives working on your father's murder—told me that homicide is either for the wallet or the bedroom. I'm not sure where his theory leaves your father, but I'd bet my bike Jane was shot for wallet reasons."

"Your privilege. Me, I hardly know the woman."

"She told me she was concerned about you." Olivia didn't add that Jane's main concern had been Ben's exploitation of Barb, ample sign of which she'd seen tonight in this kitchen. "She thought your father had treated you unfairly."

Ben shrugged again. "He did. But like they say, all's well that ends well."

"I'm starting these eggs," announced Barb. "Look at the time."

"Nothing for me," Ben said. "My stomach's killing me."

Barb's face crumpled. "But honey—"

Ben had hauled himself to his feet. "Maybe a soak in the tub," he said without confidence.

Barb reproached Olivia the instant he was out of the room. "He *has* to eat. He's got three hours of rehearsal ahead of him. And they're always at their worst right before a performance."

"I won't stay. Sorry to waste your eggs."

"This whole thing—you've really made me angry. You should've *said* you were going to ask about that meeting. I'd have sent you on your way, and Ben would be eating his dinner in peace. I mean, he didn't even tell *me* the details. And you just barge in—where's your sense of privacy?"

"Must be contagious. The Griscoms haven't worried much about my privacy either. Look, here's my card. After rehearsal, when Ben's not so fussed, will you give it to him? And urge him to change his mind about talking to me about the meeting? Fair's fair, right? Griscoms involved me, and Ben's a Griscom, like it or not. I have a business to run and my name has to be squeaky clean."

197

Barb was sullen. Mad at herself, probably, for daring to show anger. "I'll be asleep when he comes in."

"So ask him in the morning. Want me to write a note?"

"No! I want you to *leave*."

Olivia did. She wasn't a brute.

21

The next day began dark and soggy, rain imminent. Olivia's favorite weather for designing. With no sun marking the hours, the imagination, uncaged by linear time, can soar.

She poured herself some more coffee. How to settle into real work, paid work, with her head full of Griscoms?

Yesterday's lengthy efforts—every second a debit on Chapman Interiors's books—had solved only one problem, her responsibility for Keith's financial welfare. The rest was questions.

Especially baffling was the family's connection to Woodside, where it had all begun. According to Keith, Chess had been fully satisfied by his success in persuading Jane that Woodside was no place to live. But suppose Jane, at the meeting, had declared a change of heart on this? Arnette might have gotten to her. The reason Jane had come home so visibly refreshed from her visits with Arnette might be because Arnette had no qualms about telling her exactly what to do and how to think. No qualms, in other words, about filling the vacuum left by Dr. Jonny's death.

Of all the people involved in this puzzle, Arnette was the only one who stood to gain having Jane, and Jane's money, right on Wardell Street. Against that, Keith had said that Chess didn't want

Woodside—"those people"—deriving any benefit from her father's death.

So Chess, thwarted by Jane's change of heart, hires a gun to get rid of her?

Olivia banged down her mug, sloshing the table. If everything had begun in Woodside, she'd better go there herself.

Looking for Wardell Street, Olivia had to mentally draw the new Orange Line subway and its surrounding parkland corridor on her out-of-date street atlas. Even then, she overshot the address, which proved far closer than she'd assumed to the upscale shops and hotels of Boston's Back Bay. So close she'd scarcely needed to get out her bike, much less the van.

But there is psychological as well as geographic distance; she was glad of the van. You need armor for places like Wardell Street. She was also glad she'd worn jeans instead of shorts, sure-footed sneakers instead of sandals.

The charred ruin of the burned-out building, familiar from television, freshly appalled in actuality. The house she recognized as Arnette Murfin's looked painfully derelict. The vacant lot where Dr. Jonny had been shot was strewn with trash, discarded appliances, shopping carts, and two broken toilet seats, one white, one pink. The men on their milk crates seemed listless, doomed.

A dense smell of bacon hung in the humid air. Olivia imagined it being doled out to children with dull eyes, one strip apiece. To fill their stomachs for the hazardous day ahead, thick slices of cottony bread would then be fried in the fat—groundwork for the obesity and hypertension of middle age. Assuming the kids survived that long.

She felt herself clinging to the van, reluctant to leave its puny protection. But there, moving majestically down her front steps, was Arnette Murfin with a wheeled shopping cart. A solemn little boy followed.

Olivia caught up with them just before the vacant lot. "Good morning, Mrs. Murfin. Remember me? From Dr. Griscom's memorial service?"

Arnette grabbed the child's hand, yanked him close. "No comment! No comment!"

"I'm not a reporter, Mrs. Murfin. I'm Olivia—Jane Griscom's friend."

Arnette pushed past, yanking Talton along and throwing another "No comment!" over her shoulder. To Cyrus Grier and the rest, she announced loudly that she wasn't *about* to talk to no more media people, never.

"Uh huh," the men approved. And: *"Tell* the bitch, sister."

Unnerved, dying to run, wondering what absurdity of pride prevented her from running, Olivia retreated to the van and drove off in the direction opposite from the one Arnette had taken. Turning at the corner, she doubled back, paralleled Wardell for three blocks, turned again, parked, and waited. Earlier she'd spotted the neighborhood's sole retail option, a bodega on the corner. This, possibly, was Arnette's destination.

Sure enough, here she came. Feeling conspicuously white, grotesquely privileged, Olivia stepped forward to intercept.

Arnette's handsome face twisted in fury. "Ain't I told you no comment?"

Olivia handed her a business card. "Please call me," she urged, her voice low. "I'm trying to help Jane."

Arnette ostentatiously tore the card to bits and flung them into a dying privet bush. "Outta my face, you."

Olivia watched her march away, the wide-eyed child in tow. Arnette Murfin did not wish to renew their acquaintance. Or, interesting possibility, did not wish to be observed doing so by anyone in Woodside.

Driving back to the garage, Olivia faced it. Instead of banishing the Griscom distractions, she'd burdened herself further. Against the poverty and wretchedness of Wardell Street, design, decor, the refinements of the aesthetic dimension, seemed an insult. How dare she, anyone, spend a single moment "making the most of a river view" when misery like this existed practically next door?

How had Jane Griscom managed to visit Wardell Street and come home refreshed? The woman was a saint.

And martyr. The most perfect saints, the ones immortalized in great works of art, had been martyrs.

But you, Olivia firmly reminded herself, are neither. You are an ordinary sinner who must pay two prep school tuitions, a mortgage, taxes, nursing home bills, and punishing insurance premiums for house, van, health, and life. You are a moderately successful businesswoman who has to settle down, get to work. Exchange this scattered, agitated state for the calm suspension that will intuit Steven Dunbar's happiest dreams, discover their shapes and colors.

Back in her office, she keyed the phones so they wouldn't ring, dropped in a CD of Bach's late choral music, and opened a fresh layout pad. Then she tried suggestion, a trick she'd learned from Josie, her departed assistant, back when Philip's coma was new and all-encompassing.

I want to design, she began, impersonating deep, sure confidence, I can't wait to sit at my table with a nice new piece of charcoal in my hand. Feel the charcoal? Doesn't the paper smell good? I want to do it, I can't wait to start. It's play, not work. Heedless, free play. Paper's incredibly cheap. I can use all I want, use it quickly, irresponsibly, throw away what I've doodled or save it, doesn't matter, no one's watching, no one's keeping score. . . .

At some later point, thunder cracked overhead, waking her to her normal consciousness. Ravenous, she went to the refrigerator, grabbed bread, peanut butter, a carton of milk, the last of the strawberries she'd sliced for Abbott's shortcake. His visit seemed ages ago, but then, so did her misguided trip to Woodside and everything else. Purposely she avoided the clock. Rain was falling hard, the skylights dark drums. It might be evening. She didn't want to know.

The next time she came to, it was with the certain awareness that she had reached a stopping place. Now it was important to stay ignorant of how well she had played. Tempting as it was to leaf through the day's sketches, lists, and notes, reviewing them, for the first time, with the analytical, appraising part of her mind, she must not—not at this early stage. Let it cook. Let sleep and dreaming make their contribution.

Message lights blinked on both phones. Dee would be out until late on workshop business. "Third night in a row, if you're counting. Let's break bread tomorrow, celebrate the end of this marathon." Next was Sally, sounding cross, wanting a Griscom update. "Our friends are driving us crazy with questions. Do I have to come pounding on your door?" On the business phone was an invitation from a couple Olivia had done a house for last year. Climbers, the Gillises had been, but not unlikable. A pool party, it was, next Sunday. First swim of the year; she was tempted.

Nothing from Arlington House about Philip, nothing from the boys. Nothing, in short, she had to deal with right away.

Upstairs the skylights were brighter than they'd been all day. The rain was over. It was almost eight.

Thirsty, wanting, of all things, milk, she poured a glass and carried it up to the deck. The wind was strongly out of the west—fair weather ahead. Most of the sky was still piled with thick clouds, gunmetal gray, but a wide band of saffron stretched across the horizon. Forty minutes of daylight left, she calculated. The Esplanade paths would be puddled, relatively empty of roller skaters and the like. The decorator could give herself an airing, a hard push into the wind for six or seven miles, then turn around and let it blow her home. Then a bath, a bullet or three while the chili waiting in the refrigerator heated, and early bed. Call Sally if she felt up to it, but keep the ring buttons turned off. Extra red pepper on the chili for extra vivid dreams.

When Olivia was in sight of Harvard, the sun had dropped into the cloudless band at the horizon, its slanting rays striking the collegiate cupolas, twice gilding their weathervanes. Further west of these Georgian glories, Olivia had the pathway entirely to herself. Here the river grew narrower, and soon she was in sight of Northeastern's new boathouse. This structure, a knock-off of Harvard's much older boathouses downriver, always evoked for her the irritating career of Ralph Lauren. (Was she a fool to struggle for originality when derivative was such a best-seller?)

Across the river stretched Cambridge Cemetery. Philip had said, several times, that he wanted his ashes scattered there, next to Henry James's grave. Sally and Pip would want him boxed, stuck in the family plot, earth heaped on him. There was going to be a fight—all the more acrimonious because of her heparin deception.

Beyond the boathouse, the river took the wide bend that created the vest-pocket savanna Olivia liked so much. Across its hummocky ground approached a woman, a dismounted cyclist.

Olivia slowed, ready to ask if help were needed, and then realized it was Darla. Dark mud caked her shoes and streaked her sturdy legs. She looked distraught, close to breakdown.

"Bike trouble?"

"Another goose. Cotton. She's gone."

It took a moment for Olivia to register what she was talking about. Then she remembered: The plastic tubs of scraps from Leaves* of Life in Darla's handlebar basket, Gordon needling her over her proprietary claims, Darla's insistence that the geese knew her voice. But hadn't she just said *another* goose was gone. Was it open season on geese as well as Griscoms?

"Are you sure?" Olivia asked.

"It's a *flock*. If Cotton's not with her buddies she has to be dead. And it's the second hit this week! Monday morning I couldn't find Iceberg—he must've taken her Sunday night. Tuesday, of course,

I didn't ride, and when I fed them last night there were still seven. I hung out awhile, watching, but Gordon didn't know where I was so I had to get back. Tonight's different. Gordon's prepared to wait all night if he has to. Fucking slope—he's got to be stopped."

Slope? "Could it be a natural predator?"

"Natural predators leave feathers and stuff behind. Bones. Except—what if it's feathers he's after? Some weird Oriental *pillows* or something?"

Olivia got it. Allston, which bordered the river here, had a large Asian population. "Do you think he'll come again tonight? So soon?"

"That's rational," Darla snapped. "What's rational about slaughtering tame geese?"

"If you're hungry—"

"There're programs for hungry people, loads of them. We've got one at the store—dented cans and stuff. This is something else. Some weird Oriental food number. Slopes're incredibly kinky with food. Look how they get off on that bird's nest soup they do, never mind if it decimates an entire species. And fugu fish. You don't know that one? Fugu has this tiny little sac of poison. Deadly, deadly poison. If the chef slips up, doesn't scoop out every little bit, chop-chop, so solly, honorable customer is dropping dead. And get this: the major reason you order fugu is to flaunt your wealth. It's the most expensive thing on the menu—hundreds of dollars. Totally insane, right? What I think is, something about these poor geese has attracted the Oriental mind-set. Ritual aspects even, who knows? Whatever, it's totally inexcusable. I've got to stop him. Catch him in the act. I don't care if it takes all night."

"Want me to keep you company?"

Pure impulse, this was. Also fairly nutty, loon to loon, since we're in feather mode. But Darla, reckless and feisty, seemed to have undergone a transformation as striking as the one Olivia had seen in Barb last night. Barb had clammed up at Ben's arrival. Darla, with no Gordon around to worshipfully defer to, was talky and opinionated. And might become more so, once the two of them were snuggled up together in the growing darkness.

Olivia felt a rising excitement. She might even end up with an insight into the mysterious meeting. An absorbing day of designing topped off with an end-run around Thaler and the stonewalling Griscoms—what could be more gratifying? She'd always been a sucker for having it all.

Darla, however, wasn't ready to bite. "You want to keep watch with me? Seriously?"

"Sure. You shouldn't be out here alone."

Still not ready. "It's real muddy. Mosquitoes, too."

"I'm not afraid of mosquitoes. Or mud."

Darla pursed her lips and nodded, stern, resolute. "OK. You're on."

Moving fast, they concealed their bikes inside a thick stand of sumac. Their own hiding place lay alongside the river, within the territory of the geese. The grass here was so abundantly scattered with feathers it seemed a freak snowstorm had struck and half-way melted.

"Don't run," Darla warned. "They're spooked enough. And don't make eye contact."

The geese were roosting in loose rows, breasts to the wind, heads twisted so they could tuck their bills under the feathers of their backs. They gleamed in the fading daylight as if lit from within. Olivia remembered those duck lamps that had been cute for fifteen minutes. This close, the fowl appeared magically clean, healthy, and fat. The smell, faint because of the wind, reminded Olivia of her aunt's henhouse, morning egg hunts highlighting childhood stays at that small farm near Gettysburg. Aunt Polly was a wry woman who'd never married and didn't seem to regret it. Olivia liked her. When life calmed down, it would be nice to visit, get back in touch.

Unobtrusive as she and Darla were trying to be, the three geese roosting closest to their footsteps raised their heads, extended their long, strong necks. "It's all right," Darla soothed. "She's a friend."

With a hiss and a gutteral gabble, one goose stood, revealing legs and feet that were the same bright orange as its knobbed beak. The creature's eyes (against orders, Olivia sneaked a quick look) were a surprising pale blue. "Easy, Bianca," crooned Darla, "easy does it. No one's going to hurt you."

Now, wavelike, the entire flock rose to move away from them, majestically and without haste. Same walk as Arnette Murfin, Olivia decided as she crept beneath the bushes and dropped onto the slippery ground next to Darla. And those blue eyes are Jane's. Or Keith's.

It struck her that Darla probably didn't know about Keith's imposture.

The instant the women were out of sight, the geese halted and arranged themselves, again without haste, much as they'd been before. The last to settle—her ass, comically, was still up in the air—was Bianca. "She's the guardian," said Darla in a low, breathless voice. "You can't blame them for reacting to us. Considering what they're going through."

"What're the others' names?"

"I can't point out for sure who's who unless we're interacting, but there's Star, Leche, Moon, Shasta, and Snowy. Snowy's the male. That's him at the right of the first row. See that brown flash on each side of his face? Very subtle, about an inch long?"

Hunkered down like this, sitting cross-legged, they were not, Olivia supposed, perfectly concealed. Her T-shirt was white, and they both wore shorts, exposing plenty of pale skin. A poacher with any inkling might spot a kneecap, a forehead, among the wet leaves. But once it was fully dark, the lay of the land, dropping gradually down to the river, would be decidedly in their favor. The poacher—he'd almost certainly approach from the bike path—would be silhouetted against the lighter sky. (Why *he*, though? Just as easily a *she*. Or, much scarier, a *they*.)

Dusk was falling fast. The storm having taken the humidity out to sea or wherever humidity goes, the air felt delicious. The geese were silent, luminous blobs. The fresh breeze seemed to be keeping the mosquitoes at bay. Olivia could hear the traffic on the parkway across the river, but little noise came from Soldiers Field Road, a couple of football fields away. Part of this muting was due to elevation: Sound travels upward. Steven Dunbar would learn that to his sorrow unless he sprung for windows with fancy baffling. Perverse that the two best addresses in the Back Bay—the water side of Beacon; the sunny side of Commonwealth—were among the most traffic-plagued in the city. Dr. Jonny would have no trouble producing an explanation: the architectural beauty that drew people to these streets distracted them from the reality—noxious fumes, incessant noise.

"What's our action plan?" Olivia loved using the can-do tone and language.

Darla dug in the pannier she'd snapped off her bike and produced an enormous flashlight. "Halogen flood beam," she said with grim reverence. "Thirty-thousand candlepower. My goal's a positive ID."

"What's my goal?"

"You stay hidden. Killing tame geese, he's got to be a total coward. He'll probably split."

"And if he doesn't?"

"That's why you're hiding. Any trouble, you cut along the river until it's safe to run for the road. Then you're on your own. Try to stop a car."

"Shouldn't I yell? Make like I'm a band of guerillas?"

"OK, but wait until you're out of range."

"Sounds like you're taking all the risk."

"I'm a real fast runner. Plus, I've got this." She hefted the flash. "Four batteries, you can do real damage. It's Gordon's. He made me take it."

Her pride let Olivia see the solemnity of Gordon's presentation.

Merlin to young Arthur, Obi-Wan Kenobe to Luke Skywalker. Believe and the Force is with you; Darla believed like mad.

As if she, too, believed, Olivia said, "Gordon's special, isn't he?"

"Gordon Griscom is the most giving and life-loving person I've ever known. He is a totally, *totally* unique individual."

"The first time I saw you two together, I said to myself, that's love, and if they're not married they should be."

"Oh, we love each other all right. But Gordon's kind of allergic to marriage. On account of his parents and all. He says if a man like his father had so much trouble staying married he'd have some nerve expecting better."

Olivia pretended to weigh this. "Marriage does take work," she then said. "For me, it's been well worth the rewards."

"You don't have to convince *me*. I'd marry Gordon like that." She snapped her fingers.

"I'm curious, do you cook at home, too?"

"Most of the time. I'm vegetarian, so if Gordon wants meat or fish, he'll usually grab himself something from the store."

"But that wonderful chicken after Dr. Jonny's service—wasn't that your recipe?"

"Sure. Work's different. Don't think it's a religious thing for me. It's more like vegetables and grains are cleaner."

Olivia tried to imagine what it could be like to handle what you could not bear to eat. Fish eyes, she tried. Tripe. Raw chicken livers aswim in their thick, dark juice. Her gorge rose in sympathy. "It doesn't bother you? Tasting it and everything?"

Darla shrugged. "It's my work, I do it. Like Gordon says, we have to serve all the people, not just a limited faction. We confine our dedication to using totally fresh ingredients, the very best and purest we can possibly find. We're not in the business of imposing belief, Gordon says. Food isn't a club to beat people with or make them feel bad."

"How did you get into cooking?"

"I always wanted to work professionally in food. Ever since I was a little kid. My mom was an alcoholic (that's something Gordon and I can really relate on) so I had free rein in the kitchen. I cooked for my brothers and sisters—there were five of us—and my stepfather too, if he happened to be around, which he usually wasn't, the shit. He made some moves on me when I was fifteen, so I ran away, ended up in Miami Beach. I lied about my age and got a job in one of the hotel kitchens. For a long time there, I thought I'd died and gone to heaven. It's terrible, but you know what I loved best? The food they wasted. Mountains and mountains of it, everyday. It made me feel safe, that food. How'd you get into decorating?"

"I wanted to be an architect but I couldn't handle the math."

"You like it?"

"Often. But even when I don't, it pays the bills."

"Gordon says the average American is totally unrealistic about work. They expect to have fun on the job. Especially at a place like Leaves* of Life. It's our image. You know—countercultural, cool. We had this bagger, she got all pissy because there was no creative outlet. A *bagger*. Gordon uses her as an example when he interviews prospective hires. He says to them, what was the bagger's mistake? Usually they just go, duh, so he has to answer his own question. She failed to understand, he says, the great division between the realm of work and the realm of play. You and I may regret that division, he says, but if you can't accept its absolute and fixed reality you won't like working at Leaves* of Life."

Gordon says. How sensually Darla repeated her lover's pronouncements! As if his very tongue, not just his words, filled her mouth. But they'd strayed far from Olivia's intended agenda. "Fun in work," she said, as if musing. "That's a Griscom ideal, isn't it? Anne being the exception who proves the rule, of course."

"Yes, but the people I'm talking about, the hires and all—they're nothing. The Griscoms are different."

"Oh, definitely. Look at Jane, right on the verge. In a way, that's the saddest thing about her getting shot."

"I don't follow."

"Fun in work. The preschool."

"Mm," said Darla.

"You don't agree?"

Darla gestured angrily. "I'm fed up with Woodside. Woodside the world over. People having all these kids and expecting the rest of us to pay for them."

"It's pretty discouraging. The amazing thing about Jane was how she hung in. Especially when it came to kids."

"Gordon says—"

"What?"

"Nothing. Forget it."

Olivia waited, then tried something different. "Great that Barb's pregnant, isn't it?"

"Barb . . . ? Oh. Them. I didn't hear that part."

A slip. What was the "part" she had heard? "I went out to see Barb and Ben last night."

"Yeah? How come?"

Too casual. She already knew how come. Thaler must have made some calls. Had he touched base with the entire family? Told them the Chapman woman was snooping around? Taking care not to seem as nerved up as this was making her feel, Olivia pressed ahead. "I was hoping one of them could tell me how my name got in the news."

"And?"

"They didn't know."

"You believe that? They hated Dr. Jonny. No problem for them if the investigation's wrecked."

"That's another thing. I keep hearing that this phone call can hurt the investigation. How? What's the connection?"

"All I know is, the cops said don't talk about it. And we haven't. Gordon and I, I mean."

"The other night, when Detective McGuire told me not to talk, I didn't question him either. I assumed it was to keep things as cool as possible, especially in relation to Woodside. But that was when there was still some possibility that Woodside was involved in Jane's shooting."

"Still? What're you talking about? Don't tell me you think Woodside's out of it."

Darla was forgetting to keep her voice down. Olivia steeled herself to press harder. "Woodside's out of it. This was family."

Disgustedly: "Oh please. Spare me."

"Friday's meeting exploded something. Keith told me Jane came home so upset she didn't even enjoy her nice write-up in the paper. And I don't have to ask you if Gordon came home upset. I saw that for myself, in the store."

"Big difference between being upset and ready to shoot. Gordon's a gentle giant. Wouldn't hurt a fly. Plus, you forgot: Tuesday night he was with me."

Still that exultant note. Must've been one royal rogering. "You know what surprises me? Ben didn't even tell Barb what happened at the meeting. His own wife. That's going pretty far, isn't it? I'm sure Chess told her husband—what's his name again? Boyd, right. I mean, sharing life's burdens along with the joys—that's the whole point of loving someone, being close, right? I'm sure Gordon had to tell you."

Prideful, eager to demonstrate how much she was loved by a totally unique individual: "Course he did."

"I'd give a lot to know the details."

"Never. Not in a million years."

"I figure money's involved. Lots of money. Jane had to have taken a position that meant less money, so much less she had to be eliminated."

"You're out of your mind. Totally insane."

"So who tried to scare her off? Or kill her? One of the two rich Griscoms, Chess or Gordon? Or a poor one, Ben or Anne? The poor, you'd think first, never mind that they both have good alibis. Guns can be hired. But wait, you'd think next, it's the rich ones who're tight with Dr. Jonny—contacts in the case of Chess, philosophy of life and promotional luster in the case of Gordon. Gee, you'd have to wonder, what if Jane's somehow interfering with those goodies? Hatching something contrary to Dr. Jonny's values, say. How could that be, though? Here's Jane, ready to give her all to Woodside, and here's Dr. Jonny, who already has. Or so it seems."

This last phrase, white noise, a high lob meant to maintain the pressure while Olivia gained thinking time, electrified Darla. "What're you saying? Dr. Jonny wasn't mowed down in cold blood?"

"The way I see it, he stopped a bullet meant for the other guy. Jamal Sutton. Happens all the time, catching a stray bullet, though not usually to Nobel winners. But I was speaking metaphorically."

Sneery: "What's that supposed to mean?"

"I'm suggesting Dr. Jonny didn't *give* his life in the same sense that Jane plans to."

A silence built. Olivia waited, then broke it. "No one's claiming that Jane's dedication to Woodside isn't the real thing, right? So, just following the path of these ideas, let's say Dr. Jonny's dedication *wasn't* real. He dropped in on Arnette Murfin once a week and encouraged her to start a rent strike. Period. Terrific benefits to his credibility, of course. Firsthand reports from the war zone. The Harding Hill disciples lapped it up. But compared to Jane's preschool, peanuts."

Darla obliterated this with an impatient slice of her hand. "Jane was an unemployed, totally supported woman, no conflicting claims on her time. Dr. Jonny was an extremely busy world-famous scientist. Slight difference."

Wondering where they were headed and hoping they'd get someplace real before it was too dark to track Darla's reactions, Olivia hit another lob. "He was also a world-class sexpot. Right? One look and I was a goner."

Stiffly: "I never met him personally."

"No? How come?"

"Gordon and I weren't that close yet."

It still hurt, Olivia saw. Of course it did. You move in with someone, you expect to meet his family. Especially the man who supposedly inspires your beloved's every move and thought—and who is a highly accessible public figure. So. Fan this wound? Uncork so much resentment that Darla will betray the family secret? Fat chance.

"Actually," Olivia tried instead, "Dr. Jonny was far from a great *man*. A great scientist, yes. So much of a star that Washington wouldn't fund his crack blocker with him gone."

Time was running out. Darkness might bring a second problem, interruption from the poacher. Olivia decided to risk some embroidery. "It's that stardom that Chess draws on, of course. All those connections into the scientific community. Which means that Chess had no reason to shoot Jane."

As she said this, Olivia realized its full truth. "Chess's career," she continued, her confidence now genuine, "relies on aspects of her father's life that would hardly form the agenda of an explosive family meeting. Whatever else he was up to, there's nothing wrong with the man's science. Too bad. I wanted it to be Chess."

"You wanted. Where do you get off *wanting*? Why's it your business in the first place? Your name's on the radio, big deal. Like Gordon says, they spell it right, you chalk it up to free advertising."

"I've got the goods on Chess. *National Enquirer* stuff, believe me. No, no, I can't say any more about it now. It'll hit the fan soon enough. Right after I finish getting the goods on the rest of them, Gordon—you better face this—included. And I doubt anyone will cheerfully chalk it up to free advertising."

Sneery again: "You got the *goods*. What *goods*? Gordon was upset by a meeting. So what? If they killed your father in cold blood you'd be upset too."

"Look, Darla. You love the man. Fine. But I'm the only one

fighting on Jane's side. One way or another I'm going to find out who shot her and why. It's just a matter of time. Besides, Jane may recover enough to speak for herself. What then? More bullets, better aim? At which point do you seriously think I won't tell the police everything I know about Chess and the meeting? Where're you going?"

Darla had clutched the pannier to her chest and scrambled to her feet. Just beyond Olivia's reach, still hidden from the savanna and the geese by the bushes that concealed Olivia, she dropped to one knee, arms braced forward. The gun she held was pointed right at Olivia's heart.

22

More bullets, better aim. Olivia had made a serious mistake. Seduced by the logic of the wallet, she'd left out love.

Stall. Say anything. "How can this help you, Darla? And Gordon—how's it going to help Gordon?"

"Easy. They find the gun in your hand. You couldn't handle the guilt so you shot yourself."

"What guilt?"

"This is the gun that did Jane, smart ass. After you lured her out." A grim laugh. "Not so much fun like this, is it? You should see yourself. Scared shitless."

"Scared isn't suicidal. I've got two kids. I'd have left them a note."

"Nope. You'll be like my mom—five kids, no note. Which I happen to know is standard. Like Gordon says, nothing we experience is wasted."

"He's right. That first time we met out here—that's when you found out I was a regular on the bike path. Then all you needed to get me out of the public view was a plausible story—the geese."

"What? You think I made that up? You think I could just *use* them like that? Totally innocent creatures? What do you think I am, anyway?"

Scared as she was, Olivia had to blink. "The gun was for the poacher? Not me?"

"Duh. Where'd you get this reputation for brains, anyway?"

Now Olivia remembered Darla's hesitation when she'd offered to keep her company. "So tonight, if I'd kept my nose out of Gordon's business—"

"None of that. Too late for that."

"Could you just explain one thing? The gun—if you'd shot the poacher, wouldn't ballistics trace it to Jane?"

"Who says I was going to shoot? Ever hear of backup? Intimidation?"

It struck Olivia that she didn't know for sure whether Gordon or Darla had shot Jane. The one thing she must not do was to provoke Darla's admission. The more she knew, the more necessary her death. A plan began to glimmer.

"It won't look like suicide, Darla. You're too far away. How am I going to have powder burns on me? Besides, the angle's wrong. I'd have to be a lefty. And a contortionist."

It was too dark to see Darla's features clearly, but her silence suggested these were new ideas, possibly confusing. Olivia grabbed at her fragile advantage. "Shit, Darla! Cut it anyway you want, you're taking a terrible chance. Much safer to just let me go. I swear I'll never say a word about any of this. You can trust me because of my kids. Their father's dying and they need me alive. They'll be like your hostages."

"Shut up." And then, after a long moment: "Keep facing me and get to your knees. Like you're saying your prayers."

Make me, a woman without a plan would say. "Might fix the angle," Olivia said. "Doesn't do a thing for the powder burns."

"Shut up and do what I say."

Olivia kneeled, thighs alert and springy, toes bent forward, balls of her feet braced against an arm-thick section of exposed root that had been jabbing her throughout their vigil. Frog, she instructed herself, think frog.

Darla stood, the gun wobbling only a little.

Now. Olivia twisted sharply around as if the corner of her eye had caught movement on the horizon. "He's here," she gasped, no trouble at all sounding eager for deliverance. Instantly, no time or heart to confirm that her ruse had shifted Darla's attention, she sprung. Flew froglike through air, through shocking, sudden noise. Then the slap of the river.

She'd hit flat—no knowing how deep the water was, how many shopping carts waited below to break her bones. Jackknifing into a surface dive, she heard or imagined a second shot. Frantically she pushed ragged breaststrokes downward, downriver, away from the bank, away, it first seemed, from the pain blooming fiercely through her right leg.

She reached down, slid her fingers to her calf, the center of the pain, and found jelly. Panic snatched the air from her lungs. She flailed blindly, came up gasping and choking. Darla fired again.

Another jackknife. Fortified by the oxygen she'd gulped in, by the sheer fact that she was still alive, she was able to steady herself, to stroke more evenly. Gauging a safe depth by the pressure in her ears, she began concentrating on an old choral exercise—releasing air in a small, gradual stream. Whatever current there was would help her escape, she reminded herself. Her kicking was lopsided because of the pain, but she could compensate for that by working her right arm harder. This dark, Darla would need sound—another panicky, choking breach—to find her. Out in the middle of the river, her surfacings quiet, she'd be safe.

She turned the white target of her face to the opposite shore and slowly rose to breathe. The water smelled like stale spit.

Diving deep, she stripped off her shirt and stuffed it into the waistband of her shorts. The wet cloth might catch air, form a white balloon.

The best thing she'd done was to yield to a fussbudget afterthought on the bikes. When Darla went to retrieve her own, the better to track her prey, she'd find it immobilized, yoked to Olivia's by Olivia's Kryptonite lock. Also, it was important to remember that Darla had no way of knowing she was injured, possibly crippled.

More air. No shots. Ahead, profiled against the sky, was the derivative boathouse. Olivia sank again, recalling the two wings of high Cyclone fencing that extended from this building's river-face into the water. Could this fence, meant to protect the landing from vandals, protect her too? No matter how much her leg hurt, she could crawl up the gradual, smoothly planked slope. There might be a security phone. Or a watchman who made regular rounds. And God knows the less time spent in an urban river the better.

But suppose Darla was expecting her to do just this? Suppose she was positioned right by the fence, waiting to shoot?

Goodbye Northeastern, Olivia thought, hello Harvard, Boston is a college town. A giggle broke loose, wasting air. She rose, breathed, felt a buzzy, lightheaded languor. The aftereffects of shock and fear? Loss of blood?

Underwater again, she focused all her willpower on the singer's exercise. Steadiness returned, and she thought to unhook her bra, to wrap and tie it tightly around the jelly place on her leg.

She knew she was almost exactly midway between bridges. If she swam to the opposite bank, Darla might not be able to see her climbing out. But even if she were spotted, she'd still gain some lead time. Time to crawl or hobble to the parkway, stick out her thumb . . .

Yes? And who's going to stop his nice clean car to pick up a dripping, bleeding, muddy woman?

She stroked angrily into the thought, pushing it away.

At the opposite shore the dark bank rose dauntingly high. The abrupt drop-off that had saved her when she'd made her dive meant there were no shallows where she could stand to test the strength of her leg. There was, however, a narrow ledge of gritty muck. She crawled onto it, felt around, found a tangle of exposed tree roots. Taking a deep breath, she reached high, grabbed a pair of roots, and pulled herself upwards.

A panting, scraping scramble, her good leg providing purchase, and she'd done it. She was on her hands and knees in a little copse, the familiar realm of bike path, streetlights, and parkway no more than twenty feet away. Using a tree trunk as a crutch, she stood and let her weight settle evenly. Her leg hurt in a different, deeper way than it had in the water, but it was not unbearable.

She wrung out her shirt and put it on, wincing as the fabric glued itself to her scratched skin. Then, parting branches as quietly as she could, she took some exploratory steps.

Good Christ. She could walk. She'd survived.

Invigorated by the realization, she decided to forget about hitching a ride. Looking like this, the nut-house entrant in a wet T-shirt contest, her chances were dim anyway. Worse, she'd have to wait, no telling how long, under a streetlight—a perfect target for Darla.

Who might have hitched her own ride. Who might be sitting in that car just coming now, about to pass the streetlight she herself would be standing under, thumb extended.

Another car passed, going in the opposite direction, its headlights showing the fringes of the cemetery. Beyond it, she knew, no more than a half-mile away, was the western entrance to Harding Hill. The only house on Harding Hill sure to be unequipped with a burglar alarm was within walking distance. Even if Keith weren't home, she could climb in through a window, clean up some, call herself a cab, go home, and pull the covers over her head. Maybe Gerry Rothfarb would make a house call. Bring her a shot of penicillin, clean and bandage her leg.

Wait. Where was Darla? What would keep her from staking out Joy Street?

First things first. She'd stick to the narrow verge between the bikeway and the river, duck into the safety of the bordering brush whenever a car approached. Deal with the rest after she'd made it to Harding Hill.

A white van stood in Jane's driveway, lights on, motor running. Gordon, Olivia thought, her heart sinking.

She hid behind some shrubs—getting good at this—for a closer look. And almost laughed aloud. It was a pizza delivery. There was Keith, handing the guy his money.

When the van left, she made a peg-legged dash for the door. Hampered by the pizza, Keith hadn't finished locking it.

"Olivia! You're all—what happened to you?"

She pushed past him and banged the door shut behind herself. "Darla tried to kill me. She's still out there, so pull the shades down."

"Darla? Gordon's girl friend?"

"The same. *Shades*, Keith."

"We only have them in the bedrooms. Accounta Dr. Jonny's openness number."

"Hit the lights then. *Run*. Lock the doors and windows. Eat up in your room. Anyone phones, don't answer, anyone comes around, you're not home. I'll grab a shower. Save me some pizza, OK? And beer—got any beer?"

Jane's medicine cabinet was almost empty—more Griscom minimalism? To clean the raw-meat furrow the bullet had ploughed across her calf, Olivia had to be satisfied with soap and water. Sitting backwards in the tub, her head and shoulders breaking the force of the shower, she massaged the suds in gently. When she could tolerate no more of this painful therapy, she eased herself to her feet, washed her hair and soaped all over. More stinging—her hide was a road map of scratches.

She blotted herself dry and wrapped the towel tightly around her still-bleeding leg. Guided by the bathroom light, she opened the nearest closet.

The powerful exhalation of Jon Griscom's smell made her gag, and she gave the door a reflexive slam. From the other closet, Jane's, she chose a loose Indian-print dress with a fairly long skirt. She put it on and, searching further, found a dusty box of maxipads on the shelf. Cut down, one of them would make an adequate bandage.

What else? Underpants? No. Facing down a gun was one thing, but borrowed underpants went too far.

She ran Jane's comb through her tangled hair and surveyed the bleak marriage bower. The bed was a mattress on a rough plywood platform supported by cinder blocks. There were two bureaus, ugly, heavy things exfoliating their cheap veneers. A perpetuity of stuck drawers, those bureaus, a small, penitential struggle built into the routine of every single day. There were some shabby scatter rugs, and, carelessly nailed to the wall, two pinup lamps for reading. For uncomfortable reading—no headboard, two anorexic pillows. The one on his side of the bed would smell like his closet.

She pulled herself together, and called to Keith. "I need some scissors and tape, but don't use any lights finding them. And some disinfectant. No? What about rubbing alcohol? Jesus. Gin?"

"So here I am," Olivia finished, "more or less in one piece."

They were hiding out in Keith's room, light from the hall only. Everything in the room was new: the paint, the Conran's furniture, the colorful dhurrie on the floor. Keith sat in his pale oak desk chair, Olivia in a blue-and-white-striped easy chair, her legs propped on its matching footstool.

"When you yelled like that?" Keith said. "In the bathroom? I went, oh no, she's back. Darla, I mean. Like Glenn Close in *Fatal Attraction.*"

"Sorry. Gin smarts." Olivia admired the neat bandage she'd contrived. "I like the duct-tape look. It's futuristic."

"All that blood—shouldn't you go to the doctor? Don't you need stitches?"

"Later." She polished off her pizza slice, drank some beer. Once she'd gotten her leg up, she had started to feel surprisingly good. As if that spacey spell in the water had been nothing more than hunger. And why not? She'd hardly eaten all day.

"This whole thing is totally incredible," Keith said, not for the first time. "I can't say I know Darla well, but I never figured her for something like this. I mean, whoa. You know? Like, *wait* a minute."

"Yes."

"You think she shot Mom?"

"Unless it was Gordon."

"Wow. Gordon. Mom liked Gordon the best of them all. Not that she'd take sides or anything, but you could tell she felt closest to him. I guess because he was the most like his dad."

Passing on this one, Olivia helped herself to another slice.

"So what're you gonna do?" Keith asked. "Call that McGuire?"

Before she could answer, the phone on his desk rang. "Don't pick that up," she said.

"No prob. It's set to monitor."

The tape whirred, then: "This is Mrs. Ober at Mount Auburn Hospital. I wanted to let you know that Mrs. Griscom has responded to my voice. You can visit after nine tomorrow morning."

Keith's hand shot out to grab the receiver. "Don't," Olivia yelled.

"Why not?"

"Maybe it's a trick."

"But I know her voice, Mrs. Ober. She's the charge nurse, nights. She's always real nice to me."

"You're sure? OK, call her back. It's wonderful news, Keith."

He nodded soberly. "Mom's gonna find out about me, Olivia. So, OK, I can live with that. I mean, I never shoulda said yes in the first place. But does that help her? The shock?"

"We have to buy some time. I'm pretty sure it's still Chess's secret. Ask Mrs. Ober if she's talked to the others yet. She says no, tell her you'd like to do it yourself. Offer to save her the trouble."

"Really?"

For a key player in a fraud, Keith could be remarkably obtuse. "I said offer, not guarantee. Later you can claim you tried, got busy signals, whatever. Do it, Keith. We're running out of time."

23

en minutes later, Olivia was en route to Gordon's house on the other side of Harvard Square.

She was driving Jane's old Volvo, a bag of bolts with a death-wish attraction to potholes. Keith had been dropped at the subway kiosk; by now he'd be on his way to Nanda and Drew's.

Poor Keith, poor, scared, weak guy. When she'd told him to lie low until further notice, his relief had been pitiful to see.

Then, rallying: "You really don't need me?"

He was saving face, but more than kindness prompted Olivia to say yes, of course she needed him. "You're my insurance. Once Gordon knows you're set to tell McGuire about Darla and the meeting, I'll be safe."

"Why don't we turn it over to McGuire right now? Make him earn his pay."

"Without cops, there's a prayer we can keep you—the real you—a secret. Worth a try, yes?"

"Yeah, but what about Darla pops another shot at you?"

"Who says she'll even be there? Probably she's still hanging around the river. Anyhow, we control Gordon, we control Darla. No sweat."

Brave assertions. But before she could step out into the shadowy dark that lay between house and garage, cross the line of fire that had caught Jane, she had to steel herself. Keith, hiding behind her, let out a little whimper. "Put your arm around my waist," she whispered. "Be my crutch and we'll run like hell."

Gordon's house was a Queen Anne beauty, clapboard amplitude flanked by two giant beeches, their pale elephant bark catching the streetlight.

Olivia was on foot, having parked the conspicuous Volvo two streets away. Her leg hurt. Stiffening's natural, she told herself. Walking's the best medicine.

The front windows of the house were shut tight; Gordon must have central AC. Only one light showed, and it was upstairs. A setback.

She crossed the shadowy lawn and climbed the front steps. The windows on either side of the door were curtainless, but all she could see was a slice of light at the rear of a wide, center hall. Olivia knew these Cambridge rehabs; there'd be a huge new kitchen back there, she'd bet anything, state-of-the-art appliances, fireplace, bookshelves, comfortable chairs, and a glass wall giving onto a terrace or deck.

She made for the side yard and ducked under the beech tree.

Just past the tree's shelter was a dense yew hedge, higher than her head. Meant, obviously, to protect the privacy of the backyard, it appeared to press snugly against both the house and the tall fence that divided Gordon's land from his neighbor's. Cautiously she pushed her way into it—more scratching and a fearsome crackling of leaves underfoot—until she could see something of the backyard. The predicted deck, raised and floodlit, curved away from the back of the house in a broad arc. Its farthest reach brushed what looked like an impervious evergreen screen—probably the rear boundary of the lot.

A distant sound system emitted an aggressive, industrial beat, but otherwise it was very quiet. No one occupied Gordon's expensive teak chairs, but a wineglass and plate had been left on one of the tables.

Olivia tried to push through the hedge but was repelled by the thick, springy branches. Reasoning that the lower growth might be more sparse, she squatted to investigate. Sure enough, her groping hands soon found a gap. The ground here was bare of fallen leaves—swept, perhaps, by neighborhood dogs in hot pursuit of rabbits, cats, each other. She knotted the flaring skirt of Jane's dress to get it out of her way and wriggled through to the other side.

Hugging the shadows, she made her way to the deck. Bent low, protected by its elevation, she crept around until she was directly opposite the house. The slope of the land meant that she had to stand on her toes to see, but the anticipated glass wall gave her a full view of the kitchen.

It was a beautiful room, one she'd have been proud to have designed. Functional to the max, no techie-mechie chill.

Gordon was at the head of a refectory table that might be the real thing, although the heavy chairs with their leather backs and seats were probably recent copies. Just as well; his chair was tipped recklessly back, his crossed legs propped on the table.

Most of the light in the room was coming from ceiling spots over the table. This, and her floor-level vantage, gave the scene a captured, monumental quality. Edward Hopper, without Hopper's despair; Gordon was reposeful, calm. No one would ever guess, from the look of him, that Jane's blood might be on his hands. He seemed the absolute master of himself and all he surveyed.

Was this how Darla was used to seeing him? A looming god with infinite claims on her gratitude and service?

More to the immediate point, he had to be still ignorant of the extreme measures his servant had just attempted in his behalf.

So Darla hadn't come home yet. Impossible to imagine otherwise. No woman, no matter how devoted, could have returned from that riverbank pretending all was well.

Olivia shivered. It was like one of those stories of childhood—

227

the frozen moment immediately before Pandora opens the box or Bluebeard's wife the door to the secret closet. Reaching these moments, she'd have to put the book down, screw up her courage before she could continue reading.

A sharp report shattered the quiet. Olivia's heart banged. Gordon was on his feet, streaking for the hall. Olivia ran too, found the steps that gave the deck access to the driveway. She hoped the glass door had been left unlocked.

Blood, a great spattered explosion of it. The ghastly remains of Darla's face in the center of the heaped, soaked pillows. Her long white nightgown soaked too, its demure lace neckline clogged and dripping. Both bedside lamps on, every detail fully illuminated.

Darla had laid herself out. Had chosen her gown, sat straight-legged in the center of the king-sized bed to arrange its folds just so. Had rested against the white-cased pillows and—what? Wept some final tears? Said a prayer? Relished the high of it, the glorious, throbbing imminence of ultimate sacrifice?

Gordon, sandbagged, moaned at the doorway. Olivia made herself approach the bed and press her fingers into Darla's neck.

No pulse. Not a flicker. Swallowing hard, she pushed past Gordon, found a bathroom, washed the blood from her hands. No automatic glance at the mirror. Whatever horror was doing to her face, she didn't want it stuck in her memory.

She'd seen a phone by the bed, but she couldn't bear to use it. "I'm going downstairs to call 911," she told Gordon. "You come too."

Snuffling, he made a childlike pass at his eyes with the back of his wrist. "She told me you were dead," he said in a high, strained voice. "She said she'd shot you."

"She overstated. And in case you're getting any ideas, Keith knows I'm here. By now he'll have told my lawyer the whole story." Then, her voice deadly cold, she asked the big one: "Did Darla shoot Jane? Or was that you?"

"Me? You can't be serious. You think I'd—"

"I was out back before, watching you. You had your feet up, not a worry in the world. So spare me the shock and protestation. Who shot Jane?"

A flash of pure hate. He hated Olivia for catching him out. But she was too angry to back off scared. "Who?" she asked again.

"Darla," he muttered.

"How long have you known?"

"How long? What do you mean? She just told me tonight."

"You take bad news well. She explain herself? Give you any reason?"

A snort of disgust. "Reason isn't on the screen here. Jane wanted all the foundation money going to Woodside. I was furious with her. We all were. Darla took it into her head . . . oh God. It's horrible! She thought she was helping me! She actually believed I'd be grateful!"

"And she was the one who called Jane about the house, of course. You didn't hear her doing that?"

"The truth is, I was out Tuesday. She offered to cover for me."

"What did she do, impersonate me?"

"She said she pretended to be your assistant."

"Last question for now: Why did she kill herself?"

"You can't pin any of this on me, you know. It was all her idea, from start to—"

"Save that for the police. I'll take the short answer."

"I told her I'd help her financially, but she had to get out of my life. Go underground, disappear. Which she accepted. Took real well! Like she, you know, saw the logic of my position. She didn't give me the slightest inkling she'd—"

"Right. Downstairs. You first."

While Olivia talked on the phone, Gordon fell into his place at the head of his beautiful table, buried his head in his arms.

By the time she'd hung up, Olivia had come to a decision. The

229

temptation to reveal Darla's role, to have her own name cleared tonight, had to be resisted. Ballistics would clear her eventually, and by waiting, keeping the police out, she stood a good chance of solving the rest of the puzzle. She'd have to do plenty of faking and bullying, but the gamble was worth it.

"The police will compare the bullets," she told Gordon. "They'll figure out by themselves that Darla must have shot Jane. When they do, you might have to hazard a motive. But you don't have to tell them anything tonight. Ignorance implies innocence, right?"

He snapped to. The hope flooding his face told Olivia how guilty he felt, how eager he was to wall himself away from this guilt. How often had he fantasized with Darla, imagining how simple life would be if Jane, and then Olivia herself, were magically eliminated? He might have joked about hiring a hit man. And certainly Darla had witnessed the full measure of his fury and frustration. He knew she doted on him, would do anything for him. And he knew, in ways Olivia could only guess, how precisely he had planted the seed of violence, fertilized its rank growth.

Now suspicion warred with his hopefulness. "Aren't you going to tell the police she shot you?"

"And explain what prompted her to do such a wicked thing? Depends. When the police leave, you and Chess and I are going to have a talk. I'll decide after that." She passed him the phone. "Call Chess now. Say that Keith's in hiding, ready to expose everything I've found out about the family meeting to Detective McGuire. Don't say what I know or how I learned it. Just convince her I've got enough of the story for the police to uncover the rest. Tell her to be here inside of twenty minutes, ready to cooperate with me. That way she'll arrive before the police leave, all on the up and up. What's wrong?"

"You've got me all confused. What do I tell the police?"

"Any story you can stick to. Use the truth as much as you can, is my advice."

"And what should I tell Chess? About Darla, I mean."

"On the phone? Whatever you want. Remember that she won't know Darla shot Jane—or me—unless you say so. Pretend it's rehearsal for your conversation with the police?"

"But why's Chess coming here? What's her, you know, cover? Her story for the police?"

Olivia let her disbelief show. "She's your sister, isn't she? Come to offer a woman's touch, help bundle up the sheets?"

"*Chess?*"

"You asked for a cover, not a character sketch. And Gordon? Better fess up on Tuesday night right away. Ballistics will make a mess of your alibi."

24

When the police came, Olivia hacked way back, became the accidentally involved bystander, the sympathetic acquaintance ready to help the grieving lover compose himself enough to tell his story. That it was Cambridge was a lucky break for her. Presumably these police would communicate later with McGuire, but at least tonight she'd be spared his scrutiny.

The investigator and his team handled Gordon with care, their deference grating on Olivia. Gordon had treated Darla too roughly to deserve better himself. Of course he must pay, between this house and the store, some fairly serious local taxes. And he provided employment—two shifts, seven days a week; most of his employees town, not gown. But that's neither here nor there, she reminded herself. She and Gordon were conspirators. Indignation, for now, was a luxury she could not afford.

The grieving lover leaned on truths Olivia already knew or had guessed, bending them well short of obvious breaking points. Darla, he said, had set out late for some cycling exercise and been caught by darkness. "Night riding spooked her. Those paths along the river can be real hazardous, tree roots humping right through the pavement. She took a bad spill out there once, and that was in broad daylight. At any rate, she called me from a pay phone, insisted I pick her up. I wasn't in the best mood; I'd just come home after one of those days, you know, true zoo from the opening gong. We had words in the van, more at home. I'm sorry to say these fights were getting to be an old story with us. Darla is—was—an extremely needy person. Sometimes I just couldn't placate her, no matter what I said or did. Tonight, me being so exhausted and all, it was just plain too much. Like I'd hit some kind of limit. I told her we had to cool it awhile. Have a trial separation."

He sighed heavily. "I guess that did it. She didn't say anything, just stood there kind of staring at me. Like she was amazed it had come to this. I should've talked her down, I see that now. At least I should've tried. Though considering where her head must've been—"

He stopped talking, swallowed hard, drew some deep, ragged breaths. Then he went on. "Finally she asked me was I sure that's what I wanted. All I could think of was how tired I was, how great it would be to get some peace and quiet. So I said yes, I was sure. She said something like, I guess I have to believe you and went upstairs. I heard the shower running and then it got real quiet. I thought she'd fallen asleep. That's when you showed up, Olivia. A minute later we heard the shot."

He gave his head a punch-drunk shake. "It's terrible," he quavered. "Just terrible. Not only have I been living with this woman since winter, we worked together. Side by side, practically, day in, day out. And now it's like I didn't know her at all. You have to wonder, you know? How can someone be so close to the edge and give no sign of it? How's that possible?"

His bewilderment sounded genuine, even to Olivia. She had to admire his technique—emoting over what he hadn't known until tonight to cover what he'd known very well: his profound contribution to Darla's violence and final despair. Listening to him, Olivia was struck again by Darla's singlemindedness, the power of her will. A woman that strong—the realization caught Olivia's breath—might even have been able to keep to herself the events of the riverside if not for her immobilized bicycle and the incriminating key that had to be in Olivia's pocket, ready to be found along with her dead body.

"Did you know she had a gun, Mr. Griscom?"

"Yes, but I thought she'd gotten rid of it."

Stop right there, was Olivia's advice, but Gordon had obviously prepared more. "She was from Florida, you know. Miami. She told me guns are no big deal down there, everyone has them. She claimed they sell them in Woolworth's, but I didn't . . . Really? Unbelievable. What's this world coming to?"

You don't shut it right now, thought Olivia, you're cooked.

"I mean really," he sputtered, every inch the outraged citizen.

The investigator waited, but Gordon, at last, was finished.

Politely: "Anything else you can tell us, Mr. Griscom?"

Gordon hung his head, shuffled his feet. "Actually there is something. When I said I was here Tuesday? When my stepmother was shot? That's not true. I'm ashamed to tell you, it's so grotesque in light of what's happened."

A brusque scrub of his forehead with the back of his hand, a shamefaced grimace. "OK. The truth is, I was with this woman. A very old friend. Well, actually she's married to another old friend who's very much the jealous type. The kind of guy who goes to extremes about it, you know? So when Darla volunteered to cover for me, naturally I grabbed it. I mean, I knew *I* hadn't shot Jane, so what was the harm? A white lie's all I thought it was. I told it for the sake of my friend—my two friends, I mean. The woman and her husband."

The inspector frowned.

Gordon frowned too. "Is something wrong?"

"You made a false statement to the police, Mr. Griscom. That's not advisable. Other people who've tried it have ended up getting charged with compounding a felony, which in this case would be the attempted murder of Mrs. Griscom. Now take it easy, Mr.

Griscom. I'm not saying you qualify on that score. For one thing, you'd have to profit from the shooting. Gain in some way. But what I said stands. You'd be well advised, now and in the future, against making false statements to the police."

"I hear you," said Gordon.

Olivia didn't know whether to admire his cool or start worrying about her own vulnerability in the false statement department. As if reading her mind, the inspector turned to her. "And what brought you here tonight, Mrs. Chapman?"

"I'd gone to Harding Hill to visit Keith. Jane Griscom's son. While I was there, he had a call from the hospital about her, so I thought I'd swing by and tell Gordon in person."

Gordon's astonished reaction was all Olivia could want. Might Jane be dead? He was too clever to show hope, but she knew how brightly it must be dawning. Darla, the only outsider who knew the details of the famous meeting, had just removed herself as a witness. If Jane were dead too, he'd be home free.

She let him hang a bit, retribution for his godlike repose in the face of Darla's collapse and her own reported death.

"Sorry to spring that on you, Gordon," she said. Then, to the inspector: "Darla's death put it right out of my mind. It's what we've all been hoping for—Mrs. Griscom has responded to the nurse's voice. I guess the old saying's true—bad news drives out good."

Chess, elegant in taupe slacks and white shirt, murmuring sisterly commiserations, arrived while the ambulance crew was bumping the wheels of the gurney down Gordon's graceful staircase. The body was sheeted, anonymous, unbloody, but Olivia saw Chess turn pale.

The uniformed cop following the gurney downstairs handed the inspector Darla's gun in a plastic bag. The two drew aside for a brief conference. Olivia caught a phrase: *cadaveric spasm.* She'd have to ask Gerry Rothfarb what it meant.

The investigator told Gordon and Olivia to come to the station in the morning, when their statements would be typed and ready to sign.

"I have an early appointment," Olivia said, not adding that it would be an emergency consultation with Mary Jane Hughes for legal advice.

"Come as soon as you can," the investigator said.

Gordon asked when the room could be cleaned.

"Whenever you want," the investigator said. "We're done."

And about time, Olivia heard in his voice, that something involving you Griscoms turned out simple, open and shut.

The waiting minicams recorded the body's transfer to the ambulance. Olivia and Chess stayed in the kitchen, listening but keeping out of sight. Gordon stood at the top of his stoop, humbler than he'd been the night Jane was shot, allowing the cameras their flashbulbs, their measures of footage. "I can't say much," he apologized, mindful, perhaps of how well the media had treated him all these years, no end of terrific free publicity for Leaves* of Life. "I'm devastated. Totally. We weren't getting along that well but I had no idea she was—look, I can't tell you anything more. Please try to understand."

But the reporters wouldn't quit. "Was there a note, Gordon? Well then can you give us more of a why? A theoretical?" And: "Was there any advance warning, Gordon? Something she said, maybe? Did she say good-bye, anything like that?" And: "Was she depressed, Gordon? Would you say she seemed depressed?"

Shoulders heavy and low—"A movie buffalo," Dee later told Olivia, "taking a lethal hail of redskin arrows."—Gordon shook his head in refusal. Sad, shaggy head refusing them—good, true friends though they were—saying no, please, I can't, please don't. . . .

Finally he had to run. Slam himself into the privacy of his house.

He strode into the kitchen and pressed a switch. Heavy white draperies swished across to cover the window wall. He sagged into his chair, his gaze fixed and blank.

Chess was on her feet. "I think we all deserve a drink."

"Vodka on the rocks, please," said Olivia. "A big one."

25

Chess sat at Gordon's right. Olivia propped her bad leg on the empty chair at his left, positioning herself so she could see both Griscoms at once.

She drank gratefully. Bullet to bullet. Homeopathic medicine.

"All right," said Chess to Olivia. "What's your real connection here?"

"In good time," said Olivia. "After we hear from Gordon."

"Oh?" But Chess's rebellion was brief. "Suit yourself," she capitulated, shrugging.

Gordon showed Olivia his empty palms, nothing to hide. "I'll tell you everything—soon's I talk to my lawyer."

"No," said Olivia. "Me first."

Gordon stood. "I'll only be a minute."

Olivia considered standing too, but it felt too good to have her leg up. "Sit down, Gordon. Unless you want me to leave right now and tell the police what I know."

"You can't. You lied as much as I did."

"Hardly. Anyway, I can repent. I didn't gain from the attack on Jane. I didn't compound any felonies."

"What?" said Chess. "What felonies?"

Intent on Olivia, Gordon paid her no attention. "I told you, that was one hundred percent Darla. I'm totally clean on that."

"What's going on here?" Chess said.

"Darla shot Jane—for Gordon's sake and Gordon's gain." Olivia paused while Chess made noise and thrashed around. "Yes," she then continued. "It *is* an ugly story. I wonder how his customers will take it. And the jury. Will they side with him? Or the lovesick woman he drove to suicide?"

Gordon sat down. "Talk," Chess ordered.

The full story emerged slowly. Just as Gordon had told the police, Darla had called from a pay phone and he'd picked her up. The parts he'd kept quiet began with his alibi for Tuesday night— more venting and thrashing around from Chess—and Darla's attempt on Olivia.

"I don't believe this," Chess finally said. "This can't be happening."

Olivia helpfully displayed her bandage. Then she told a bare-bones version of her own story, emphasizing that Keith not only knew everything she did but had by now passed the information to her lawyer. To conclude, she told Chess about Keith's call from the hospital. "Jane's responding. They say there's real hope."

Chess wasn't a hypocrite, give her that. No fake joy and relief. "Real hope for what? Medicals tend to confuse life with meaningful life."

Olivia cut to the central point. "It doesn't matter if Jane comes out of this with a flawed memory. You're going to tell me all about the meeting yourselves."

"No we're not," said Chess.

Olivia sighed. "Is it law-and-order time again? Want me to point the police in the direction of the meeting? Want the D.A. calling a grand jury? You two will doubtless be among the first subpoenaed. So leaky, grand juries. So talkative. Some jurors even write books."

The Griscoms weighed it.

"That stupid, *stupid* Darla! And you, Gordon. How could you?"

"How could I what?"

"Blab to Darla about the meeting."

"She had me by the balls! That guy whose wife I was with—you have no concept. Possessive doesn't even get on the screen here. This is your fire-breathing, rampaging, green-eyed monster. I couldn't risk it. No way."

Olivia controlled a shudder. In exchange for giving her lover an alibi, Darla had driven her bargain, forced him to hand over what he'd been determined to keep secret. And—this was the worst part—managed to con herself into believing he'd offered his secrets freely, as proof and demonstration of his love for her. "Having your secret meant the world to Darla," she said to Gordon. "She literally glowed, talking about it."

"For the last time, none of this, repeat *none,* is my fault. What she did, she did on her own."

"I just realized something," Olivia said. "The reason you looked so calm before was that Darla's confession put her back where she belonged, under your thumb."

"So? Every relationship has its power thing. It's not like I *used* my power on her. I didn't crank her up to blow people away."

Businesswoman Chess had a terrible thought. "Did you pick her up in the store van?"

"Oh yes indeed. Logo right out there for everyone to see while I wrestled in the bikes."

"Bikes plural?" Chess asked.

"I'd locked them together," Olivia said, enjoying herself. "One of those inexplicable impulses."

"I just pray," said Gordon, "no one noticed there were two of them. But you see how totally innocent I was? Advertising my presence with the van?"

Now Olivia had a thought. "How did Darla explain the second bike?"

"She said she couldn't tell me until we got home. She was in such terrible shape I was afraid to pressure her. On top of everything else, while she was off phoning me, the goose killer or whatever made another hit."

Again Chess had to be filled in. Then she had to jump up, pace around, yell.

"She loved those geese," Gordon said, as if awed by the discovery. "She really, truly felt for them. I wonder if that's what pushed her over the edge."

He did his wounded buffalo thing with his head, sighed, and turned to Olivia. "The bikes are in the garage. Give me the key and I'll get yours over to you whenever you say."

Olivia flipped an impatient hand. "Keith has the key. Forget the bike. You and Darla are in the van. What next?"

"We didn't fight. We hardly even talked. Once we got home, we had a glass of wine and she told me everything. I had a fair amount of trouble taking it in, you can imagine. And when she was done, it seemed crystal clear to me that the only viable option was for her to disappear herself. Go deep underground, new identity, everything. It's been done before, right? By people with far less resources than she'd have. I offered her my Saab and a gas card and the thousand or so cash I keep in my safe here. And more money, I told her, anytime she called—whatever she needed to get back on her feet. She had to leave, though. Right away. Not negotiable."

He gave both women a beseeching look. "You see that, don't you? I couldn't have her in the house any longer, could I?"

"Of course not," said Chess. "I hope you've learned your lesson, Gordon."

Gordon's face hardened. "What lesson?"

"To take more *care*. You and Father between you have introduced some rather bizarre females into the family circle. I'm sick of putting up with them."

"Are you by any chance including my mother?"

"I meant Jane, actually. But yes, Bonita too—since you mention her."

Olivia, mother of sons, wanted Gordon to leap to Bonita's defense. Or be pulled up short by the grim parallels between Darla's plight and his mother's. Instead, he counterattacked. "In that case, let's mention what *you* introduced into the family circle. Let's mention Boydie-pooh."

"Boyd behaves himself, darling. Keeps his pants zipped. Too bad you didn't Tuesday night."

"What should have stayed zipped was Boyd's big fat mouth," Gordon observed to Olivia. "He's the one who called WBX."

"Boyd?" Olivia didn't get it.

Chess sighed. "I distinctly remember telling him don't say a word, but the silly old bear mixed it all up. What stuck in his mind was, oh boy, here's how to fix that Olivia Chapman. You know, for pissing me off that day at lunch. Remember? You got all starchy and high-horse on Jane's Woodside lunacy."

Gordon gargled his disgust.

"Boyd," Chess frostily informed him, "acted out of misplaced chivalry. Your Darla was a thug. A common criminal."

Gordon's meaty forefinger stabbed close to Chess's eyes. "Darla didn't saddle us with Olivia's snooping. That was Boyd's doing. Ask her yourself."

"No need to ask," Olivia said cheerfully. "Jane's become a friend as well as a client, but I doubt I'd have pushed so hard without the impetus of false accusation. I certainly wouldn't have driven out to Framingham to pester Barb about the meeting. Which of course got back to you, Gordon. How? Thaler call you?"

"Course he did. He called us all."

Chess pounced. "But only one of us told a thug."

"Still," Olivia scrupled, "if Boyd hadn't talked, I'd probably have let matters take their course."

Gordon's finger stabbed in triumph, but Chess wouldn't give him the satisfaction of flinching. "Can't you see she wants us fighting? She thinks we'll spill things in the heat of argument. Shall we bear that in mind? And shall we wind this up? It's past my bedtime and I've got an important breakfast tomorrow."

"Wind away," said Olivia. "Tell me about the meeting."

"I'm afraid you're in for a disappointment. It's all quite humdrum. Uncle Mort, as trustee, put my father's Nobel winnings in with some other funds and bought a bunch of real estate. What we met for was essentially a status review of this particular investment. Jane wanted to go one way on it and the rest of us another. End of story."

Olivia had to contain herself. Heavily as she'd counted on the meeting's agenda to lay mystery bare, she hadn't bargained for the rocker that was almost surely coming. Better start slow. "Had Jane known about the real estate before the meeting?"

"No," Gordon was quick to say. "None of us did."

"And were these properties in Woodside?"

Silence. Then Chess, belligerent: "Does it matter?"

Olivia reached for the phone and dialed information. "Cambridge," she said to the operator. "The number of a taxi company."

"Hey, slow down," said Gordon.

"No," said Olivia. "You two speed up or I'm out of here. My leg hurts."

They speeded up, but it was still a long story, rooted back in Morton Thaler and Jon Griscom's college days. Chess did most of the talking. "You have to understand that Uncle Mort adored Daddy and would do anything for him," she explained. "I mean that quite literally—anything. In addition, the man has this pathological desire to impress people like us. People who normally don't pay a whole lot of attention to the Uncle Mortsies of the world. You've met him, haven't you? Well then, you know what I'm talking about. But to give him his due, he's *fiendishly* clever on taxes. So when Daddy dropped his prize check on him and said, what on earth am I supposed to *do* with this thing, the instrument Uncle Mort concocted was full of nifty tax angles. Which is why, considering its relatively moderate beginnings, it has performed quite nicely."

"Nicely and secretly," Olivia said.

No, no, both Griscoms protested. There was nothing furtive or secretive about their father. He was open, totally without guile. He lived his life like an open book. He wouldn't even have curtains on his windows!

"It's very simple," Chess said. "Daddy had an entirely legitimate fear that people, his tenants and whatnot, would overreact to the Nobel aspect—you know, see him as a magic wand for all their troubles and woes. He had to protect himself from that kind of distortion—and protect them, too, of course. He explained it to me years ago, how important it was to shield people from their own unrealistic expectations. Enter Uncle Mort's nifty offshore trust, absolutely no paper trail."

Gordon was blinking in disbelief. "Am I hearing right? You knew about the property before the meeting?"

"Daddy turned to me." Chess was still proud to have been the chosen one, the indispensable favorite. "When Bonita checked out. Thank God I was there for him. I hate to think—"

Gordon interrupted, his face dark red. "Why didn't you tell me?"

Chess backed down fast to keep her ally. "I couldn't, Gordon. Please understand. Daddy had taken me into his confidence. How could I betray that? Besides, what difference would it make?"

"Lots," said Olivia. "Gordon trades on his father's good name, his pretensions to altruism. He might have tried to discourage this sideline. Looks bad on the resume, slumlord."

Stung, Gordon rounded on Olivia. "Don't you *dare* call him a slumlord. This whole business—Uncle Mort made it crystal clear at the meeting. Dad's interest in Woodside was entirely and exclusively humanitarian. He was going to plough back his profits, bring the housing stock up to a decent level, charge fair rents, the whole schmeer. Other landlords, people who really *were* slumlords, would see how well it worked and follow suit. Unfortunately real-estate law in Boston is totally biased toward the tenant. Dad was stuck with all these deadbeats left over from the former owners. Uncle Mort said with the rent delinquency they racked up, you'd think Dad was a gouger too."

"It was a beautiful, beautiful dream," Chess said. "And hardly Daddy's fault it failed. The sad fact is that no amount of fair treatment and fresh paint will deny people their constitutional right to piss in the hallways, tear out plumbing, or fall asleep with lighted cigarettes. Finally Daddy gave up. He stopped throwing good money after bad and began to give it to people who'd appreciate his generosity."

Wonderful, thought Olivia. Dr. Jonny had taken from the downtrodden poor to comfort the temporarily strapped. "Was some of the property on Wardell Street?"

"Yes." Chess might have been confirming the time of day.

Olivia set the pliers to pull the next tooth. "Arnette Murfin's house?"

"Yes."

Gordon leaped on this. "You know why Dad picked up on Arnette? Visited her and all? Because of her rent strike. This was what he'd been waiting for: the first sign that Woodside might be getting its act together. Taking responsibility for itself."

"You mentioned falling asleep with lighted cigarettes. Did he own the burned house?"

"Yes." Go ahead, Chess was challenging her, make something of it.

Olivia did. "The twice-burned house, I should say. The drug house. You seem familiar with Boston real-estate law. Landlords, you probably know, can summarily evict for drug activity."

"I didn't know, actually," said Gordon.

"Neither did I," said Chess. "Why would we? More to the point, why would Daddy? Once he realized his dream was doomed by forces beyond his control, he cut his losses, psychologically speaking. From then on Uncle Mort handled everything—until that wretched Murfin woman surfaced. Daddy heard about her entirely by accident, you know. I wish to God he hadn't. He'd still be alive today."

Gordon nodded in ponderous agreement. "She's got a lot to answer for, Arnette Murfin."

Olivia could slap them. "Interesting that Mort Thaler sprung for alarm systems the minute your father was no longer around to say no. Must've cost a bundle. Old houses have all these jigs and jogs in the framing. By the way, how long did Dr. Jonny last as a model landlord?"

"No idea," said Chess, much too quickly for credence.

"Bonita died about two years after the Nobel. Was his dream still intact then? When you first heard about the properties?"

Chess's silence was answer enough.

Gordon, fierce, cut in. "What are you driving at?"

"He didn't have much sticking power, your saintly father. Except with—what did you call them, Chess?—people who could appreciate his generosity."

The Griscoms studied the table, trying to hide in the depths of its antique graining.

"Tell me more," Olivia continued, "about Mort Thaler's *instrument.* Nice word. I always pay attention when I hear specialty words. Usually something's being hidden, and it's fun to figure out what. OK. Mort's instrument and that offshore trust you mentioned—could it be unraveled by a determined sleuth? An investigative reporter, say?"

Chess laughed, a dry bark. "I told you, Uncle Mort's impressive. The trust is registered in Delaware, of course—no big deal, Delaware's your basic garden-variety flag of convenience. But that's just the beginning. Incomes go to the Netherlands, into a charitable trust with a different name, and then into a third trust in Liechtenstein. Distributions come from Liechtenstein. It sounds complicated and it is. A couple of years ago a reporter from the *Phoenix* opened a crack in the Delaware entity, but she hit solid rock right after. And of course everything's set up to survive Daddy and his beneficiaries. Probate, if anyone's paying attention, will reveal the existence of the Delaware entity, nothing more."

Olivia moved to the central reality. "And that was just ducky with four of his five heirs—you kids. The profit that used to benefit your father's research assistants would start coming directly to you."

"Profit!" Chess had to laugh. "Try pittance."

"For you two, it's extra walking-around money, the rich getting richer. But Anne can stop pretending to look for work, and Ben and Barb have started their family. Besides, there's the future. Wardell Street's near the new subway line. Gentrification strikes, the goodies drop right in your laps. So everything looks great—except that Jane refused to go along. Sickened, perhaps, by her discovery of her husband's hypocrisy."

"Totally without relevance," cried Gordon. "The purchases were made long before Jane came on the scene. We tried to make that clear to her, but she wouldn't listen. She was determined to liquidate her share. Give it away, zip, just like that. With absolutely no appreciation of the effect on the rest of us."

"Ah," said Olivia, understanding. But she made them go through it, made them articulate every last detail.

In all, the trust owned three hundred and twenty-three separate buildings—well over two thousand separate rental units. Jane was claiming not her legal share but only the Wardell Street buildings—forty-two in all, including the burned building for the pre-school. Strictly speaking, Jane was not proposing to give these buildings away. She had already engaged Arnette Murfin to help her find four trustworthy people (Arnette herself making five) who would live at reduced rents in exchange for supervising the first five buildings. Rehabilitation would begin in earnest, drawing on the Griscom Foundation for funds. The supervisors and Jane would meet every week, exploring ways to boost the street's morale, ensure safety, and encourage personal responsibility. Each year following, if all went well, five more buildings would enter the process, with five more tenant supervisors, and so on until the street was fully rejuvenated.

Olivia pretended to consider Jane's plan only on its merits. "Sounds like it's worth a try," she said. "Nothing else has worked there, so why not? Anyway, it was her legacy that funded the foundation. She ought to be able to use it as she pleases."

"That's preposterous," said Chess. "What about my father?"

"Jane's his star pupil. She seems to have taken everything he said about personal responsibility and community involvement right to heart."

"You don't understand," Gordon began.

"Of course she does," Chess interrupted. "Can't you see she's playing with us?"

There was nothing playful in the look Olivia gave her. "Keith told me Jane came home from the meeting weighed down by life's complexities. The great altruist she admired and struggled to emulate had just been exposed as a slumlord. My guess is she was worried about you two as well, given the importance of your father's reputation to your careers."

"Bully for Jane," said Chess.

"Be fair, Chess," Gordon said. "She hasn't gone public yet." Then, to Olivia, "Chess has this funny little problem with Dad's wives."

"*What?* You set *Darla* on her and you have the nerve to—"

"I didn't *set* anyone. Darla was in the twilight zone. Purely and utterly."

In the silence that followed this spasm of bickering Olivia felt her tiredness, the late hour, an overwhelming desire to get far away from these two cutthroats.

First, though, she had to insure Jane's safety. "Jane may be recovering. Nothing would please me more. And I'm sure you'll both agree that pleasing me on this particular score ought to be a high priority."

Chess was scornful. "What are we supposed to do, stage a laying-on of healing hands?"

"Rallying round with kind words and offers of support will suffice. You can tell her you've rethought your position on Woodside—that you're ready to endorse her plans as retribution for your father's mistakes."

"Never," said Chess.

"Impossible," said Gordon.

"Don't worry," said Olivia, deliberately misunderstanding. "Jane won't look askance. She's an innocent, sees only the good in people. OK. Suppose someone acts to interrupt her recovery, a family member causes her some kind of shock, for instance. I will then tell Detective McGuire all I know. But if Jane gets well, I'll take whatever secrets are left to my grave."

"Why should we trust you?" Chess needed to know.

"Only because of Jane. She held off exposing your father, so I will too. All clear, then? We all agree we want Jane to get well and spend the foundation's money on Woodside?"

Sullen silence from both Griscoms.

"Cheer up. Six or seven months from now someone like that *Phoenix* reporter might start wondering how Wardell Street was so effortlessly detached from an invisible trust. The slumlord might get unmasked. Great shock and outcry, but by then the four of you kids will have started to clean up your act as landlords, yes? Sure you will. And it's much the lesser of two evils. Gordon won't be pilloried as a man who induced a woman to kill for him not once, but twice. A woman whose real fault was loving him too much. Shut up, Gordon, you know perfectly well that's how it'll play. Especially when they bring the geese in. Heartwarming visuals, those geese. And Chess, I haven't forgotten your secrets."

"What secrets?" Gordon asked.

Chess gestured airily. "Boyd's call to WBX, I suppose."

"That's one. She said *secrets.*"

Less airily: "Don't ask me, ask her."

"He can ask all he wants, I won't tell," said Olivia. "It's a beauty, though."

Chess shot her a quick searching look.

Olivia's agreeable nod had the effect on Chess of a punch to the midsection. And thus, at last, the Keith card was played.

26

Olivia's cab arrived promptly, but the man waiting on the sidewalk blocked her way.

"Hi, Olivia. Jerry Costello, *Boston Herald*. Got a minute?"

Medium height and build, anonymous features. Medium for the media. Her enemy. She had to be polite. "Sorry. It's too late."

"The police said you were with Gordon when he heard the shot."

"Yes. I'm tired, Mr. Costello. Let me pass."

Costello stepped aside. Olivia opened the cab door, checked the driver. He was large, young, and black.

"How come you're always on the spot, Olivia?"

She leaned toward him, dropped her voice. "What's *cadaveric spasm?*"

The reporter blinked, surprised, perhaps, that she'd claimed the questioner's role, and lowered his own voice. "A certain indication of suicide. The deceased has a tight grip on the gun, knife, whatever. It's not always present, but when they find it they trust it."

"Thanks." Olivia slipped into the cab.

Costello yanked the door open, stuck his head in after her. "My turn, right? How come you're always on the spot?"

She tugged on the door handle but Costello had the advantage. She met the driver's eyes in the rearview mirror. "All set," she said. "Let's go."

"Your friend coming with us or what?"

"He's not my friend. Let's go."

The driver swung his big shoulders around to face Costello. "Shut the door, Bud. Less you wanna wipe up the street."

Costello got out of harm's way, but not without the last word: "See you soon, Olivia."

When they were underway, Olivia spoke to the driver, whose name was Terrence Latchem. "You handled that well. Thanks."

"No problem," said Latchem. "Some guys, they can't take a hint."

"You said it," said Olivia.

The next morning began early, with an agitated call from Keith. Olivia told him exactly what she and Gordon had told the police and arranged a transfer of bike and car keys. Then she remembered he'd be seeing Jane soon. "I think Jane should hear about Darla from you," she said. "Not today, maybe, but as soon as she's stronger."

"Yeah? You want me to tell her everything?"

"Think, Keith."

"Oh," he said after a time. "OK. Just what the cops know, right?"

"Right. The public story. From now on, it's all you know, unless you see something in the paper or on TV."

Olivia's next conversation was with her lawyer. To her astonishment, she learned that she had broken no laws last night. "One, you didn't gain materially," Mary Jane said, "and two, you weren't under oath. But don't conclude I'm happy about any of this, Olivia."

"I won't," Olivia promised.

* * *

Gerry Rothfarb scolded her too. "It's much too late for stitches," he said as he swabbed her leg. "I can't think why you didn't see to this right away."

"I said, Gerry. It didn't hurt that much."

She had been talking fast since her arrival in his office. She couldn't hide from him how she'd spent her evening; he'd already caught the news on Darla and would learn more very soon. She gave him the public story with one embellishment: before getting involved with the Griscoms, she'd spent the afternoon visiting friends in New Hampshire. "We drank lunch, sort of, and used the empties for target practice."

"Brilliant."

"Local custom. It's our wild west, New Hampshire."

"Their license plates say 'Live free *or* die,'" Gerry said. "Not *and* die."

"Everyone thought the gun was empty."

"Everyone was stupid."

"True."

"Does Philip figure in this?"

"Was I playing dangerously because he's in danger? I don't think so. But just in case, I'll watch myself."

"Good."

He bandaged her up and planted a tetanus shot in her bottom. As she was leaving he gave her a look that made her think he hadn't swallowed her story whole. But that was all right. Clinicians should be skeptics. Doctors too easily conned aren't worth their hire.

Dee's workshop over, he stopped by her office that afternoon. Bursting with questions, of course. "Enough," she finally had to say. "I'm sick of talking about it. Tell me about the workshop."

"Went well, I think. At a minimum they learned what Diego Quintero, leading Bay State Latino scribbler, considers good writing. A couple of them sprouted wings and may actually fly. I'll miss the winged ones, but two weeks is a long time. Are we on for tonight? Takeout OK? Pizza or chicken?"

"Chicken, please. I'll do a salad."

"Call me ghoulish, but this suicide—. Let's watch the six o'clock news. Unless you're doing your bike thing."

Gerry had said to lay off biking for awhile. "It's too hot for exercise. My place?"

"Fine."

Imagining how speedily Dee would demolish her target-practice tale, Olivia wore pants that hid the bandage on her leg. He arrived in a state of high excitement. "I know something you don't know."

"Been listening to the radio?"

"Glued. You'll see."

She gave him a beer and poured herself a bullet. Hard to believe it was just last night that she'd cracked her little homeopathic medicine joke.

Settled on the sofa, the picture on and sound off, she had a pretty good idea why Dee was so excited. And she hoped she was equal to what was sure to follow.

"Sound!" he cried.

First the anchor told them that ballistics tests proved that the gun Darla Anderson had used to kill herself with last night had been used on Jane Griscom. Triumphant chortling and a told-you-so sock in the arm from Dee; cut to the investigator who'd been on the scene last night. "Mrs. Griscom regained consciousness yesterday. She has now remembered that a woman called her the night she was shot. This woman claimed to be the assistant of Olivia Chapman, an interior decorator widely known to be working with Mrs. Griscom. Since Mrs. Chapman has no assistant, we're looking at the strong possibility that Darla Anderson made the call herself."

Cut to the anchor, who told them Gordon Griscom would read a prepared statement.

Cut to Gordon. "So pale," Dee murmured. "Is that stress or too much brown rice?"

"Persons who take their own lives are so deeply in despair they can see no other course. Darla and I had not been happy together for some months, and recently she had begun to blame our problems on my stepmother, Jane Griscom. The night Jane was shot, I had no clear-cut alibi; I'd been driving around aimlessly, not wanting to come home. Darla offered to cover for me, and it seemed the simplest thing to do. Now that it appears she was covering her own criminal action, I see how wrong I was to lie to the police. I regret this very much, and I deeply regret the apparent outcome of Darla's mistaken belief that Jane was her enemy. Jane is enemy to no one, never has been. I also regret the false rumor that Olivia Chapman played any part in my stepmother's shooting. Mrs. Chapman has been a good friend in these dark times, and I'm very sorry she has been troubled. Thank you."

Cut to commercials. "That boy's been talking to his lawyer," Olivia said. "I wish the part about me would rerun as the sound bite."

Dee had been watching her closely. "You knew Darla did it."

"I guessed."

"You knew. One of those Griscoms told you. What else are you sitting on?"

"What *else?* I made a guess. No *else* about it."

"And me thinking we were friends."

"You really want to fight about this, Dee?" Don't do it, she silently begged him, don't drag out knee-jerk gay paranoia: *what, you're not telling me things because queers are notorious security risks, can't be trusted to keep their mouths shut?*

The commercials over, the news turned international. "I have to say it," Dee drawled, "Russia bores me blue."

Olivia muted the sound. "Me too."

"This development's going to help Jane Griscom with Woodside, you know."

255

"How so?"

"She was preyed on by her own, so are they. Puts them on common ground. Forces everyone past the rich white lady stereotype."

Slam-bang into the victim stereotype, Olivia thought but didn't say. Dee, a minority on two counts, was not above claiming for himself the problematic privileges of victimhood. They'd argued about it before and probably would again, but not, if she could help it, tonight.

Would Jane embrace victimhood? Concentrate on the injuries dealt her, deriving identity and esteem from them? "Common ground" sounded good, but if this was its basis, you had to wonder.

A few days later, in the relative cool of late afternoon, Olivia, not yet ready to cycle, boarded the subway for Cambridge.

Plenty of cabs at Harvard Square, the plus side of recession. "Mount Auburn Hospital," she told the driver. "Sorry to stick you with such a short ride."

"Oh please, Madam," the driver protested with a smile that looked real. "No problem."

Olivia read his name: Francois Debouyer. His accent, his thin dark arms and neck, suggested Haiti; his smile and the little American flag on the dash suggested he was still glad he'd left home. Still happy with what America offered: subsistence jobs, lousy pay, limitless opportunity for hope. She wondered how long this would be enough for Francois Debouyer. It wasn't enough for much of Woodside. It wouldn't be enough for her.

She felt keyed up, butterflies in her stomach. This, her first visit to Jane, would entail some performing. According to Keith, Jane was relieved that Darla had been identified, that no faceless, nameless menace still lurked, waiting for the next chance to strike. "And it was great for her," Keith had added, "to know Woodside was in the clear. Then she was like, uh-oh, Gordon. Poor Gordon, she goes, this is awful for him. Really meaning it, you know? Really feeling for the dude. She's something, huh?"

The young nurse at the desk was the second cheerful immigrant of the day. Eileen Finneran, her nametag said. "You'll need to wait," she said in her nice Irish voice. "Mrs. Griscom's allowed just the one visitor. But it won't be long—we're telling people ten minutes. Less if she becomes too excited or tired out."

"Have there been lots of visitors?"

"Oh indeed. The son especially, and all four stepchildren. Gordon's grand. He brings us presents—the best strawberries and blueberries you ever tasted. But isn't it a terrible shame about his girl? I still can't take it in, him such an openhearted and friendly fellow and all. You never know, do you?"

"Never. Who's with Mrs. Griscom now?"

Eileen Finneran dropped her voice. "Her colored friend. Oh—here she comes."

Olivia moved to intercept. "Hi, Mrs. Murfin."

"How do."

The sovereign graciously acknowledges one of her humbler subjects. "How's Jane?"

"She good. Be good three days running now, praise the Lord."

"Amen." Olivia might have been born to such response.

Something—wariness?—flickered across Arnette's impassive features.

"I'm sorry I disturbed you the other morning," Olivia said. "I was trying to help Jane."

"We *all* trying." Not arguing, just stating a fact. "The good Lord, He guiding our hand."

"I hope so."

"You got to have the faith."

"Yes. Well. I'll go into Jane now. Talk to you again soon, Mrs. Murfin."

"*Uh* huh."

* * *

257

"Olivia!" Jane's voice was weak and scratchy, but there was no missing her pleasure.

Tears stinging, Olivia bent to embrace her friend. "I'm so glad you're back, Jane."

"It's wonderful to be back."

It was a private room, small but sunny. Olivia sat in the visitor's chair, and the two women beamed at each other. The bandaging around Jane's head bulged fearsomely, her face looking yellow and drawn beneath its absolute whiteness.

"Oh Olivia, I don't know where to begin. You've had all this trouble because of Darla, and you sent those lovely flowers, and you've taken such good care of Keith. He told me how much you've done for him."

Olivia chose her words. "The Darla trouble is over, Jane. And as for Keith, that was no trouble at all. I like Keith." This last was almost fully true. Most of Keith's sidling, evasive quality was gone, blown away along with the root falsehood.

Jane's hand was on her arm. "He's *really* told me, Olivia. Everything. But don't think that he . . . I knew, you see. Almost from the very beginning. Remember how nervous I was the night you first met him? Please don't be too angry with me. I knew it was wrong to keep pretending, but I couldn't stop myself. I so much wanted him to be my son that it seemed he really was. Can you understand that?"

Olivia hid her relief. "Of course I can."

"It never occurred to me that Chess was involved. I thought Keith had seen our resemblance and charmed the birthdate out of some clerk—you know, wherever they keep the records. Over the years I'd heard of other searchers doing that sort of thing. The people responsible for these records must have a soft spot, and thank goodness. Adoptees today shouldn't have to be penalized by the beliefs of the past. Well, there it is. Keith deceived me, but I forgive him. I know he feels the same hungers I do—to belong, to have the comfort of close family ties. What's wrong, Olivia? You look so worried."

Olivia didn't want to introduce her views on close family ties. "I'm afraid it'll distress you, talking like this."

"Oh, I'm fine. Really. Keith and I have talked it all out, you see. Little by little we've separated the lies from the truth, which is that we care for each other very much and want to go on together. Also, I need your advice. Poor Olivia, I'm always asking your advice, aren't I? But what do you think? Should I tell people that Keith's not—" For all her assertions of confidence, Jane had to stop and marshall herself. "Not really my son?"

"That's a tough one. What's your basic impulse?"

"Oh, to hold off. Very much so. Mostly for Chess's sake. She's been in to visit morning and night, you know, ever since I woke up. A busy woman like Chess taking all this time to cheer me up—I'm sure she's sorry she tried to trick me. And think how embarrassed she'd be if the papers got ahold of it."

"Anything persuading you on the other side?"

"This will sound funny. I think Keith wants it over and done with. It's been hard on him, living a lie."

"I'm sure." Olivia wasn't, though, not entirely. Keith's new likability aside, he seemed fundamentally a taker, capable of lying to get what he wanted. Doubtless his childhood losses were part of this propensity; the question was whether he would grow beyond it. Before she could trust him as serenely as Jane seemed to, Olivia would have to know him longer and better.

"Chess will lose the most," Jane went on, "if the truth gets out. And of course she's already suffering terribly from the loss of her father. His death, I mean, not the shock of knowing he'd profited from slum housing. I think Gordon was hardest hit by that part." A wan smile. "Harder than me, even."

Nothing to say, Olivia hugged her.

Jane spoke first. "Would it be all right with you if we put off talking about poor Darla? Good. I know you can't stay long, and

I really must decide about Keith. Do you agree with me that Chess took Jonny's death most to heart?"

"Yes."

"So her needs should come before Keith's. Yes. I'm sure that's the proper way to settle this. Thank you, Olivia. Goodness, how sleepy—can hardly keep my eyes . . ."

The remarkable woman had dropped off.

Olivia checked her watch. She'd been in this room about eight minutes. Hard to imagine the map of reality could change so completely in eight minutes.

Jane, clearly, was tougher than she had seemed. Tough enough, it was suddenly obvious, for Woodside. It would not be a matter of wading in, forcefully wrestling socioeconomic demons to the ground. Instead, there'd be endless dithers while everyone screamed for decisions. The people she'd choose to trust would probably fail her. She'd forgive and forget without a shred of caution or prudence. But in her holy-fool way, she might be able to pull off some significant changes.

And show Dr. Jonny all to hell. Mop up the floor with him and his hypocritical altruism. Not that Jane herself would ever see it that way.

Studying art, and on her travels, Olivia had seen countless depictions of Judgment Day. Every single one showed the damned as infinitely various in form and behavior—and infinitely more interesting than the saved in their cooky-cutter parade to Heaven, each wearing the same prayerful expression, the same white robe. Good people are boring, these frescoes and tympanums had seemed to illustrate, evil ones fascinating.

But there was nothing cooky-cutter about Jane. Her goodness was quirky, subtle, idiosyncratic. You could miss it altogether, as Olivia initially had.

You had to wonder. Can some of humanity's badness be blamed on our wimpy, partial, bloodlessly conformist notion of good? It made a kind of rough sense. Why struggle and strive to incline the heart in a direction that guaranteed certain boredom?

But why had we set it up that way, done such a dumb number on ourselves?

Most human stupidity, Olivia believed, was due to failures of imagination. Here too? But why should the imagination, fertilized so thrillingly by scaly evil, quit cold, shut down, grab for formula, when it came to good?

She thought about it all the way home but found no answers.

At Washington Station, Arnette Murfin had not immediately transferred to the Orange Line, the splendid new subway that was expected to enhance the Griscom properties. Instead she made for the concourse, a busy, anonymous place where there was a long bank of phones.

She chose a cubicle isolated from other callers and moved all the way into it, rounding her shoulders for additional privacy. Thus barricaded, she consulted Detective McGuire's card and dropped her dime.

McGuire picked up right away. *Soft desk job,* Arnette reflexively began, *air condition office sit the livelong day on his big white ass—*

"Thanks for calling, Mrs. Murfin," McGuire said, interrupting her mental tirade.

Dr. Griscom, he'd do that same thing—thank her before she even told why she was calling. Before she could say it was good news or bad.

Arnette took this coincidence as a sign of where she ought to begin. "Dr. Griscom, he shot by mistake. They really after that Jamal Sutton, counta he burn down that drug operation, you know, number twenty-two Wardell, right cross from me. They fighting over turf, see. One bunch pay Jamal for torching the house, other bunch pay them gunmen to take him out. Dr. Griscom, he just in the way."

"That's very interesting, Mrs. Murfin. I'd like to hear more. How about I swing by and—"

"No you don't. Chance enough I be phoning."

"I appreciate that, Mrs. Murfin. But the thing is, we need some names and faces. Like, who paid Jamal?"

"You ax Jamal."

"You know where I can find him?"

"You ever try Newark? Down New Jersey? His mama's family, they Newark people."

"You know his mama's family's name?"

"Name? Why, Sutton."

"Fine. I'll try Newark. You heard arson for sure, Mrs. Murfin? You got a name or face might say arson to me?"

"Two kids live round here, little kids, they seen Jamal the night of the fire. He park by the alley, run behind that drug house. Then he get outta his car toting four a them milk bottles, you know, that big plastic kind. Two each hand. Dark like that, they ain't swearing, but *something* in them bottles making them heavy. And ain't no *milk* gon burn up a house that way."

"I'll need the kids' names, Mrs. Murfin."

"*Uh* uh. They talk for *me*. It get out, they dead meat."

"Believe me, Mrs. Murfin, I appreciate the problem. But I really need your help on this. Whatever you tell me, I swear it'll go no further. Honest to God."

Arnette could hardly breathe. They'd reached the place she'd most been fearing. Ain't no way you survive the livelong years without you keep your head down and your mouth shut. Always and always and always. But she'd made her promise, her solemn vow. And Jane, praise be, was getting well, coming right along.

Old nigger woman start in gaming with the Lord, she a stone *fool.*

"From my window?"

"I can't quite hear, Mrs. Murfin."

"Gunfire stop, I run over to look out my window. I see Jamal

Sutton kinda raise hisself up and hand Cyrus Grier that bag he been wearing. Cyrus, he shove it under his belt quick as quick. Pull his shirt down, you can't see nothing there. What I say, that bag gotta be holding Jamal's money from the fire. Cash money. He show up in the Emergency with money, you people gon come down hard on him. Ax him questions he ain't gon like."

"You actually see some money, Mrs. Murfin? Some bills?"

"What I *see*, I see Cyrus Grier drinking like a fish five days running. Offering his bottle round and things."

"He drank up Jamal's arson money?"

Arnette had to laugh. "Cyrus a *drunk*, not a crazy man. Jamal musta give him a tip, see, for minding it till he come back from the Emergency. Jamal *know* Cyrus, you know. Cyrus, he live with his mama once."

McGuire took a moment to sort out syntax. "Jamal's mama," he then confirmed. "Mrs. Sutton from Newark. What happened to her?"

"Oh, she dead long ago. Cancer."

McGuire clucked his tongue.

His sympathy was wasted on Arnette. "Girl smoke like two chimneys, what she expeck?"

"I wish you'd seen the money, Mrs. Murfin."

"It in that bag, don't you worry. Woman round here, she waiting on Jamal Sutton the same morning he got hisself shot. They gon trade cars. Jamal gon pay her extra cause her car more fancy. It really her son's car, see, and he doing time. I ain't saying where, so don't be axing. His mama, she can't be meeting no payments and things. Repo man hadda pick it up, she tell me. Jamal Sutton, he break the deal. He hadda use his money for running. He don't run, them gunmen try again."

Talking to Arnette, McGuire had put heart and soul into persuasion. Now that they'd hung up, he allowed himself a small rush of optimism.

Ever since Jamal Sutton skipped, McGuire had begun the day monitoring NCIC, the National Crime Information Center, punching FIND without much expectation of pay dirt. Two days ago, Sutton, Charles M., had come up on the screen, a warrant default in Newark. Yesterday and this morning he was still there.

Now, just to be sure, he checked again.

There it was, no change in the listing, no other Suttons in Newark. Course, Charles M. might be no relation whatsoever. Sutton wasn't exactly an unusual name. And not—he thought of Willie Sutton—necessarily a black one, either.

Worth a long-distance call? McGuire thought yes. He found Newark—get this thing properly alphabetized one of these days—on his Rolodex. Oh yeah, Mike Squires.

The check mark next to Squires's name said Boston owed him rather than the other way around. Not ideal, but what in this sorry vale of tears ever is? Arnette had offered conjecture and hearsay. To get more out of her, he'd have to bring her in, work her over pretty hard. For days, probably. Which'd be death to his long-range goals for her. A lady like her, smart, motivated, respected rather than popular, you wanted her on your side. Someone has to be worked over, let it be in Newark.

Dialing, McGuire dropped back into persuasion mode.

Fifteen minutes later he had some of what he'd hoped for. Charles M. Sutton, Mike Squires had assured him, was "black as myself," also chronic. Petty stuff—*B* and *E,* larceny. This current *B* and *E* default was par for the guy; he'd been caught lifting two Eddie Murphy videos and failed to show for his court date.

The Newark courts were as backed up as Boston's. Squires could promise only to ask for a *capias* first chance he got, tomorrow morning unless some hell broke loose overnight. Weather like this, you expected the worst. "Bright side," Squires then added, "finding him's no problem. Guy's a fixture, you know? I saw him yesterday, hanging at his usual corner."

Squires let out his big-chested laugh. "We pick him up on this nickle-dime, he'll shit a brick. He has anything on your man Jamal, guarantee you he spills before we get to the station house."

27

Looking back, Olivia saw the events following Jamal Sutton's return to Boston in the form of a film montage—not surprisingly, since much of her information came from the tube. She and Dee often watched the news together, which inspired further what-did-you-know-and-when-did-you-know-it questions.

"Stop that," she'd say.

"It's not fair. I'm stuck at my desk, scribbling and grading papers. You're out in the world. It's your *duty* to tell me things. How else can I fertilize my imagination?"

(He'd even persuaded himself that she had, through Arnette, the inside track on Jamal Sutton. But McGuire kept true to the secrecy he'd sworn. No one, not even Jane, ever discovered Arnette's crucial role. McGuire's honorable behavior was, of course, more than its own reward. It allowed him to claim the case had been cracked by good, thorough police work—chiefly his own.)

The montage's dominant motif was what Olivia and Dee called the Giant Bug—Jamal or some other "alleged" criminal being hustled up the courthouse steps, uniforms and plainclothes cops pressing in closely on all sides. Clambering, urgent, they looked especially buglike in a long shot. "Snipers," declared Dee at the

Giant Bug's first appearance. "They don't want some Jack Ruby wrecking everything."

Jamal arraigned and stowed in protective custody, the second Giant Bug brought in the functionary who had paid Jamal to burn the drug house. After that, the Giant Bug's center was Latino instead of black. First came the wholesaler who had supplied the drug house with raw materials and processing equipment, then the executive-level operative who had ordered Jamal punished, and, finally, his functionary, the man whose careless aim had killed Griscom.

What spliced the sequences together, naturally, was plea bargaining. Olivia couldn't get over it. "I thought those blindfolded statues were Justice, not Lady Luck."

Dee liked this. "And the lawyers have turned croupier."

"Why does it run out of steam, though? Look at the trajectory: petty criminal, functionary, middle-manager, boss, then back to functionary and bye-bye, case closed. Why don't the courts go for the super-boss, keep bargaining up and up until they nab the source?"

"By source do you mean the human condition?"

Olivia brushed this away. "The architects of this infernal machine. The ultimate kingpins."

"Plea-bargaining must be like a rubber band. Stretch it too far, it breaks."

"Or we don't want drugs solved. Drugs keep places like Woodside down. Out of our mainstream hair."

Dee lifted a skeptical eyebrow. "The genocide theory? My paranoia likes it, but the rest of me says no. For one thing, the drug industry's tax-exempt. Every other national lunacy—our worship of automobiles and guns, our shop-till-you-drop materialism—at least that stuff nourishes the tax base. Anyway, if genocide's the goal, why bother with blunt instruments like crack? We put a man on the moon, we can do elegance. We can do surgical. Griscom's lab could ring some changes on sickle-cell anemia, make it wildly contagious, black-on-black. Something like that starts coming down, I'll buy genocide, but not yet."

Sally had called right on the heels of Gordon's televised statement. "Thank heavens you're out of that terrible mess," she said. Olivia didn't bother saying aren't you ashamed you doubted me, and Sally didn't bother to apologize. Instead: "I'm giving a luncheon party next Saturday and we'd all love to see you. I know that's your day for Pip, but he'd understand if you were early. Or late."

"Thanks, Sally, but I've made other plans."

"Are you sure, darling? It's been so long."

"It's another lunch—with some old clients." Olivia wasn't exactly lying. One lunch per weekend was quite enough.

And as always, Sally's priorities could be trusted. "Oh in that case. Have fun, darling. We'll catch up another time."

Am I really going to this thing? she kept asking herself as she drove north in the van. The Gillises, Al and Joanne, lived in Manchester-by-the-Sea. All Boston had emptied out for the mountains or seashore. Even Dee had left for a week in Provincetown, where cute, dumb Kevin and some other friends had rented a house. Herd behavior, herself in the thick of it. For no better reason than a pair of social climbers had dropped an invitation on her.

She wondered if the Gillises' friends would be snobs too. This led her to a related question: when Philip died, would she keep herself listed in the social register? Keep herself, that is, in a position to appeal to people like the Gillises, people with money to burn and ladders to climb? Probably. Business was business. A decorator's gotta do what a decorator's gotta do.

It wasn't all bad, the party. The hot, windless day had actually prompted people to change into bathing suits and splash in the pool. Two women were even getting their hair wet, an all-time first in Olivia's experience of pool parties. Instead of joining them, she dropped a long caftan over her bathing suit and crossed the rocks to swim alone, in the ocean. Salt water was healing. And the ragged stripe across her leg had gone a lurid red, likely to provoke curious questions.

"Wasn't it *freezing?*" Joanne cried when she came back.

"Pretty cold," said Olivia. Whenever had North Shore water not been cold? "Nice, though."

Joanne laughed with enough volume and delight to insure an audience. "You old-line Yankees! If it hurts, it's got to be good for you, right?"

Olivia joined the laughter. Business. They wanted her to be Boston and social, not the daughter of a failed insurance salesman from Media, Pa.

Lunch was served late, to tables of eight. "Festa!" announced Joanne, summoning her guests from pool and bar. "Festa Italiano!" They began with prosciutto and sublimely ripe cantaloupe and ended with a take-no-prisoners tiramisu, everything washed down with quantities of very cold Orvieto.

Al, on Olivia's left—she'd been given the seat of honor—brought up the Griscoms right away. "No surprise to *me* the doctor was accidental," he said. "He was just too damn important to be mowed down like that on purpose. Too big a man. And the black guy, what's his name, yeah, Sutton—he was too damn *un*important for it to begin and end with him. So it didn't surprised me a bit when they bagged the rest. But that Gordon Griscom—something fishy there. How can a man live with a woman and not know she's crazy?"

The man on her right, a lawyer, smooth and flirtatious, said much the same thing in his different style. Then: "I gather from Al they implicated you. Must've been rough."

"Not really. It didn't last long. And innocence is fortifying."

He had his card ready. "See how you feel in a week or so. I've achieved quite a nice record with libel cases, invasions of privacy, that kind of unpleasantness."

269

She smiled, put the card in her pocket. Business. Give him hers in return? No. *Basta.* Flirtatious men were OK to work with if you liked them. This guy wasn't likable.

Al again: "Joanne's got a bee in her bonnet on the living room."

"What kind of bee?"

"Don't worry, she'll tell you."

"Changes ahead?"

"You have to ask?"

Anything for peace, his resigned sigh said. World-beater Al was, at home, an abject coward. A fairly common male type, Olivia had discovered over the years. Still, each fresh demonstration startled. And disturbed. On some level, every family member understood that power wasn't being shared in any genuine fashion. Rather, a busy man had to pick his fights, and the domestic sphere was simply too dinky to bother about. Peace, now; nothing dinky about peace. Peace at home let a man recharge, gather energy for the next round of world-beating.

For a time. Breakdown was inevitable, though. Wives and children could be disregarded, shunted aside, for only so long. Sometimes their angry resentments erupted of their own accord, sometimes wife or child took decisive action. Joanne's discontent with her nearly new living room could be either the first rumblings of the volcano or a calculated provocation.

Pursuing peace, Gordon Griscom had played on the hungers of a woman who loved him to the point of obsession. The more he could convince Darla to blame Jane for her troubles, the less she'd fret at him for not loving her as she yearned to be loved. And there was a vital side benefit too: the more Gordon dumped on Jane, in Darla's sympathetic hearing, the better he could ignore what had started everything—his beloved father was a slumlord. Peace at any price.

"You see what I mean, don't you Olivia?"

Olivia and Joanne were standing in the living room, facing the vast sweep of window wall that gave them a panorama of garden, sky, sea, and rocks.

"It's not a *room,*" Joanne went on. "It's a *view.*"

Last year, early in the planning stage, Olivia had repeatedly made this very point. "I paid three mil for that view," Al had argued. "Joanne wants to feature it, I say feature it."

"A splendid view," Olivia now demurred.

"I hate it. No really, I do. Winter's the worst. Brrrrr!"

Olivia had made this point too. And predicted that in any season people would come into the room, say wow, what a view, and then need something—color, arrangement, works of art—to draw them happily back indoors. "Otherwise," she remembered saying, "everything you're trying to do in here, have a conversation, even, has to compete. Also, it's not unusual for people to feel a bit uncomfortable with so much glass. Not consciously, perhaps, but it's there. We started out living in caves, remember. We still crave enclosure. Solidity."

Deaf ears. Joanne had wanted everything in shades of off-white. No curtains or blinds. No antiques. She hated antiques. She hated oriental rugs. Then: "Al bought this humongous seascape. You'll love it, Olivia; it really complements the view."

Today the seascape was gone, nothing in its place. The low fireplace that had been designed not to crowd it looked very low indeed.

"How about trying some color?" The decorator, listening hard, heard no hint of told-you-so in her question.

"Oh, this is way beyond *color,* Olivia. You know what I want? Some friends of ours just bought this adorable little house up in Maine. It belonged to this real old-timey lobsterman who never did a thing to it. Well, a flush toilet, but you know what I mean. Anyway, it's right on the water, just like this, same rocks and everything. But the windows! They're teeny, Olivia. Darling little panes of glass . . . I felt so *cozy* there. So, I don't know, *safe.*"

"You want to change the windows here?"

"Exactly."

"How big was the lobsterman's living room, Joanne?"

"Oh, teeny. And you know what was on the floor? Linoleum! With flowers on it! Of course I wouldn't want *linoleum,* but the *look!* It was wonderful, Olivia. I could have the same effect with a flowered rug."

"You could. Or you could buy a cottage."

Joanne's features hardened. "No I can't. Al refuses to even consider it. He loves this house."

So the price of peace had its limit for Al.

Joanne made a face. "Course, I might love it too—if I spent as little time here as he does."

Ah. The volcano's first rumblings? Deliberate provocation? Either way, the decorator had better get cracking, set the hook. Joanne's dilemma was not without precedent. Finding Versailles too large and chilly, Marie Antoinette had built herself a hamlet of cozy cottages where she could play milkmaid, have fun for a change.

Joanne Gillis, contempo Queen of France. She'd love it. Hook and then some.

But Olivia couldn't get the words out. She'd gag on them. "Joanne? What do you call this room?"

Warily: "What do you mean? It's the living room, isn't it?"

"Yes. Why's it have that name, do you think?"

Still wary: "Because . . . I don't know. People're supposed to do their living in here?" An embarrassed laugh.

"And when you say *living,* what kind of things come to mind?"

"Is this a game? Because I've never been one for word games."

"It's not a game. I'm trying to say there's more to living than endlessly tearing out windows and putting in new ones. Or re-creating Maine cottages."

"Well of course. You don't have to play word games to know that."

"True. But unless you can tell me, in specific terms, what you mean by *living*, I can't help you change this room."

"This is unreal. Are you saying you don't want to work for me anymore?"

"Not unless I know a good deal more than I do now."

"I thought you had to be licensed to do psychiatry in this state."

"Nothing to do with psychiatry. We old-line Yankees have a horror of waste. I'm not going to help you clog some landfill with this"—Olivia's gesture gathered in the clunky but expensive off-white, butter-soft leather sofas and chairs, the off-white carpeting, the off-white bare expanse over the fireplace, the yards and yards of top-of-the-line insulated glass—"unless its replacement will stay put. For the foreseeable future."

"Well la-di-da! Do you talk to all your clients this way?"

"Yup." A lie, but she hadn't gone this far for Joanne to grab the easy way out of taking everything she'd said personally.

"It's a wonder you can stay in business. Though I guess you really hauled it in on that Griscom auction."

Olivia answered this with her nicest smile.

Joanne stamped her foot. "This is ridiculous! You're as good as sending me to your competition, you know."

"If that's the way you see it. But if you have some specifics for me and want to talk, you know my number. I've got to run, Joanne. The food was delicious and so was the swim. Thanks for including me."

Once home, Olivia couldn't settle. She wasn't hungry, and she certainly didn't want anything to drink after swigging all that wine. She flipped through magazines, clicked around the TV dial, went up to the deck, deadheaded half the petunias, came back down, paced some, considered putting on some music, calling a friend.

Then she had an idea.

* * *

It was almost dark when she reached the vest-pocket savanna. She removed her headlight, hid her bike in the same bushes she and Darla had used before, and ran through the dry, crunchy grass to the riverside.

As before, the geese lifted their heads at her approach, hissed, and moved a few feet away before they roosted again. But the poacher had been busy. The flock was down to three.

The poacher or a natural predator. A feral dog. A fox. Against Darla's conviction that natural predators leave remains was the fox Harry Belafonte had sung about. The night that fox had been on the town-o he'd grabbed a goose by the neck, throwed a duck across his back and run for home, the legs all dangling down-o.

It was too dark to see the face markings that indicated the male. Snowy, she remembered. What other names had Darla come up with? Bianca, Milk, no, Leche . . . Moon . . .

A mosquito whined at her ear. Lots of traffic noise from the Cambridge side, but the river itself lay flat and shiny, not a ripple.

Here was the lifesaving root she'd braced her feet against. The smell of the water brought everything back—the sickening, heart-thumping fear, the bounding joy of survival.

Suddenly, footsteps. Shocking in their loudness, their absence of caution. The geese lifted their heads, hissed, stood. The intruder squatted, rummaged in a plastic sack. The geese stopped their evasive fussing and came running, shouldering one another in their eager haste.

It was dinnertime. Tonight's menu smelled Chinese: onions, garlic, soy sauce. *Fucking slope, he's got to be stopped.* But was it a he? Olivia couldn't tell. A kid, maybe. Under five feet tall.

The buffet laid out, the intruder strolled to the riverbank and squatted not far from Olivia's hiding place. There was a scratch, a Bic's flare of light. Olivia saw a small, sharp chin, wide cheekbones like polished knobs, deep squint lines, gray hair in a cropped bob. A woman, quite old, almost certainly Vietnamese. A country-woman who liked her smoke in deep, greedy drags.

That brief glimpse sent Olivia straight back to the period when what America did in its living rooms was watch war on TV. Women with faces like this were rarely seen enjoying a tranquil smoke, though. The western cameras preferred them in states of terror or grief. Olivia could bring that part back too. She could jump out, loom hugely tall over the woman, blind her with the headlight. Yell in a big western voice about cruelty to animals or city codes, slaughtering geese without a permit or some such.

Presumably that's what she did: wrung their necks, plucked them, and cooked them for dinner.

To find out more, Olivia would have to show herself, start asking questions. The woman was sure to be frightened, sure to misunderstand. And the risk was great that she, too, would be thrust back in time, back to the rolling thunder of the bombers, the maddening thup, thup, thup of the helicopters. To Agent Orange and napalm.

Olivia couldn't do it to her. Much better to fill in the details herself.

Dropped into this new world, the woman was likely to have missed being useful, missed her contribution to the family rice paddy, the vegetable garden. She'd have puttered aimlessly around her son's—her grandson's?—apartment, as unable to settle as Olivia had been tonight. She'd have ventured outdoors, restless still, until her wanderings led her to the little savanna. Instantly she'd have seen its potential as a poultry yard. She'd have appreciated its remoteness, its access to water.

A low-overhead, low-maintenance operation. The dinner the geese were now gobbling could easily be restaurant scraps.

The woman rose with a little grunt, took a final drag, and tossed the butt into the river. In a language Olivia didn't understand she spoke to the geese, finishing with something that made her laugh with amusement. Bending from the waist—classic rice-paddy stance!—she gathered up the food containers, stowed them in their sack, and left. Melted, as they'd said during the living-room war, into the night.

What had she said to the geese? Tonight you eat Brother Pig, tomorrow we eat you? Or maybe, you're hungrier now there's not so many of you. Because she must have wondered, during Darla's tenure as rival caretaker, how her geese could have so little appetite and still be nice and fat.

Headlight bright, eyes peeled for breaks in the pavement, Olivia rode thoughtfully home. The Asian woman's earthy enterprise and Joanne's sterile discontent; Jane's holy-fool tenacity and the rotten core of Dr. Jonny's altruism; true peace and peace at any price; rooms for living and living-room wars—the colliding pairs seemed to join hands and dance in the beam of her headlight.

Their movements were slow and stately. A court dance, perhaps, though Olivia failed to detect any obvious pattern or design. The music was unmistakeable: the gravely lilting first movement of the requiem that Benjamin Griscom's chorus had sung so beautifully. The Kyrie.

She unlocked her office for a routine message check. On the personal phone a light blinked.

"It's nine Sunday night, Olivia," said Fran Concannan's voice. "Please call me at work."

At nine she'd been at the savanna, about to leave. It was now nine thirty-five. Her hands shaking, Olivia pressed the auto-dial button for Arlington House.

Fran picked up herself. "He's gone, Olivia. He slipped away between checks, God love him. Quiet as a dear little mouse, he was, or I'd have heard."

"I'm coming right now. I'm so grateful it's you, Fran."

"I thank God I'm here for you. You'll call a friend or a cab? I don't like to think of you driving or taking that train. I'm off at eleven, so I can bring you home. I've called his mom and dad, but there wasn't any answer."

Olivia asked her to keep trying them, and they hung up.